Sam Hawken is a native of Texas now living on the east coast of the United States. A graduate of the University of Maryland, he pursued a career as an historian before turning to writing. *The Dead Women of Juárez* is his first novel.

THE DEAD WOMEN OF JUÁREZ

Sam Hawken

First published in this paperback edition in 2011 by Serpent's Tail
First published in 2011 by Serpent's Tail,
an imprint of Profile Books Ltd
3A Exmouth House
Pine Street
London EC1R 0JH

website: www.serpentstail.com

ISBN 978 1 84668 774 7
eISBN 978 1 84765 655 1

Designed and typeset by folio of Mayfield

Printed and bound by CPI Group (UK) Ltd, Croydon, CR0 4YY

10 9 8 7 6 5 4 3 2 1

MIX
Paper from
responsible sources
FSC® C020852

Acknowledgements

Regardless of what it says on the cover, every book is a team effort. With that in mind, I must thank Dave Zeltserman and my agent, Svetlana Pironko, for championing my work when even I had my doubts. Thanks also go to Pete Ayrton and John Williams of Serpent's Tail for taking a chance on me.

Most of all I thank my wife, Mariann, for allowing me the opportunity to pursue a career as a writer, for being my first reader and prime defense against bad writing, and for being the cornerstone of our family. Without her, there would be no novel for you to read.

For *las mujeres muertas de Juárez*

PART ONE

Bolillo

ONE

Roger Kahn wrote, "Boxing is smoky halls and kidneys battered until they bleed," but in Mexico everything bled in the ring. And there was also pain.

When Kelly Courter fought in the States he was a welterweight, but he didn't fight Stateside anymore and he was heavier. No amount of sweating and starving would take him out of the middleweight class now. This mattered little to the man who paid the purse. If pressed he would call these catchweight fights, but they were really just demolition without a weigh-in or any formality beyond money changing hands.

The Mexican kid was leaner and harder than Kelly, and that was the point; Kelly was here to be the kid's punching bag. Mexicans liked to see La Raza get one over on a white guy. It was twice as good if the white guy came from Texas like Kelly did.

They circled. Kelly's blood was on the canvas because he was gashed over the right eye and his nose was dripping. Vidal, the cut man working Kelly's corner, wasn't much for adrenaline and pressure alone couldn't stop the leaking. The crowd wanted to see the *bolillo* bleed anyway.

Kelly worked the jab to keep the kid at a distance. He connected, but he wasn't putting enough hurt behind the punches to make a difference to the outcome. His shoulders burned and his calves threatened to cramp. He started the match dancing, but now he was shuffling.

They traded punches. Kelly soaked up the kid's straight right with his cheekbone and when his head rocked he heard and felt his neck bones crackle. He hooked a punch into the kid's ribs, but his follow-up left windmilled. And then they were apart again, circling. If Kelly could keep the action in the center of the ring, he might manage to stay on his feet through six rounds.

The bell rang. The crowd was happy. Under the ring lights a layer of tobacco smoke was as thick and gray as a veil.

Vidal wiped the blood off Kelly's face and pressed an icy-cold enswell where it would do the most good. In the other corner, the Mexican kid's trainer talked the boy up while he got all the best stuff, from ice packs to adrenaline hydrochloride. Kelly didn't have a trainer with him because he wasn't that high-class; he was just the designated sacrifice. Vidal came with a ten-year-old boy who worked the bucket and iced down Kelly's mouthpiece. Kelly paid them both ten bucks a round.

"Can you do something about my nose?" Kelly asked Vidal after his gum shield came out. "I can't breathe right."

"Don't get punched in the face no more," Vidal replied, but he stuffed a soaking Q-tip up Kelly's left nostril and swabbed it around. "Here, suck it up."

Kelly snorted and his sinuses flushed with the stink of alcohol and blood. Kelly felt nauseated. The boy held up his plastic bucket. Kelly spat into it instead of throwing up.

"You going to make it?" Vidal asked.

"What round are we in?"

"You can fall down any time now. Fall down or get knocked down."

"He can knock me down."

"Then you're stupid."

The bell rang. Vidal yanked the Q-tip out of Kelly's nose too roughly, but the bleeding didn't start again.

As far as smokers went this one wasn't too big: about forty men surrounded the ring and the walls were close. Everybody had something to drink and there were lots of cigars. Old Mexican faces heavy with wrinkles and extra chins and dark eyes grew darker in the shadows of a fight so that looking out beyond the ropes a fighter saw only dozens of dead, unblinking holes.

"*¡Délo a la madre!*"

Give him to the Mother. Roughly it meant *kick his ass to death*.

The Mexican kid came straight at Kelly and so did the first hard jab. Maybe Kelly was distracted, or maybe he was slower than he thought, but the punch came through his hands and cracked him right between the eyes. It shouldn't have rocked him, but it did.

Kelly took a step back. A left hook took him flush and the combo right to the body made his guts shake. He had his hands up, but they weren't where they needed to be, so the kid battered him left-right, left-right, and he fell while all the old men cheered the blood.

Back in the States the ref would step in once Kelly's head bounced off the canvas, but this wasn't the States. Kelly's nose was gushing again. The Mexican kid was over him. Another punch slugged down from the heavens and blocked out the ring lights. Only then was the bell rung. The ref raised the Mexican kid's hand and Kelly Courter disappeared for everyone in the room.

TWO

IF THE PLACE HAD DRESSING ROOMS, they weren't for *bolillos*. They set Kelly and Vidal up at the back of the men's room. While drunken *viejos* wandered in and out to use the piss trough, Vidal helped Kelly get the tape off his fists and get changed. He cleaned up Kelly's face the best he could, but he worked corners and wasn't a doctor.

Green and white paint on the walls peeled from neglect and humidity. The men laughed at Kelly and insulted him in Spanish because they didn't think he understood them, but he did. "His face looks like a bowl of *frijoles refritos*," one of the old men said to another. Kelly might have argued, but he saw himself in a mirror coming in and knew they weren't far wrong; the Mexican kid did a dance on his face.

Vidal put his thumbs on either side of Kelly's nose and pressed until cartilage crunched. Needles of pain stabbed through Kelly's forehead then and when Vidal put tape across the bridge of his nose to keep things stable. Kelly would have two black eyes for a while.

Ortíz came in. The room reeked of urine and shit. There wasn't a breath of fresh air inside four walls. Ortíz didn't look like the kind of man who'd wash his hands in a place like this even if the sink worked. He took a wad of American bills out of his jacket and counted out $200.

"What did you think of Federico?" Ortíz asked Kelly.

Kelly gave Vidal two twenties. The old cut man put the money away and packed up. "I think he punches hard," Kelly said.

"Oh, yeah," Ortíz agreed. "Without gloves on, he could kill you."

"Then I guess I'm lucky he had gloves on."

Outside the bathroom the crowd revved up again. Kelly's match wasn't the only fight on the card, but the rest of the fights were all brown on brown. Now that the spectators had their appetites whetted, good matches would go down smooth.

"You want I should call a taxi for you?" Ortíz asked.

"I don't want to waste the money."

"Hey, it's on me, Kelly."

Vidal was already out the door. Kelly got up. His bag and jacket were inside a stall with a broken toilet. Ortíz's money went in Kelly's pocket. "You already paid me. And I'm not fuckin' crippled," Kelly said. "I'll take myself out."

"Hey, *amigo*," Ortíz said, "I might have something for you next month, you heal up okay. You want I should let you know?"

A month would give the cuts time to close and the bruises to fade. Every dollar in Kelly's pocket would be gone, too. The only constant was the demand for gringo blood.

"Yeah, okay," Kelly said, and he left.

It was hot and still light on the street. Kelly could have gone right to bed. People outside the fights — too proper to care, or too sophisticated to admit it — didn't understand what a fighter gave up in the ring. Every drop of sweat had a cost and every punch thrown or taken did, too. Kelly was tired because he was all paid out.

He left the smoker behind. Old cars crowded the broken curb on both sides of the street. Rows of fight notices were pasted up beside the entrance. Even out here Kelly still heard the spectators hollering.

Kelly didn't have a car, old or not. He drove a slate-gray Buick down from El Paso five years before and sold it for a hundred bucks and some Mexican mud. He was already so bent that the *culero* paid him half what he promised and Kelly didn't notice until it was too late. So he walked, bag over his shoulder, and kept his swollen face pointed toward the pavement. Juárez had plenty of buses.

He stopped two blocks down to spend some of his money. A little bar with a jukebox playing *norteño* beckoned Kelly inside. He had six bottles of Tecate, one after the other, and that took the hurt off some. The alcohol stung a cut in his mouth. He was the only white man in the place; the rest were rough brown men who worked with their hands under the sun or with machines in the *maquiladoras*. They ignored Kelly and that was fine.

"*Oye*," Kelly asked the bartender. "You know where I can find some *motivosa*? *¿Entiende?*"

The bartender pointed. The bar was long and narrow and lit mostly with strings of big-bulb Christmas lights. Posters for the *corridas*, the bullfights, were on the walls beside pictures and license plates and any other junk they could put up with a nail. Booths with high backs marched all the way back to the *baños*.

Kelly checked each booth until somebody made eye contact. He put his bag in first and sat down next to it. "*Motivosa*," he said to the woman.

"How much you looking for?" the woman asked. She was flabby and braless and wore an unflattering shell-pink top that showed too much arm and neckline.

Kelly put a couple of Ortíz's twenties on the table between them. "Keep me busy."

The woman took Kelly's money and stuffed it into her shirt. From somewhere under the table she produced a shallow plastic baggie of grass. Kelly put the baggie away. "You that white boy they like to knock around at *el boxeo*, eh?" the woman asked.

"What of it?" Kelly asked.

"Next time you around, come see me."

"What for?"

The woman smiled. She had even, white teeth. Kelly realized they were dentures. "I like *boxeadores*," she said. "Next time you come around, I get you relaxed."

Kelly got up. "That's what I get the herb for."

●

Kelly Courter wasn't a good-looking man. He'd seen uglier, both inside and outside the fight world, but he wasn't a model and that was okay with him. Kelly's nose had a crook in it and bent slightly. Even when he didn't have raccoon eyes he always looked tired because he always felt tired; his body was older than he was.

At thirty he felt like a grandpa getting out of bed in the morning—all aches and protesting joints and sore muscles—and more decrepit still on the day after a fight. He carried too much weight around his middle and his hair was falling out, so he shaved his face and head once a month and let it all grow at the same rate.

He lived in an apartment building ten minutes away from the border crossing into Texas. Just a few miles, a line of police and a mostly dry riverbed separated Kelly in Ciudad Juárez from El Paso. Standing on a street in Juárez with closed eyes, just listening to the sound of Spanish, the rush of cars and smelling exhaust, it was easy to pretend the cities were the same, but Kelly didn't go north anymore.

His apartment had a concrete balcony. Kelly kept a heavy bag there, though he rarely hit it. For Ortíz's smokers Kelly didn't need to be in shape and didn't need to keep his skills sharp; all he had to do was show up more or less at weight and take a pounding. That he could do. That was what he had left.

He put his stuff in the bedroom and because the air was still went out on the balcony to roll a magic carpet. Sitting in a folding lawn chair with an old, chipped plate for an ashtray, he had a perfect view of a *maquiladora* that turned out automobile seats for GM. Night and day the seats came off the assembly line and went into truck-portable cargo containers for shipment back across the border. Wages started at a buck an hour and topped out before hitting three.

Mexican weed bought away from the tourist traps was always better than anything a man could find on the other side. Some Canadians told Kelly once that their marijuana was primo, but he didn't believe it. Call it *malva*, *chora* or *nalga de angel*, Mexico grew the best shit; if Kelly was going to *acostarse con rosemaria*, go to bed with rosemary, he would do it south-of-the-border style.

The marijuana took the edge off. He didn't even feel his heartbeat in his nose anymore. Kelly kicked his shoes off and let his bare feet rest on the cement. The car-seat *maquiladora* was lit up like a parade float at Disney World and was pure entertainment.

Once upon a lifetime ago, Kelly got mixed up with heavier stuff and learned to love the needle. He kept it up until he couldn't even think straight anymore and ended up sweating and puking and shaking in a Juárez hospital for four weeks. On the outside and broke all over again, he swore he wouldn't touch that shit for the rest of his life, and he hadn't. Now he stuck with the *mota*.

The smoke wanted to put him to sleep, but Kelly was a soldier; he finished the joint before he went to bed. Without bothering to change out of his street clothes, he sprawled across the mattress, pulled the sheet over his chest and slept.

THREE

OVERNIGHT THE SWELLING CAME up on his face and his nose was more bent than usual. Under a lukewarm shower, Kelly straightened it out as best he could and let fresh blood swirl down the drain. He ate a monster breakfast to make up for lost calories. The sliding glass door to the balcony was open and he heard the whistle for the morning shift. Working Juárez had places to go and things to do, but Kelly Courter had some free time.

For a fighter it was better to run, but Kelly walked because he didn't have stamina for anything else anymore. He put on his sneakers and locked up the apartment and headed out. He saw no one because everybody was at work. The only people without jobs in Ciudad Juárez were the very old and very young and sometimes they worked, too, if there was money to be had.

Deeper into Mexico the people got poorer and living conditions rotted away with them. Juárez was a little better because since 1964 it had the *maquiladoras*: factories turning out everything from tote bags to engine parts, mostly for American companies. Like most fighters on the Mexico side, Kelly used Reyes boxing gear, and all that was made in the *maquiladoras*, too.

Wages in the factories were criminal and the cost of living in a city like Juárez was higher than the interior, but for the most part it evened out. Ciudad Juárez had its shantytowns and hellholes in the *colonias populares*, but the *maquiladoras* kept them from taking over. A family could live here. The air was dirty and the city was crowded. There was crime and death, too — more now than ever before — but there were parks and schools and paved roads. Even though many *maquiladoras* were losing business and their production heading to China because even Mexican goods weren't cheap enough for Wal-Mart.

Kelly had been to Tijuana and didn't like the filthy streets and circus atmosphere. Over in Nuevo Laredo it was nothing but whorehouses and bars and places to buy worthless tourist bullshit. He settled in Ciudad Juárez because it seemed enough like home, but wasn't, and partly because it worked out that way. Things were changing with all the bloodthirsty *traficantes* moving their business farther and farther north and east, but Kelly wasn't going anywhere.

He walked a mile and then two. He sweated under his shirt, took off his jacket and tied the sleeves around his waist. His face was hidden under a cap and sunglasses, but anyone looking closely would see the beating he took. Fresh tape on his nose was a dead giveaway.

Kelly walked all the way to El Centro, skipping the buses in favor of roadwork, though they roared by at regular intervals and blasted him with hot exhaust. Kelly hadn't been behind the wheel of any kind of vehicle since he sold that Buick. Driving was no good anyway, especially when the streets were so thick with traffic that he passed block after block of cars and trucks baking in the sun and sweating out the people inside. On foot he could move. On foot he was free. He didn't want to be trapped or singled out, and pedestrians seemed to be invisible to everyone with wheels.

El Club Kentucky was his stop. He dashed across the street and got a horn and a curse for it. It was cool under the bar's green awning and milder still inside. The ceiling was high and lined with heavy wooden beams. A few chandeliers with yellow lights, fake candles, dangled overhead, but most of the light came by way of the street glare.

Only a few men were there at this hour in the middle of the week. Kelly took a stool at a dark-varnished oak bar that stretched all the way to the back. A TV showed *fútbol*, but the screen was over Kelly's head so he couldn't watch even if he wanted to.

The Kentucky was almost a hundred years old, but it was in good shape because customers and money kept coming in. They said Bob Dylan drank there and Marilyn Monroe, too. The bar fixtures were as old as the place: big, serious-looking wood and glass and age-foggy mirrors. The bartender was an old man wearing an apron. He gave Kelly a Tecate in the bottle with a little bowl of lime slices.

"*¿Dónde está Estéban?*" Kelly asked the bartender.

"*¿Quién sabe?*" the bartender replied.

Kelly had beer and lime and waited. If it were later in the year, he'd see what tickets to the bullfights were available and lay out for cheap seats he could hustle to drunken *turistas* who didn't know they could just walk in and get better views for less money.

Estéban didn't show for over an hour and two beers later. He passed Kelly without seeing him but when Kelly called his name, Estéban turned around like he wasn't surprised at all. "Hey, *carnal. ¿Que onda?*" Estéban asked. "Where you been, man?"

Estéban took the stool next to Kelly. He was lighter than Kelly and shorter, but his skin was blasted deep brown by genes and time in prison work crews on the American side. He wore sunglasses, but took them off inside. Kelly kept his on.

"I been around," Kelly said. "Lookin' for you."

"Hey, I ain't hard to find. What happened to your face? You been at *el boxeo* again? When you going to learn, man?"

"I guess never," Kelly said. "What you drinking?"

"Gonna spend big today, huh? I'll have a *cerveza* if you're buyin'."

Kelly ordered a Tecate for Estéban and another for himself. The bartender brought fresh limes.

"It's that *puto* Ortíz," Estéban complained to Kelly. "People he knows... you don't want to be no part of that world."

"I just want to lace up my gloves," Kelly said. He wished Estéban would stop talking about it. "I don't want to fuck the guy."

"Everybody he fucks, you fuck," Estéban returned.

"That doesn't make any goddamned sense."

"To you, maybe not."

They drank. Finally Kelly asked, "You got someone else carrying for you?"

Estéban put his hand over his heart. "What you thinking, man? I been on vacation for a few days, you think I forgot all about you? I ain't some asshole; I know about loyalty."

"Well, I took that fight because I couldn't find you. Rent don't pay itself," Kelly said.

"I was down in Mazatlán for a while to see my cousin get hitched. Me and Paloma both. You offending me, man."

Kelly finished his beer. "I don't want to argue; I want to get some work."

"What, like Ortíz gets you work?"

"Shut up about him."

"Hey, all right," Estéban said. He clapped Kelly on the shoulder. "Listen: I'm back in town and I gots plenty of stuff for you. In fact, I was goin' to call you today and see if you wanted to carry some shit for me."

"What kind of shit?"

"The usual kind of shit. Don't bust my balls, okay?"

Kelly signaled the bartender for another beer. He put some money on the rail and the old man made it disappear. A fresh bottle of Tecate came, still sweating water from the cooler. "Okay," he told Estéban. "Tell me when and where."

FOUR

MORE THAN CHEAP FACTORY GOODS crossed the border from Ciudad Juárez into the States. Too many trucks and too many people meant too many places for dope to hide. The cops tried their best to catch the crooks, but it was a losing battle. More than that: it was a rout. Now the hardcore *traficantes*, the ones that came up in places like Mexico City, were even taking their fights and their weapons into Arizona, New Mexico and Texas.

Estéban's product was weed, but he handled a little *gumersinda* from time to time. He knew Kelly was off the hard stuff, so when raw heroin came through he had one of his brown runners take care of it. Estéban showed respect for Kelly that way, and that was why they kept on together. That and because of Paloma.

Kelly carried a Reyes gym bag with boxing gear on top and a kilo of weed underneath. A setup like that could never make it past the border guards with their dogs and checklist of suspicious parcels, but for a gringo walking around here it was nothing a cop would glance at twice. Maybe not even once when Kelly had been through the grinder like the night before.

He came north, this time by bus, and then walked the rest of the way to a neighborhood so close to the border that he saw the lights of El Paso clearly. Every night was party night on these blocks, with white-boy tourist trash circling around the strip clubs and legal brothels getting drunker and drunker until they staggered back across the downtown bridge with their wallets and their pockets picked clean.

People knew Kelly here; at least enough to let him pass without trying to sell him fake Cuban cigars, flowers, Mexican fly and everything else under the sun. While the rest of Ciudad Juárez settled down for dinner and bed, these blocks hopped. This was where the city came close to being like all the other *turista* carnivals along the border, and why Kelly only came here when he was being paid.

The place was La Posada del Indio, the Inn of the Indian in English. A large animated neon cartoon Indian, complete with feather headdress of the kind never seen south of the border, marked the door. Inside it was no inn and was barely a saloon: tiny stage for a single dancing girl, a compact bar with two men doubling as bartenders and pimps, plus a dozen tables around which girls constantly circulated.

Kelly bought an overpriced *cerveza* from the bar. He didn't attract a swarm of girls, either because of his looks or because they knew the score; La Posada del Indio was a good place to get business done, and the men who came for money instead of pussy had a certain air about them.

"*¿Usted está buscando el hombre gordo?*" the bartender asked Kelly.

"How did you know?" Kelly asked.

"He was waiting. You're here."

Kelly shrugged, but now Estéban would have to come up with a new place for a drop; they knew Kelly too well here. "So where is he?"

"He was waiting a long time. He got a girl."

Kelly looked around the place for a fat man. Because it was midweek, most of the faces here were Mexican brown and bodies working-lean under the florid lights. Coming closer to the weekend the complexion would shift and the men would get doughier. There would be more cash changing hands, too.

"You want to get your dick sucked?" the bartender asked. "There is a girl, she's new. She won't mind your face."

"No, thanks," Kelly said. He unconsciously touched the tape on his nose. Even now, after a handful of aspirin, his face throbbed with his heartbeat. "What room did the fat man get?"

The bartender told him. Kelly finished his beer and went out the front door. A narrow alley brought him to the next street where a ramshackle apartment building with rusty iron balustrades sulked in darkness. Women and girls moved up and down concrete steps, leading men in and sending them away.

Kelly ignored the women and they did the same for him. In the bar they were selling, but back here it was business. He went to the third floor and rapped on the last door. He heard nothing from inside until a short, dumpy prostitute opened the door and then the sound of a television game show reached Kelly's ears.

The woman was topless, dark skinned and had a heavy-featured, almost Indian look. She didn't smile at Kelly. "What do you want?" she asked.

"He's lookin' for me, honey."

Kelly saw the fat man on a little bed in the room. Light from the television made him seem pasty and blue. He reclined with his pants down around his knees and his cock was somewhere under a heavy pudding of fat.

He covered himself up when Kelly came in. The man wore a Texas State shirt half buttoned with a sweaty white tee underneath. Everything about him was large and fatty, including his hands. The woman put her blouse on.

"You want me to come back when you're done?" Kelly asked the fat man.

"Nah."

The fat man paid the woman off. They squabbled about the price because he hadn't popped his nut. Kelly stood in the corner of the little room and stared into the bathroom; too small for a tub, it had a standing shower infested with roaches. A thick, brown carpet of shiny palmetto bugs gathered in the center around the drain. Kelly wondered whether they would scatter if he turned on the light over the sink and if they did, where they might go.

"You only going to pay *me* half?" Kelly asked the fat man.

"You got the full kilo?"

"Sure."

"Then I got no complaints. Let's see it."

They left the television on and didn't switch on a lamp. In the flicker of the tube, Kelly brought out the *motivosa* tightly wrapped in four flat packets of plastic film. He put the packets on the bed. The fat man took a roll of hundreds out of his pocket and counted out twenty. Then he took off his Texas State shirt.

"Want me to call the girl back?" Kelly asked.

"Funny," the fat man said. He removed his T-shirt. His body wasn't hairy, but it looked like it was melting; great folds of pallid flesh drooped from his frame. He had breasts bigger than a stripper.

Kelly took the two grand and recounted it. He put it in his breast pocket, zipped up his bag and prepared to leave. This was the awkward part; some buyers liked to chat, others were all about getting the hell out of there. Kelly preferred the latter. "You're not gonna put it in a belt, are you?" he asked. "They watch for that."

"Nah," the fat man said. He palmed one packet of weed in one hand and lifted a roll with the other. Kelly imagined a musty smell. "Got my own safety deposit box."

The fat man stowed the weed and put his shirts back on. Kelly couldn't tell the difference.

"It's a pleasure," Kelly said at last. "I'm gonna go."

"See you next time," the fat man said. "I'm Frank."

"Good luck, Frank," Kelly said and he left.

His chances of seeing Frank again were slim. Every white guy with a dream of making a quick buck on a hop across the border had to try running a little *motivosa*, and the odds were good, but when the first batch sold and it was time for another run, nerves got the better of them. Would they make it? Could they make it? What if they didn't make it? And that was that; the head game was harder than the deal.

Smart buyers and sellers used cutouts to divide the risk. The ones that came over themselves, like Frank, were amateurs. But so long as the money was good, there were no complaints from Estéban.

Kelly took a taxi home because it was late and he had money in his pocket. The ride was only five bucks.

In this neighborhood people went to bed early and got up before sunrise. All-night parties were for gringos and losers; around here people worked for a living, and they worked hard. To stay out of the city's temporary suburbs of particleboard, cinder blocks and plastic everyone in a family had to work hard. It was the way.

He put the outside light on, just a bare yellow bulb without a fancy cover, and went inside to wait. He had beer in the little fridge and drank until his legs felt heavy and relaxed.

Paloma knocked after midnight. Kelly let her in.

Maybe she wasn't beautiful, but she was everything Kelly liked. She had wide hips and a full body that stupid men up north would call chunky. Kelly liked her short hair and her tan skin. He liked the way she smelled.

"Hi," Kelly said.

"*Dinero*," Paloma replied.

Kelly gave her the money. "You owe me extra for cab ride."

"Pay your own cab fare," Paloma said. She counted out the cash. She wore snug jeans and kept a wallet in her back pocket like a man. The two thousand went up front. She paid Kelly from the wallet.

Kelly found extra for the cab, after all. "Thanks," he said. "I don't like the buses at night."

"Cabs are a rip-off," Paloma said. "You got any more of that beer?"

"Help yourself."

Kelly sat on one end of a ratty convertible couch. Paloma sat on the other. They drank and looked at each other for a while. Kelly felt her eyes on his bruises.

"You look like shit, Kelly."

"I got to make a living. You and Estéban were out of town."

Paloma nodded. She drank beer like her brother: hard from the bottle and no flinching. Kelly hadn't ever seen her smoke a joint or touch a needle. These were also things he liked about her. "Our cousin Ines got married."

"That's what Estéban said. How was it?"

"Better than *your* weekend."

Kelly laughed. Paloma smiled. She had dimples and white, white teeth.

They sat a while and Paloma told him about the wedding. Mazatlán was on the Pacific coast and was beautiful all year round. Kelly saw cliff-divers there once and ate so much fresh fruit over a weeklong visit that he felt like a health nut gone wild. Compared to Ciudad Juárez it was tiny, but the air was cleaner and the streets less crowded. Kelly might have lived there, but Mazatlán was a retreat, not a place to make a home. He didn't really understand why Juárez was one and Mazatlán the other, and not the other way around.

Paloma talked about vows taken in the shade of a white tent on the beach with a view of the old lighthouse. Dancing and drinking and eating followed. And family arguments and embarrassing drunkenness. "I would have invited you," Paloma told Kelly. "But Estéban said you wouldn't come."

"Not my thing," Kelly lied.

"Next time," Paloma said.

"Sure."

The beer didn't last and neither did the wedding stories. Paloma got up to turn off the light and came to Kelly on the couch. He lifted her blouse in the dark. Paloma had small breasts and when Kelly put his mouth on them he felt the little steel barbells in her nipples on his tongue. She had other piercings elsewhere — in her tongue and at her navel. The stitched wool of a green scapular around her neck fell against him when they kissed.

Kelly was sore, but Paloma was careful. She did the work, put him inside her and set the pace. Kelly loved the sound of her breath in his ear when it quickened, and her hair in his face. He put his hands on her hips; let his fingers sink into her flesh. The smell of her was stronger than the fresh scent of beer.

"I'm close," Kelly said.

Paloma lifted herself off Kelly and knelt between his legs. Her grip on his was tight, insistent and her mouth was searing. He felt her tongue stud on him. When he came, she swallowed. Afterward they lay together on the couch. Drying perspiration kept them cool.

For the first time that night, Paloma touched Kelly's face, but delicately. "When are you going to stop fighting?" she asked him.

"Whenever they stop paying me."

"I don't like it when you get your nose broken. How are you supposed to eat my pussy?"

Kelly smiled in the dark. "Who says I was going to?"

Paloma hit him on the shoulder, but not hard. "You better, *cabrón*!"

"I know. I'll go down for an hour when I'm better."

"If you got to do it more than ten minutes, you're not doing it right," Paloma said, and laughed. "Maybe that's the problem."

"Oh, fuck you."

He was tired and the alcohol was working on him. His mind drifted and he fell asleep. When he woke up, the sun showed through the windows and he was alone. A quilt from the closet was draped over him from the waist down.

Kelly showered and had beer and eggs for breakfast. Paloma didn't leave a note, but she never did. Later he would call her, or maybe he would catch a bus and surprise her for *comida corrida* in the afternoon. Mexicans ate late and so did Kelly. In the meantime he walked. He had money in his pocket and nowhere to be.

At the end of the long row of apartment buildings a telephone pole was painted pink halfway up its length. Black crosses of electrical tape were fixed to it and below them a forest of multicolored flyers stirred whenever the wind blew.

Kelly saw a woman at the pole tacking up a new flyer. She was gone by the time he reached her and he stopped to see what she left behind. A photocopied picture of a teenage girl on green paper smiled out at him. Her name was Rosalina Amelia Ernestina Flores. She seemed too young to work, but that was the *Norteamericano* in Kelly thinking; in Mexico there was hardly such a thing as *too young to work*. Rosalina made turn signals in a *maquiladora* for a German car company. She had been missing for two weeks.

¡Justicia para Rosalina! the flyer said.

Other flyers overlapped Rosalina's, other girls and other faces. Flyers were two or three deep. All pleaded for *justicia*: justice for Rosalina; justice for Yessenia; justice for Jovita. There were so many that the city had a name for them: *las muertas de Juárez*, the dead women of Juárez, because they were all certainly gone and gone forever.

"*Excúseme, señor. ¿Usted ha visto a mi hija?*"

Kelly turned away from Rosalina and her sisters. He saw the woman again. She had a fistful of photocopies on green paper. She looked old in the misleading way the working poor of Juárez often did; she was probably not forty.

"*¿Usted ha visto a mi hija?*" the woman asked again.

"*No la he visto. Lo siento.*"

The woman nodded as if she expected nothing different. She walked down the block and stopped at another telephone pole. A flyer there would be torn down by the end of the day, but she had to know that and Kelly didn't feel right saying so. Only the notices on the pink-painted pole were untouchable.

FIVE

MUJERES SIN VOCES HAD A SMALL office on the second floor of a ramshackle building housing a pharmacy, a chiropractor and a smoke shop. Bright pastel-colored paint chipped and peeled from plain concrete walls. Signage was blasted white by endless days of sun. Somewhere along the line the foundation settled unevenly, so the whole structure leaned.

The office door was painted bright pink and had three locks. The word *justicia* was stenciled at waist height in rough black. Self-adhesive numbers marked the address, but no sign or label announced the occupants.

Kelly knocked once and let himself in. Two desks and a trio of battered filing cabinets crowded the small front room. The back of the office was used for storing paint and paper and wood and signs. Once a month the members of Mujeres Sin Voces – Women Without Voices – dressed in black and gathered near the Paso del Norte International Bridge crossing into El Paso. With posters and banners on sticks, they paraded silently along rows of idling cars waiting to enter the United States. They reminded the *turistas* that while *they* came to Mexico for a party, women were dying.

Paloma used the desk closest to the office's single window. She was here four times a week, sometimes alone, sometimes with another member of the group. When Mujeres Sin Voces marched, she marched with them. A dusty box fan turned in the window, circulating warm air. The group had one secondhand computer with an internet connection and a bulky, hideous IBM Selectric typewriter, the kind with a golfball-shaped element. Ella Arellano was the group's typist, though she could only hunt and peck with two fingers.

The women looked up when Kelly entered. Ella was younger by a few years than Paloma and skinnier. Her sister was one of the dead women of Juárez, gone for more than ten years. She smiled at Kelly. She spoke no English. "*Buenos días*," Kelly told her.

"*Buenos días*, Señor Kelly," Ella said.

"What are you doing here?" Paloma asked Kelly.

"I thought maybe we could get something to eat."

"We're busy right now; the president's coming next month. We have to be ready for him."

The walls of the office were like the pink telephone poles, littered several layers deep with flyers demanding *justicia, justicia, justicia*. By tradition, missing women were never referred to as *dead*, but this was just a way of keeping the faith. Sometimes families kept on the charade even after the bodies were found. Some part of that annoyed Kelly, but he couldn't say why.

"I just want an hour," Kelly said. He sounded more irritated than he meant to, and the swelling in his nose pitched his voice up a notch.

Paloma frowned at him. "*¿Tú tendrá todo razón sin mí*, Ella?"

"I will be fine."

"One hour," Paloma told Kelly sternly.

She got her purse. They left the office. Out in the sun, Kelly saw she'd put dark red highlights in her hair. She wore a bright yellow pullover that blazed against the color of her skin. Kelly realized he loved her, but he couldn't say so; Paloma wouldn't want him to.

"You should call first before you come," Paloma said.

They walked up the block to a restaurant popular with the locals. The place and the neighborhood were too far off the beaten track to draw tourists.

The restaurant had no menus for the big meal. The inside was too crowded, but they found a place outside in the semi-shade, sharing a picnic table and benches with a quartet of men wearing street-construction vests and hard hats. They talked to each other in rapid Spanish. Kelly and Paloma used English.

"I wanted to surprise you," Kelly said.

"I know."

"*Sorry*," Kelly said, though he wasn't.

"I know. Forget about it."

A short, apple-shaped woman brought them deep bowls of *pozole*. Mexicans had plenty of different ways to make the stuff, but the base was always hominy. This cook prepared *pozole* with pig's feet, slices of avocado and raw onion and a garnish of chilis. A wedge of lime took away the heat when the spice got to be too much.

They ate in silence for a while. The men at the table seemed to sense the tension and they left as soon as they could. No one took their place, though the restaurant bustled.

"You look better today," Paloma told Kelly at last.

"Yeah?"

"Yeah. But your nose isn't going to heal right. I can see it now."

Kelly resisted the urge to touch his face. He shrugged. "It was fucked up already."

Paloma sighed and shook her head. Kelly didn't have to ask what she was thinking; they had argued over it enough times.

Empty bowls were replaced by a serving of tortilla soup. The heat and the spice of this and the *pozole* made Kelly's nose run and he could feel his bruised sinuses opening up. Food like this was good for the belly and good for healing. Watching Paloma eat was a pleasure because she ate heartily, but still like a woman. It was the same way she made love.

"Estéban wants to know what you're doing tomorrow night," Paloma said.

"I'll have to check my calendar."

"Don't be an asshole."

"Okay, I'm not doing anything. What does he want to do?"

"Get drunk. Smoke *hierba*. What else?"

"Weed pays the bills," Kelly said. He used his napkin to wipe his lips. A fresh throbbing started in his nose, but it was the good pain of swelling going down; he'd been through this often enough to know.

"He should sell it, not smoke it."

"I'll tell him that."

"I said don't be an asshole."

Kelly finished his soup. He changed the subject: "I saw a new flyer today."

"Rosalina?" Paloma asked.

"You know about her?"

"We heard."

"Do you think—"

"Kelly," Paloma interrupted, "you don't have to talk about that if you don't want to."

"I'm just trying to be interested."

"I know, and that's good, but it's… don't worry about it."

A shadow passed over Paloma's expression and Kelly realized it had been there all along, only he hadn't noticed. She seemed distracted, but not by the food or his condition. He was angry at the office and the flyers all over again; Paloma was meant to shine.

"I was thinking about Mazatlán," Kelly said. "Maybe next month we could go together. Get a room at that one hotel on the beach. You remember that one? It has those two swimming pools by the restaurant?"

Paloma reached across the table and took Kelly's hand. Kelly imagined he could feel her darkness in her touch. "I remember," she said.

"It doesn't have to be too long. Just a couple of days if you want."

"I'd like that."

"You would?"

"Yes, okay?"

"Good."

The little fat woman came to their table with the main course. The *corrida comida* wasn't called "the big meal" for nothing. Paloma pulled away from Kelly and for the rest of their time together they were more concerned with eating than talking.

SIX

Estéban came by early, driving a dusty white truck with a flat bed. Kelly rode shotgun and they started drinking cold bottles of Tecate from a Styrofoam cooler before they got to where they were headed.

Kelly didn't know whose idea it was to build a massive skate park in Ciudad Juárez, but it was built and the skaters came. It was a broad, open space at the edge of the city that looked like a moonscape of cement craters. A massive tower of concrete stood at the center, looming sixty feet into the air alongside a winding framework of metal and wood steps. All day long climbers mounted one side while others rappelled down the other to the echoing sound of clattering skateboards and shouting.

White concrete blinded and reflected heat. In the middle of the day Parque Extremo was punishingly hot. It was possible to lose pounds just sweating it out in the half-pipes and skating ponds.

Neither Kelly nor Estéban skated, but this was their drinking spot. The politicians who celebrated the park's grand opening had a lot to say about health and safety and keeping kids off drugs, but the smell of *motivosa* was as common as the odor of wholesome perspiration. Skater punks from the US came to show off their skills and score at the same time. Sometimes Kelly and Estéban sold here.

They bought some tamales from a snack vendor and sat underneath a metal awning to watch a trio of Mexican kids run their BMX bikes up the sides of a nine-foot practice pond. The kids hit the upper lip and caught big air before crashing down wheels-first for another run. Kelly liked the rubbing buzz of the bike wheels on cement, but not the bone-jarring rattle of metal returning to earth. *That* took him back to something he would rather forget but could not. A part of Kelly wondered whether he agreed to come here for the reminder.

The tamales were good: spicy and filling. Kelly and Estéban ate with their hands, spinning the packed, corn-meal cylinders of the tamales out of their cornhusk jackets. Some people liked to pour sauce over theirs, but Kelly enjoyed a tamale eaten plain and Estéban shared his tastes in most things, including this.

They filled up and had some more beer. The BMX kids moved on. Kelly and Estéban stared at the empty practice pond. "Why did you tell Paloma I wouldn't come with you to Mazatlán?" Kelly asked at last.

"You know why."

"No, I don't, or I wouldn't ask," Kelly said, and he looked right at Estéban.

"Hey, don't to make me feel bad, man. You know I love you. But *nuestra familia*, they got some – how do you want to call it? – they got some old-fashioned ideas in their heads."

Kelly turned away. He looked over to the next practice pond, where a group of skateboarders, Mexican and white, traded stunts on steep concrete walls. He considered getting up and moving closer, but there was no good shade there and he was comfortable already.

Estéban continued: "I see you, I see a good guy. Paloma, she loves you. But you know how some *vieja gente* can get with white boys. And my sister is *una mujer fina*; she deserves the best."

"I know," Kelly said, and he knew before Estéban explained. He wondered why he asked in the first place, knowing the answer was just going to make him feel lousy. The tamales didn't sit right anymore, huddled in the pit of his belly.

"Maybe next time," Estéban said.

"Next time. Sure," Kelly replied. It was as though he were talking with Paloma about it all over again. He stood and stretched, but put his hands on the wooden crossbeam rather than on the corrugated aluminum roof of the awning; the metal was hot enough to sear meat.

"I tell you one thing," Estéban said after the silence grew too long, "you got to stop putting your face in front of those young *boxeadores*. Ain't you ugly enough?"

"I got to be *handsome* now?"

"No, but you can't get nobody's respect looking like you got hit by a truck. I don't know how Paloma can look at you. I wouldn't kiss nobody look like you do. People talk, man. They call you 'Frankenstein.'"

"That's funny. What people?"

"Ain't no joke, homes. Just people. Paloma, she has *respecto*. More than you or me."

Kelly nodded, but said nothing. He finished off his bottle and rooted around in the slush of the cooler for a fresh one. Bending over he felt the booze in his head, a good kind of sleepy and stupid that a strong batch of *motivosa* could bring on in a hurry. It was where he liked to be.

"But I tell you," Estéban said, "you two get married, no matter what no one says on their own, they won't disrespect you on your wedding day. That's not the way we do it."

"You won't take me to see some cousin get married, but I can be your *cuñado*?" Kelly asked.

"No, no, listen to me: that will show them: when you put on a white suit and get your blessing from the padre under the eyes of God, you'll be as brown as my ass," Estéban said.

"That's pretty goddamned brown," Kelly said. He sat down again.

"Fuck you, man," Estéban said without malice.

"Yeah, fuck me," Kelly said.

SEVEN

HE WOKE BEFORE THE SUN CAME up and lay on his bed in the dark thinking about everything and nothing. Usually when he stirred out of sleep this early he'd bumble around with the lights off, and smoke a cigarette (or something stronger) until the day really started. This time when he rose, he brushed his teeth and washed his face. He looked at himself in the mirror. "Frankenstein," he said out loud.

Kelly put on some sweats and went outside.

Mexico is hot and the border is no exception, but Ciudad Juárez is a city in the desert and deserts grow very cold at night no matter what the season. The dirty exhaust of the *maquiladoras* trapped heat and grit close to the ground, but even dozens of smokestacks couldn't defeat the forces of nature; Kelly saw his breath in the air.

Stretching made his legs and back hurt, but not so badly that he felt like stopping what he was doing… whatever he was doing. His calves were especially tight. He had muscle from walking, but no flexibility. He couldn't remember the last time he could touch his toes without having to bend his knees.

Lights were on and people were on the street. There were many women traveling together for safety as much as company. Some wore surgical masks, an echo of the swine flu scare. Occasionally a *maquiladora* bus rumbled down the main thoroughfare splitting Kelly's neighborhood. In the States the buses would be lit up from the inside, but this was Mexico and pennies mattered, so riders sat in the dark.

Kelly sucked in deep lungfuls of air through his busted, healing nose and blew out through his mouth. He did this twice before a coughing fit snaked up from the bottom of his lungs and doubled him over. He hacked up a glob of something nasty and spat it on the sidewalk. The sky in the east turned red.

This time when he breathed deep he didn't cough. His lungs felt shallow, and though Kelly tried to let the air fill him up from belly to sternum, he could tell he'd lost a lot of his capacity. Five years seemed like ten.

He forced himself to breathe in and out, hard and full, until his ribs ached and early-morning colors grew vivid at the edge of hyperventilation. When his lungs were as saturated as he could get them, Kelly ran.

Compared to his memories of running, this was nothing; he picked up an earnest, low-speed shuffle that wasn't much faster than a brisk walk. Almost immediately he began to sweat and his body demanded more air to feed his rapid heartbeat, but he knew he had to keep his breathing even for as long as possible, or everything would spin out of kilter and he'd have to stop sooner rather than later.

The pink telephone pole came up quickly, aglow in the first rays of the sun. The numberless flyers demanding *justicia* fluttered as Kelly passed, as if trying to draw his attention away from silly pursuits and into their world of the dead. Kelly managed to make it to the end of the block before he had to stop, the telephone pole twenty yards behind him and a broad street busy even at this hour with the traffic of business.

Kelly put his hands on his knees, his sternum throbbing with his struggling heart. A wave of nausea passed over him, but it wasn't as bad or as long as he feared it would be. A few feet away in a concrete bus shelter a dozen woman in *maquila* uniforms – neat, plain blouse and pants and rubber shoes – watched him as the sun chased away the veiling shadows. They didn't laugh or point; Mexicans were not as rude as gringos.

He straightened up and ran some more, past the bus shelter and along an uneven sidewalk in the shade of apartment blocks just like Kelly's. Again he had to stop, this time in the parking lot of a tiny convenience store beside a *taquería*. He coughed like he had before and spat up another gooey mouthful of something foul. The taste made him gag.

Three more times he pushed himself to run until he felt his pulse beating in his gums and everything hurt too much to continue. He finally came to rest on a low bridge crossing a broad concrete flood ditch. Sitting on a cement buttress, he let the wind from passing trucks whip him. The sun was free of the horizon now and the night chill evaporated.

If there was a constant in Juárez, it was trucks: going to the *maquiladoras* or coming back from the *maquiladoras*. When the streets jammed up with American cars trying to escape north from their holiday destination, the trucks were always with them, spewing black diesel smoke as they idled, sweaty drivers behind the wheel, lungs turning to asphalt with every breath.

From where Kelly sat he could see the same line of factories just visible from his apartment. From a distance they were all the same, but stamped on the boxes in the backs of all those trucks were American names. Kelly had GM practically on his doorstep. Out there it was easy to find General Electric, Honeywell, Du Pont, even Amway. Kelly thought maybe *this* was why he stayed here; so much of America lived right across the border that it was possible to be in two places at once. Kind of.

In the end his pulse stilled and his stomach settled. His lungs no longer burned. Kelly hopped down from his perch. The urge to run had passed, so he walked like he always did, aware of new pains in his joints and muscles that hadn't been there before but feeling better about having them. He wondered whether this was what giving a shit was like; it had been so long, he didn't remember.

EIGHT

THE NEIGHBORHOOD WAS QUIET when Kelly returned. He heard a radio playing *norteño* somewhere. Kelly recognized the song: "Un Rinconcito En El Cielo," by Ramón Ayala y sus Bravos Del Norte. The song was called in English "A Little Corner in the Sky." It was about a man separated from his woman, and because they could not be together they would look on the same spot in the stars and be together in spirit.

Kelly thought it was sappy as hell, but Ayala and his band were huge in Mexico and in the States. They did their recording Stateside and lived there, too. Mexicans bought their own music back from American companies. Kelly didn't understand that, either.

He climbed the steps to his apartment and heard the voice of Eliseo Robles, Ayala's singer during the band's boom years, crooning over the bouncy accordion:

> *Un rinconcito en el cielo*
> *Juntos, unidos los dos*
> *Y cuando caiga la noche*
> *Te daré mi amor...*

Breakfast was as burly as if Kelly had fought the night before. He'd forgotten how ravenous he got after running. He ate to fill the hole in his belly and even washed dishes afterward.

He still had energy when normally he'd be tired. He prowled

the apartment and realized just how little he had to do; he was too keyed up for television and he hadn't listened to music since his CD player broke.

In the end he wrapped his hands and stepped out onto the balcony out back to hit the heavy bag. His first punches weren't much; just enough to put fist to leather and feel the firmness and weight behind it.

Kelly paid more attention to form than power. A real punch came from the hips, torquing the whole body behind the shoulder to apply mass that two knuckles on the punching hand didn't have. A good punch sounded a tone in the flesh like a deep, ringing bell. Out in the ring for Ortíz, taking hits and bleeding, he never felt the magic of a punch well thrown, but he could have it here if he could make his muscles remember the way.

Sweat came fast, and hard breathing, just like on his run. Kelly found himself holding his breath when he punched, and he reminded himself *breathe, breathe* after that. Punching without air sucked oxygen right out of the muscles. A fighter lost all his power without breathing right, and he could even pass out. Kelly wiped his forehead with the back of his arm.

He didn't want to punch himself out, but it felt good to do something the same way it felt good to get out there and run even though his lungs weren't up to it and his legs didn't have the power they ought. He worked the heavy bag until he felt weight in his arms that made it hard to throw punches correctly and then he stopped.

Across the plain of roofs he saw a line of trucks come out of the GM *maquiladora*. Below, at the foot of Kelly's building, a cat rummaged through tall grass and discarded junk – tires and boxes and half-broken cinderblocks – looking for a mouse or a lizard to eat. Kelly sucked air greedily. It was only when he stopped blowing that he went back inside, put his wet wraps over the back of a chair to dry and started a shower.

In the summer even the cold water wasn't completely cold.

Kelly soaked the oil and sweat from his body, stood with his hand underneath the spray and let his skull hang forward until the ligament at the base of his neck popped.

Endorphins still skidded around his system. He wouldn't feel any of this until tonight or tomorrow. Right now he only had the good tired and the pleasant ache of exertion. He enjoyed it for the same reason he avoided it all these years: because it reminded him of before.

After his shower he toweled off and lay on the bed letting the still, dry air wick away the last moisture from his skin. This, too, he'd forgotten for good or ill. He drowsed for a little while and then fell asleep for less than an hour before waking to a room that looked and felt exactly the same, as if time hadn't moved forward at all.

He felt different, and it wasn't just the mixture of energy and tiredness that followed a good workout and a better nap. Kelly vaguely recalled dreaming of Paloma and Estéban, too. The place and the happenings were mixed up in his memory and fading quickly, but he knew that everything he'd done this morning had to do with them.

The telephone rang. Kelly got up naked and left the bedroom. The thin carpet felt oily and gritty on his clean soles and he resolved to borrow a vacuum cleaner from Paloma to do something about that.

"Hello?" he answered.

"*Hola,*" Estéban said on the other end. "*¿Qué tal?*"

"Nothing," Kelly said.

"Hey, listen, I'm going shopping tonight. How's your face look?"

"All right," Kelly said. The bruises were pretty much gone, though his nose was still healing up on the inside. He didn't look like a zombie anymore.

"That's good. That's good. Hey, listen: you up for shopping?

Two, three hours and I'll cut you in for the usual. What do you say?"

Kelly looked around the apartment. It seemed too small to him now. Something was going on in his head and maybe getting out would cure it. "Okay," he said. "What time you want to meet?"

"Meet me at nine," Estéban said.

"Nine," Kelly said. "All right."

NINE

ANY NIGHT IN CIUDAD JUÁREZ WAS at least busy when it came to hookers and booze. It was too easy to cross the border and good times came too cheaply for workingmen in El Paso to say *no*, despite all the warnings about pickpockets and muggers and drug dealers and AIDS. They came over the walking bridge as daylight failed, sometimes straight from work, their trucks parked in clusters in lots laid out expressly for pleasure seekers headed south. Sometimes they were already a little bent and the idea of Mexico entered their brain through the bottom of a beer mug or in a shot of yellow-tinged tequila.

Shopping with Estéban happened on Fridays and Saturdays. These were the nights when the crowds were heaviest, the white faces most common, and cops had a harder time figuring out who was who and doing what.

They met outside the *farmacia* where the *turista* Juárez stopped and the Juárez of the *Juárenses* began. The place was open long hours, had broad aisles and a well-lit, clean atmosphere. A tacky green-and-red "trolley," just a bus made up to look like a streetcar, ferried Americans back and forth across the border in air-conditioned comfort and dumped them right on the doorstep. Around the *farmacia* the white people were mostly older and looking for cheap drugs to fill their American prescriptions, but there were plenty of younger folks, too, picking up steroids and Viagra and other things, things that kept the party going all night long.

Estéban came out of the *farmacia* with two plastic shopping bags. He crossed the street with Kelly and they sat down under the orangey splash of a streetlight to get ready. Kelly saw a flyer tacked to the lamppost: *justicia*.

"Put five pills in a baggie," Estéban told Kelly. "The price stays the same, okay?"

"Okay," Kelly said.

From one shopping bag came little self-sealing plastic baggies of the kind soccer moms used to pack their kids' lunch snacks in: too small for a sandwich, but just right for a serving of goldfish-shaped crackers or, in this case, five capsules of OxyContin or hydrocodone. The drugs were in the second shopping bag in clean little orange-plastic bottles with neatly printed labels.

They divvied up the score. Kelly wore loose pants cinched tightly around his waist by a belt, the cuffs turned up on the inside so he didn't look too much like a hick. The front pockets were roomier than they would be if he wore his size. He stowed the baggies in the front where they wouldn't be crushed.

When they were done with the legal stuff, Estéban passed the *motivosa*. These baggies went in back pockets that zippered shut. In the end Estéban carried nothing. He gave Kelly a wad of pesos. "You can keep the change."

"Thanks," Kelly said.

They walked north without talking. The farther they went, the more they separated, until Estéban was well ahead and Kelly had him just in sight.

Hookers were out on all the corners, standing alone or in clusters. The sidewalks were jammed with gringos, mostly young and a lot of them drunk. Kelly felt himself blend in among them; that familiar sinking sensation. No matter how many times it happened, it felt strange. He wondered whether Frank the fat man was still hiding weed in his folds and getting away with it. He wondered whether Frank was somewhere out here tonight.

Estéban picked the places and Kelly followed. Kelly passed

a uniformed policeman with a holstered gun and a baton in his hand. The cop's eyes slipped over him without a pause; Kelly was invisible to him. On shopping nights, cruising the *turista* bars, Estéban was the one who stood out. Where the *Juárenses* spent their Friday evenings the police wore body armor and carried automatic weapons, not a little pistol and a stick.

Anyone with half a brain could get bent south of the border on just about anything. The Rio Grande Pharmacy and a thousand others just like it made their livelihood catering to those who knew the score. But *turistas* were stupid: they paid too much for beers, too much for sex, too much for everything. The draw of the *farmacias* was that prescriptions were sometimes optional and the prices were low, but college kids, and teenagers especially, either didn't know this or figured the *farmacias* were some kind of trap. They'd rather pay American prices to a man like Estéban than spend five minutes doing the same thing for less in a place without the noise and smoke and crowds.

Kelly bought identical beers in identical bars with Estéban's pesos while loud American music busted out on speakers overhead. The air reeked of bodies, drink and cigarettes. Estéban cruised the crowds and from time to time he fell back to Kelly. He pressed US money into Kelly's hand and placed an order. "Two oxy, one *aracata*," he might say, and Kelly would pass two baggies of pills and one of weed.

Estéban didn't carry on shopping nights. This was the way it worked because Kelly's was the face the cops couldn't see, or didn't want to. Estéban held only on the short walk back to the buyer, and then he was clean again.

They repeated the process over and over, working north block by block until even the hardiest partiers began to thin. Kelly's pockets were almost empty. Some nights Estéban let him hold back a little *motivosa* for himself if they ended up with more than they could move. Tonight, though, they got rid of it all.

Kelly's end was fifteen percent. A member of La Raza would take less, but he couldn't glide beneath the radar the way Kelly could, either. As much as for his pockets and his skin, Kelly got paid for trustworthiness, too; he never held out on Estéban.

They sat down in a booth at an all-night *taquería*. "Good night," Estéban remarked. He counted money on the table where no one could see and gave Kelly his cut. Kelly put the dollars together with his leftover pesos.

"Yeah," Kelly agreed. He yawned into the back of his hand. The food came, they ate and he felt better.

"You coming to dinner tomorrow?" Estéban asked.

"Sure. Why wouldn't I?"

"Just asking," Estéban said. He ate, but stopped with food still on the paper plate in front of him. His eyes were bloodshot and bleary. "I'm fucking tired, *carnal*. You want a lift back to your place?"

"Yeah, okay. You all right to drive?"

"Better than a bus driver," Estéban said.

Estéban left a tip for the old lady who cleaned the tables and he and Kelly went out together. The night was cold the way it always was, and the sky was stained an ugly color from the city lights. Away from the *turista* Juárez it was quieter and the shadows were deeper. Hardly anyone was on the streets and cars were rarer still.

TEN

SHE WOKE AT FIRST LIGHT WITHOUT needing an alarm clock because it was Sunday morning and she always went to bed early on Saturday nights. This was her habit since she was a little girl, when her mother and grandmother were still alive and Sundays were the most important days.

Estéban was asleep and wouldn't wake until afternoon. Even if he hadn't gone "shopping" the night before, he wouldn't go to church. As soon as their mother died, Estéban abandoned the churchgoing habit and left it to Paloma to say prayers for both of them. He was like their father that way, and their grandfather, too, though at least he stayed and didn't slip away to another town, into a bottle and then into oblivion.

Estéban's one concession to faith was a little statue of Jesús Malverde, the narco-saint, and a pair of Virgin Mary candles to go with it.

Their house was small and old fashioned. Paloma had a white enamelware basin with blue flecks in her bedroom, which she filled from a matching pitcher. Soft light filtered through the yellowed drapes. Paloma removed her nightshirt and washed her body with a wet cloth.

On Sundays she didn't wear the post in her tongue. She put the barbell in a glass of water with a tablet that made the water fizzy and blue, as if she were cleaning dentures. She brushed and flossed and put on her best dark dress and made sure her hair looked right. Makeup was for other days, so she wore none.

On Sundays Paloma didn't drink coffee. When she left her room she prayed at a little shrine for Nuestra Señora de Guadalupe. A replica of the icon hung from a wire and a nail in the corner. A low bench with a hand-stitched pillow for the knees had supported the women of their family on Sunday mornings for decades. Paloma recited the Glorious Mysteries with her mother's black rosary.

On Sundays she walked two miles to the church. She could have taken the car, but when she was a little girl the family owned no car and the walk was even longer. This she did, like so many other things, to remember her women by.

The church was not the biggest in Ciudad Juárez, nor the richest. It was an old structure with deep roots, made from stone bricks and so traditional that it verged on the ugly. It centered a poor neighborhood of gathered homes and apartments, the streets crisscrossed overhead with thick tangles of electrical wire. Some roads were paved and others not. As Paloma walked, other pilgrims joined her. The church bells pealed.

On Sundays she met with a dozen women, all older than she. Some could have been her mother and some her grandmother. To a woman they wore black: black dresses, black hats and black veils. They gathered near the open church doors in the bright morning, speaking to no one nor to one another. Each woman's face was heavily lined from age, work and sorrow. The only time they smiled was when Paloma arrived and hugged each one of them in turn.

On Sundays this church gave the Tridentine Mass. Other churches served their flock in Spanish, but here were the Latin words recited by a pair of ancient priests with hair the color of ash and snow.

On Sundays Paloma sat with these old women and worshipped. She prayed fiercely, and when the time came for Remembrance of the Dead, she and the women linked hands and held tightly, as if the strength of their human chain was the only thing keeping them in the pew.

The air grew warm and thickened with the mingled odor of

flowers, incense and sweat. Lingering smoke drifted high in the vaults of the ugly old church, visible in the light coming through the upper windows. Sooty black stains remained on the stone where countless masses left their mark before.

When the mass was finished, Paloma and the women filed out with the other parishioners. They shook hands with the priests and emerged into the bright morning. Only now that they had said their prayers and received blessings did the women speak to one another. Paloma stayed with them.

The first question each woman asked was always the same – "Have you heard anything?" – because they had all lost someone. In Juárez the bodies of dead women were often found, but other times they vanished and never reappeared. To Paloma, these were the worst, because the women and girls could not be dead if they couldn't be buried, so they existed forever out of reach in Limbo. When the old women in black held onto each other during the Remembrance of the Dead, they held onto their hope, too.

Paloma had no news for any of them this week. She let her eyes wander the half-dirt street, past a line of battered old cars, and settle on a pick-up parked along a broken curb.

New trucks weren't unusual in Juárez; even when a family couldn't afford a proper home and squatted in the *colonias*, sometimes and somehow they could still pull together enough money for a shiny truck. This one was black and had tinted windows and a long cab with double doors for a back seat. Four men lounged against it, the rims of their sunglasses glinting. One man pointed a little camera at the women in black and the ugly church. He was too far away for Paloma to hear the click of a shutter. He lowered the camera again.

Paloma stepped away from the women. The women were talking and would talk for a long time before walking to a late breakfast. The street was littered with yellow-slate rocks. She stooped to grab one. When she straightened again, the man with the camera took another picture.

She hurled the stone. The men scattered and the rock smacked the side of the truck, bounced and hit the ground. One of the men started toward her, but another held him back. Behind Paloma, the women in black fell silent.

"Go home!" Paloma yelled at the men.

One of the women in black made a hissing noise. "Paloma, ¿qué tú está haciendo?"

The men by the truck lingered. One of them, the angry one, made an obscene gesture at Paloma. She stood in place, ready to pick up another rock, ready to yell or fight or even flee to the church. The men got into the truck. The taillights flashed, big tires in the back crushed gravel and then the truck was gone.

Paloma turned back to the women in black. They stared and suddenly Paloma felt embarrassed. At the door of the church, other parishioners were frozen in place and watching.

"Vamos," Paloma said.

She went to the women and they left together, away from the ugly church and the empty space on the curb the truck abandoned. They would have a light meal together and talk some more and pray and hope before parting ways until the next week.

On Sundays that was the way it was.

ELEVEN

KELLY WOKE LATE AND LAY IN THE slanted rays of sun casting from the bedroom window. For a while he just stayed there, but in the end he forced himself to rise and visit the bathroom for a piss and a shower. He wrapped a towel around his waist. Maybe he was a little thinner lately; he wasn't sure.

He opened a front window and the door to the balcony to let some air flow through the place. Breakfast was light because he hadn't had time to shop, but with money from the night before he could afford to splurge at the *grocería* come Monday. Some Sundays he had a beer to wash it all down, but not today.

Sunday was a day for dressing up, or at least putting on a shirt with buttons and better shoes than his ratty high-tops. He shaved his neck but left his beard-growth alone. He wore a leather belt with a silver-and-turquoise buckle that was a Christmas gift from Paloma.

It was close to noon before Sevilla knocked on Kelly's door. Kelly saw him through the open window first, leaning against the iron railing outside with his jacket open against the burgeoning heat, a holstered automatic against his side. Kelly opened up and Sevilla walked in without further invitation.

His full name was Rafael Sevilla and he was, to the best of Kelly's estimation, closing in on sixty or just past it. His hair used to be black, but now was mostly white, though the whiskers of his little beard were still hanging on. He tended to short as many Mexican men did, but he made up for it with an upright bearing and presence.

"Good morning, Kelly," Sevilla said in English. He always spoke English to Kelly, even though his accent was heavy.

"Señor Sevilla."

Sevilla investigated the kitchenette, the empty pans and dishes. He had a large nose and dark eyes and a heavy, melancholy face. He joked he was part hound. Kelly stood by the open door. He glanced outside. Sevilla was alone.

"I hear you went to the clubs with Estéban last night," Sevilla said. "All night long, club after club. You know, I wonder what the two of you are up to when you do that."

Kelly finally closed the door. Sevilla wandered to Kelly's couch and sat down. He had an old man's belly, but he wasn't fat. He always rested so his gun was available, never pinned beneath or beside him.

"Are you two selling drugs to the Americans again?" Sevilla asked.

"Wouldn't the city police want to know?" Kelly returned. He went to the kitchenette and busied himself cleaning. It was easier to keep his voice steady when his hands were busy under warm, soapy water. "Not state police."

"We're all on the same side," Sevilla said. "Besides, you know what drugs mean these days. Did you know they found six bodies without their heads outside the city limits last week? Who knows where the heads are."

"Estéban isn't cutting off anybody's head."

"Maybe I see a bigger picture. Maybe I'd like to know where Estéban gets his product."

Kelly rinsed and dried his pan. "No one cares about a little weed."

"Marijuana? Not really. Who hasn't had a little *hierba*? But drugs are on everyone's mind now. We have more federal police in the city than we have flies."

"So, what, then?" Kelly asked.

"*Chinaloa*," Sevilla said, and he looked over his shoulder at Kelly with his dark eyes. Kelly couldn't figure their color; maybe they were brown, or maybe green. He didn't like to look too long, because it was the intensity behind them that made him uncomfortable more than the mystery of their color. Kelly watched his hands instead.

"I don't handle that stuff."

"Never?"

"Never. You should know that by now."

"But Estéban deals it," Sevilla said.

"You know that, too. Goddammit," Kelly said, and he cracked two plates together in the sink. "Don't you get tired of coming around here? I got nothing for you. Okay? Nothing."

Sevilla made a gesture with his hands as if he were tossing an invisible ball back and forth. He half-smiled and turned away. "Maybe I just like to talk to you, Kelly. Nobody wants to talk English with me."

"Talk to the *turistas*," Kelly said.

"Even *turistas* hate cops. They think we're all taking money or looking to bust them for having a good time. Why do they think that, Kelly?"

Kelly shrugged. "I don't know. Maybe it's you they don't like."

"That's being cruel."

They fell silent. Kelly dried the dishes and put them away. He didn't look at Sevilla, but he felt the man at his back, eyes always searching.

"How is Paloma?" Sevilla asked at last.

"She's good."

"Have I told you I respect her?" Sevilla asked. "She does good work with that group of hers. Many families are touched by the tragedy. Some of them would surprise you."

"I'll bet."

"You're eating with her and Estéban today?"

Kelly turned back to Sevilla. The policeman's face was the same: heavy and sad looking, with a touch of flinty purpose behind the eyes. His body seemed relaxed, but somehow Kelly knew Sevilla was never at rest. "Yes," Kelly said. "I always eat with them on Sunday. And I know you know."

"Then do me a favor, Kelly: just ask Estéban the question. If he answers, you pass it on to me. When we know where he gets his heroin, we'll leave you be. It's like painting your door with lamb's blood; we'll pass by in the night and you won't be touched."

"What about Estéban?"

"If he wants to sell weed to the *turistas*, that's his business and no concern of mine. Like you say, I'm a state policeman. If the locals want to go out of their way, they can." Sevilla paused. "Well?"

"If I hear something about it, then I'll tell you," Kelly said at last.

"That's not agreement."

"It's what you get."

Sevilla nodded shortly. He rose from the couch and only then did Kelly venture out of the kitchenette into the larger room. They met at the door. Sevilla opened it. "I knew there was a reason I didn't throw you back to the police in the States," he said. "Some people think fighters are stupid, getting hit in the head all the time and not complaining, but we know better."

"I'll call you," Kelly said.

"Of course you will," Sevilla said, and Kelly knew they both understood it was all a lie; Kelly would never call and Sevilla would not deport him. This was part of a game only Sevilla seemed to understand completely. Kelly wanted him out.

When Sevilla was gone, Kelly paced the apartment. He waited twenty minutes before putting on sweats and running shoes. He would burn the agitation away.

He locked the door and was halfway down the steps to the street when he spotted Sevilla. The policeman lingered by the pink telephone pole, his back to Kelly, absorbed in the flyers. As Kelly watched, Sevilla passed his hand across the flyers as if reading them with his fingertips. He did it twice more before finally walking on. He crossed the road, got into an unremarkable blue sedan, and drove away.

TWELVE

ESTÉBAN AND PALOMA LIVED IN A
small house that once belonged to their parents. Kelly found it old
but comfortable, smelling of age and many fresh-cooked meals. He
watched *fútbol* on the little television with Estéban while Paloma
prepared the meal. When the food was ready, they gathered around
the modest dining-room table. Paloma led them in a prayer and
then they ate.

The character of their talk was different on Sundays. Paloma
did not allow Estéban's business into the house, and definitely not
around the table. Instead they talked about sports and *turistas* and
local news and even the weather. Paloma and Estéban discussed
extended family Kelly had never met, but kind of knew from many
Sundays before.

Paloma's meals were never fancy, but always hot and filling.
They ate green chile stew and hand-pressed tortillas, black beans
and rice and eggs. When they were full, Estéban went out back to
roll a joker. Normally Kelly would go with him, but today he helped
Paloma clean up.

"Don't you want to get stoned?" Paloma asked him.

"Not today," Kelly replied.

They gathered dishes and scraped them into a plastic bucket.
Later on Paloma would put the bucket outside and a trio of local
dogs, lifetime strays, would gorge themselves on scraps.

"You look nice today," Kelly said after a while. He told the truth;

Paloma always seemed lovelier on Sundays, even when she dressed down for work in the kitchen.

The kitchen was small, but Paloma knew the space well. She cleaned without wasting any effort. "You look good, too," she told Kelly. "How's your nose?"

"Better. I've been running, too. Getting a workout in. I figure I could lose ten, fifteen pounds easy."

"What for?" Paloma asked.

"To get my walking around weight down. You know."

Paloma glanced at him, and Kelly felt her instant appraisal. "For fighting?" she asked.

"Yeah. But *real* fighting, not the kind of stuff I've been doing. I've lived here long enough and I know some people. Maybe I could get licensed again."

The dishes and pans were clean, dried and put away. Paloma wiped her hands with a threadbare towel. She wore no polish on her fingernails on Sundays, and the change made her hands look different, more honest somehow.

"I thought you wanted to stop someday," Paloma said. "We talked about it."

"I know. But what else am I going to do?"

"There are things out there."

Paloma looked at Kelly and he looked back. He didn't sense disapproval from her, but he couldn't figure out the mind behind the face. Kelly lowered his head and pressed on. "I don't know what else I could do better than this. Yeah, I'm thirty, but that's not so bad; in my weight class, some decent training… I could win some fights."

She was silent for a while, and then finally Paloma nodded. "All right," she said.

They embraced in the kitchen. The smell of marijuana smoke drifted through the tiny window from the backyard and mingled with the pleasant odor of cooking and Paloma's skin. "I think I've got it figured out," Kelly said. "I'm trying."

"I believe you," Paloma said. She kissed his forehead. Kelly put his hand on her ass. Paloma pushed it away. "Not on Sunday."

"Okay."

She said the same thing every week.

THIRTEEN

He WENT TO THE FIGHTS THOUGH he wasn't going into the ring.

Vidal worked the corner of a poor young fighter from one of the *colonias* outside Juárez who couldn't be making much more than the bus fare that brought him there. Kelly raised his hand to get the old man's attention before he sat down. Vidal nodded, which was as much as he ever offered.

The card wasn't much – six fights with no one weighing in heavier than welter – but the matches were sanctioned. The atmosphere was better in the athletic hall than at the smokers: Kelly saw women and even a few kids. The crowd was bigger and there were more smiles, fewer scowls. If there was blood, then there would be blood, but it was not what brought the spectators here.

Kelly bought a warm packet of tamales and a bottle of tamarind-flavored Jarritos. Rickety pullout bleachers lined two sides of the hall and shuddered with the moving weight of Mexicans standing up, sitting down or wandering around to talk with friends. A few eyes passed over him with questions behind them, but no one crossed Kelly's path or objected when he found a good spot. Down by the ring there were folding chairs three deep, but those were assigned and the tickets cost more.

The hall packed them in until everyone had no choice but to sit down hip to hip and arm against arm. A man in a white shirt, black pants and neat bow tie swept the ring with a straw broom. He and another man, similarly dressed, would referee the fights.

When the announcer came onto the canvas things got rolling. He introduced the three judges and read a list of local sponsors. Kelly didn't know any of the names, and didn't recognize the first pair of fighters, either. One was Vidal's boy, the other a rail-thin flyweight with acne pits in his face. The crowd cheered them both the same.

Heavyweight fights got all the attention and the big money, especially in the States, but the little guys had technique. When Kelly fought welterweight, he always hit the scale at exactly 147 pounds. He had the frame to go a real middleweight back then or even super-middleweight if he wanted to push it, but those extra fifteen or twenty pounds felt like a concrete overcoat whether they were fat or muscle. Light fighters were meant to fight light.

The bell rang and the fighters closed. Vidal's kid had long arms for his size and maybe a two-inch reach advantage if his tape was applied just the right way. He worked from behind the jab and didn't keep still; he was circling, always circling, and even though the other kid blocked, those little impacts took their toll after a while.

It took most of the first and second rounds, but the other kid got his feet under him and started moving the fight his way. Vidal's boy relied on the jab *too* much, and when his opponent moved inside he danced back like he was stung even before a punch landed.

Kelly ate his tamales between rounds and sucked on the Jarritos. The Mexicans around him were excited and he was excited, too. He'd forgotten the smells outside the ring, the sound and shape of the fight when the gloves weren't on. The man beside Kelly nudged him and they traded smiles.

Round three was tough for Vidal's boy; some fighters locked into a losing game when shaken, and everything narrowed into a desperate corridor of try, try again. He kept trying with the jab even though it wasn't working anymore. A flyweight couldn't hit with the power of a heavyweight, but solid punches to the inside rocked Vidal's fighter. Kelly saw the old man shaking his head over his bucket.

The kid went to the corner with a visible kink in his side. Kelly watched Vidal rinse the kid's gumshield with one hand and press a cold pack against his ribs with the other. He talked low and quiet. Kelly had never seen Vidal talk so much. The kid nodded.

The fourth round was the final round. The fighters came forward at the referee's command. Vidal's kid circled, started to throw the jab again, but hesitated. Kelly focused on his face, the perceptible struggle to follow corner advice, break from a losing pattern and change things up.

The other kid came in hard with more body punches. Vidal's kid backed up, but with control this time. He still got hit, but he traded well and then jabbed his way out turning from the corner.

His aim was combinations, trying to put two or three punches together that would keep the other fighter guessing and off those swollen ribs. Vidal's boy was used to having his way with his arms, being able to reach out and pepper the other guy with jab after jab at distance. The other kid was hardheaded, but knew how to weave in for the sharp body shots he preferred.

The clock ticked. Each punch thrown was a half-second closer to the last bell. Vidal's kid tried to bring some technique to bear and pull some points back on the judges' cards, but he didn't have the ring smarts to keep the other kid away.

Bell and ref were in time with each other. One rang and the other stepped in. Both fighters dropped their hands. They were slick with perspiration and so was Kelly. He stood and clapped and hollered with everyone else. Corner men climbed through the ropes and the ring was crowded the way it always was at the end of a bout.

The other kid took the fight three rounds to one. The fighters embraced. Photos were shot. When Kelly settled back down he was smiling. This was the magic of the fight: no matter how small the purse, the fight mattered when it happened as much as any other fight for any amount of money.

"I forgot," Kelly said aloud.

"¿*Qué?*" the man beside him asked.

"Nothing," Kelly told him. "Good fight."

The man nodded. "*Sí, era una buena lucha.*"

FOURTEEN

EACH DAY HE WALKED LESS AND ran more. He'd quit smoking altogether and now he wasn't even drinking beer except on those nights when he and Estéban did business. Running the same route along the main roads got boring, sucking up the smog, so he changed it up with smaller streets and neighborhoods far from his usual haunts.

He found the gym this way. A pack of short, lean Mexican fighters crossed his path on the run. Kelly recognized them immediately the way fighting animals know their own kind. He fell in with them without having to say a word and they loosened their ranks to accommodate him.

Theirs was a humbler section of Juárez, well away from the bright lights and clean sidewalks of the tourist district, but not as broken or filthy as the *colonias*. Boxing was a poor people's sport, maybe poorer even than *fútbol*. Kelly saw kids playing *fútbol* in the streets with cheap plastic balls or even bags of leaves, but boxing could be had on its own terms, fighter by fighter, on the strength of the body alone.

Kelly ran with the fighters until he thought he couldn't run anymore, but he didn't fall out. He kept up with them until at last they reached the gym: a solid square of high-windowed concrete beside an attached auto yard walled high with the rusting hulks of cars behind a sagging chain-link fence.

Most filed through an open front door heavy with shadow. It was morning, but bright and there were no clouds in the sky. Inside it would be cooler and darker and it would smell of perspiration and mildew. One fighter waited. "*Bueno*," he said. "*¿Cuál es su nombre?*"

It was a formal way to ask, but Kelly was white and certain things didn't change. Kelly put his hands on his knees and sucked air. "*Me llaman* Kelly," he said after a while.

"Jacián," the fighter said. He was tiny and as lean as a strip of leather. He reminded Kelly of the hardheaded kid that beat Vidal's fighter, but he was older and his face showed the lines of premature age. "Do you fight?"

"Sometimes," Kelly said.

"Come on in."

It was better out of the sun. The gym was small but clean and the expected odor of mildew was replaced by motor oil. Dusty ceiling fans stirred the air around.

The gym had a ring with cracked-leather ropes and shoe-scuffed canvas, three hanging heavy bags and two speed bags. An uppercut bag patched with successive layers of duct tape dangled from a hook on one wall. There were pads on the concrete floor, ancient medicine balls and a pair of weight benches near neat stacks of iron. Men and boys were working, some using muscles and others their minds, student to teacher to student in an endless loop.

Jacián introduced Kelly to Urvano; a man perched on a high stool near the door, partly shielded by a desk like a lectern and piled high on one side with thin gray towels. Urvano was older, going white, but still fit. His face looked familiar, and when the old man shook Kelly's hand, he said, "I know you: Ortíz brought you around Gonzalo Lopez's place."

Kelly nodded. He was sweating and his face was already hot, but he felt his cheeks go red anyway. "Yeah," he said. "Yes, sir."

"You should stay away from Ortíz," Urvano said. "He's no good for anybody."

Kelly nodded again, but he wasn't sure what to say.

"Good run," Jacián told Kelly, and clapped him on the shoulder. "*Hasta luego*. I need a shower."

He headed for the back and left Kelly alone with Urvano. The old man didn't move from his stool; he watched Kelly the way fight men do, as if from behind a curtain. "You looking for a place to train?" Urvano asked at last.

"Depends. What's it cost?"

"Fifty-five pesos a week for towels and the shower. Eighty pesos on the first Monday of every other month."

"You got hot water?"

"For fifty-five pesos a week? Don't be stupid," Urvano said, and he almost smiled.

"I'll think about it."

Urvano shrugged.

"How about I get back to you next week?"

"This place isn't going anywhere."

Kelly lingered. A few of the other fighters emerged from the back with their hair still wet from the showers. "Okay," Kelly said. "Thanks."

"You could fight all right, you stop getting hit in the face," Urvano told Kelly. "You're not too old yet."

This time Kelly had nothing to say. He left the gym and stepped back out under the sun. His hands shook a little. He realized he didn't recognize any of the buildings here, or the names of the streets.

He was too tired to run anymore. He oriented himself by the light. North to the border was as constant as a midnight star, and all points in Juárez were judged by their relationship to Texas, though the land was no less flat, no less dry, no less hot.

A dented old working truck loaded with teenaged boys cruised past. Kelly felt predatory eyes on him and the truck slowed. He didn't look them in their faces, but he didn't turn from them any more than he'd turn from a pack of feral dogs.

The truck dragged on another twenty feet and then the driver gave it the gas. One of the boys in the back tossed an empty bottle in Kelly's direction and it smashed in the crater of a pothole. "¡Maricón!" the boy yelled and the others all laughed.

FIFTEEN

KELLY PAID HIS RENT REGULARLY and on time, which was more than many could afford even with a steady job. The men who ran the *maquiladoras* liked to say that they paid more than the average worker could ever hope to make outside the factory and that was true, but factors balanced out when apartment space grew short and prices for food and rent rose.

The landlord didn't seem to care where the money came from so long as it came, so he didn't bother Kelly back when he mounted his heavy bag on the balcony. Nor did he come around when Kelly bought a metal pipe from a scrapyard and figured out a way to make a pull-up bar out of it with nails and screws.

Today it was nearly one hundred degrees and the air was paper dry. Kelly perspired putting the pipe up, but he never felt hot; his sweat wicked away almost as quickly as it came.

He didn't hear Paloma at the front door or her key in the lock. He saw her shadow against the window and got down from the milk crate he used as a stepladder. "Hey," he said, "come see."

She came onto the balcony looking pretty and tanned and smelling faintly of something sweet. Kelly grabbed the pipe and did a half pull-up to show off. The pipe stayed in place.

"I thought you were going to that gym," Paloma said.

"Yeah, but I want to get more workout time at home." Kelly wiped his face with the back of his arm. His skin felt hot. "You thirsty? I got some Gatorade in the fridge."

Kelly served up lemonade-flavored Gatorade in plastic glasses.

His refrigerator was clean inside and the cabinets in the kitchenette were neat.

They retired to the couch. Paloma watched him over the rim of her glass. "How do you feel?" she asked.

"Good. It's working out."

"When are you going to fight?"

"I don't know. I have to talk with Ortíz."

Paloma frowned. "Why Ortíz?"

Kelly looked back over his shoulder to the balcony. He could just see the pipe. It could take his weight, so now he just had to get out there and use it. "Urvano doesn't have the juice to get me booked in sanctioned fights."

"And Ortíz does?"

"I don't know. Maybe."

"You should stay away from him, Kelly."

"Don't start with that again."

"You don't know the things about him that I know."

"Then tell me."

Paloma shook her head. "It's not time for that. Just… stay with Urvano. He's a good man. Not like Ortíz. And besides, Ortíz won't be around for much longer."

"How's that?"

"When people find out what he's into, he'll be gone."

"How are people going to find out? You going to tell them?"

"Maybe."

Kelly rubbed his eyes and pushed away a burgeoning headache. "You're just talking crazy. I was thinking I could fight under another name. Ortíz has some pull with the right people; he can get them to book me without too many questions."

"I'm telling you, Kelly, Ortíz knows all the *wrong* people."

"Will you cut it out? All I need to do is make it in. That's the hard part."

Paloma nodded as if to herself. She put her empty glass aside. "You can do it," she said.

"Yeah?"

"Yeah."

She leaned in to kiss him and everything else fell away. Kelly found wells of that sweet smell behind Paloma's ears and at the base of her neck and she breathed deeply when he kissed them. In the bedroom he lay her back and went between her legs with lips and tongue, tasting salt and wetness and feeling the heat of her. She was still trembling when he moved on top of her and pushed his way inside.

After they lay on the bed facing each other. Kelly traced the curve of her hip with his fingers again and again, the flesh pliant beneath the skin. Paloma put her hand against his chest over his heart.

"I love you," Kelly said.

"Shut up."

"You always say that."

"And you never shut up."

"That's because—"

"Hush," Paloma said. She urged him onto his back, straddled him and made a face when he entered her from below. They moved together, her breasts brushing his face. Kelly kissed and sucked her nipples. The urge overcame him. Paloma pushed her hips down hard when he came into her.

Now Kelly was quiet and they heard the sound of traffic, not so distant and never still. Kelly drifted to sleep. When he awoke, Paloma breathed deep and even in the crook of his body. He pulled the sheet over their hips. He listened and watched until she stirred.

"I love you," Kelly said.

"Fuck you," Paloma said.

"Why can't I tell you I love you?"

"Because I don't like it," Paloma said.

She started to rise. Kelly held her back. "That's bullshit," he said. "You don't want to hear because—"

"Because why, Kelly?" Paloma sat up and pulled the sheet around her completely. Her hair was mussed, but it didn't make her unlovely. Kelly didn't like it when she looked angry and she did now. "Why?"

"Because I'm white?"

Paloma's expression curdled. "*¡Pinche cabrón!*"

She left the bed and gathered her clothes. Kelly didn't move; he knew he should stop her, but he couldn't and didn't. He heard her in the front room putting her shoes on. He was sweating again.

Kelly expected to hear the door slam. Paloma reappeared. She was flushed. When she pointed her finger at him, it trembled. "You are a goddamned *baboso*, Kelly! Is that what you think of me? Are you my fucking white-boy stud? Why are you such an idiot?" Paloma demanded.

"What the hell did *I* do?"

"What did you do? What did you *do*?" Paloma ripped the sheet from the bed and threw it at Kelly. He knocked it away. He saw Paloma's eyes tearing. "I cook you food every week, Kelly. I fuck you. I bring you money. I don't say nothing when you want to get your face bashed in over and over… why isn't that enough for you? I'm not *ready*, Kelly! *¿Tú no entiende?* I'm *not ready for that!*"

Tears came. Paloma battered them with her knuckles.

"I just want you to say you love me," Kelly said. He hated the sound of helplessness in his voice.

"Of *course* I love you, *retresado!* Why do you got to make me say it?"

Kelly got up. He felt strange, naked in front of Paloma fully dressed, and he embraced her awkwardly. She hit his arms with her fists, but the blows were soft and he barely felt them. She cried against his chest until her whole body heaved.

"Don't say it," Kelly whispered to her. "You don't have to say it. Don't say it."

Paloma held him tighter and they said nothing after that.

SIXTEEN

THE SUNDAY WAS LIKE THE OTHERS: the same prayers, the same church, and the same conversations. Paloma didn't see the black pick-up this time, but she imagined it had been there while she was at mass, or just around the corner.

Their group had a new member and Paloma walked beside her to the Sunday gathering. The woman, Señora Muñoz, was the youngest of all the mothers, though still older than Paloma. A black veil framed her face. The visible strain of hard work and sorrow would turn her into an artifact like the others, a monument to loss and pain.

Señora Muñoz's daughter cleaned and vacuumed floors in the offices of a *maquiladora* called Electrocomponentes de Mexico. The Muñoz family lived in a home made of cinder blocks with no water or power. Belita Muñoz Castillo was thirteen years old, pretended to be older, and took a company bus to work at three o'clock in the morning alone.

Paloma preferred to talk about other things with new women in black, but the subject could never be changed, as the first question was always *have you heard anything?*

"We have new flyers with Belita's picture on them," Paloma told Señora Muñoz. "We'll put them all over the city. All around the *maquiladora*."

Señora Muñoz nodded. "Thank you," she said.

"Someone will recognize her."

In the beginning Paloma always said more, but she learned differently and now it was best to let simplicity be her guide. She could not say whether Belita would be found, or whether she would be alive. Sometimes a disappearance was just a disappearance. Sometimes girls found a boyfriend and vanished over the border and if *la migra* didn't catch them, they might never return. Sometimes girls found a place in the bordellos where the money was better, but the shame too much.

Señora Muñoz's mouth was so tight that speaking seemed to cause her pain. "Have you lost someone?" she asked.

"No," Paloma said.

"God bless you anyway," Señora Muñoz replied.

They walked along in silence, though the other women in black talked among themselves. Being together would not bring the dead or missing back, but sometimes even a little friendship was better than days and nights alone without cease.

"My husband," Señora Muñoz said, "he died when Belita was only six. My oldest, Manuel, he said we should come to the city for the work. He was the man for our family."

"Where is he now?"

"Dead," Señora Muñoz said, and offered no explanation.

"Someone will recognize Belita," Paloma said.

"She is dead, too," Señora Muñoz said.

The other women in black perked up. *No, no, no,* they said. *She's still out there. Don't give up hope.* Paloma let them mother Señora Muñoz in the way only they could.

The lines on Señora Muñoz's face grew deeper and deeper. She shook her head violently. They stopped in the street under the leaning face of an abandoned house, the spine of its roof broken and the ceiling collapsed. Weeds shot up through the cracked foundation. "I had a dream that she was dead," Señora Muñoz declared. "They took her from the bus… they violated her and strangled her to death. She could not even cry for her mama!"

The women in black closed around Señora Muñoz. She pushed them back. Paloma stood away from them, helpless. *No, no, no. Never say that.*

"They raped *mi hija!* They are animals! Butchers!"

Señora Muñoz grabbed at her clothes and the women in black took hold of her arms. Paloma felt something on her cheek. She touched her face and her fingers came away wet. She shivered all over.

"*Why did God take my children?* I say confession! I leave money for the offering! Where is my Belita's body? *What did they do with her body?!?*"

Hysterical tears stained Señora Muñoz's face. She collapsed in the middle of the women in black, vanishing into a sea of lined faces and dark cloth. Words became wails and wails became lung-heavy noises filled with anguish. Paloma felt weak in the legs and steadied herself against the rough stone face of the dead house.

"Give her air," Señora Guzman said. "She'll faint."

The women parted. Señora Muñoz lay crumpled in the street with white dust soiling her Sunday clothes. Señora Guzman was the eldest. She cradled Señora Muñoz like the Pietà. Instead of blood there were tears, and all the women in black cried.

"What did you say to her?" Señora Guzman asked Paloma.

Paloma shook her head dumbly.

"It's not her," Señora Delgado said. "Paloma is a good girl."

Señora Muñoz looked asleep, her face wrought by tears, but her body still jerked, also twisted within. Paloma sobbed for her.

"Hush," Señora Guzman told Señora Muñoz. She touched the woman's forehead, but the wrinkles refused to vanish. "We can't carry you; you must walk on your own. Hush now."

The women in black urged Señora Muñoz to her feet little by little. She swayed when she stood, but they were there for her. Paloma ventured closer and put her hand on Señora Muñoz's arm. The woman didn't shrink away.

"Every woman must walk on her own," Señora Guzman said.

They went on. Paloma looked back one time. She still didn't see the black truck.

SEVENTEEN

KELLY STRETCHED OUT, JUMPED rope until his calves burned and then shadowboxed in the corner of Urvano's gym. Other fighters were there – some Kelly knew by name now, and more that didn't have any words for the white boy – sparring or tossing the medicine ball or pummeling bags. Urvano stayed on his stool most of the time; though occasionally he stepped down to offer a few words of instruction to this fighter or that fighter on something he spotted.

Managers and trainers cruised through the gym at odd intervals. Some stopped to watch Kelly and he did his best to put them out of his mind. He wasn't a prospect anymore, not an up-and-comer; he was too old, too slow and just too damned *white* to make an impact anywhere south of the border. Still, just the sensation of being considered made him feel ten years younger, like he was in back in the gym on Zarzamora in San Antonio, still a white boy among the brown kids, but with fast hands and quick feet.

Urvano's only had one mirror, cracked at the corners and fogging with age. Kelly shifted his workout to a battered, duct-taped mat before this stretch of silvered glass and watched his body move. For this he didn't rely on speed or power; instead, he shadowboxed like an old Chinese man doing t'ai chi, deliberating every punch and every step.

Over five years, even with regular bouts in the ring, he'd let his form go. He didn't have to think about the perfect hook or the right toe-step when he was only meant to be hit. Going slow he could watch himself and every sloppy error leaped off the mirror. Control like this sapped energy, and Kelly's shirt soaked through with perspiration.

He didn't notice anyone moving behind him, or the sudden hush. Trainers stopped calling punches and the gym fell quiet except for scratchy music on the radio.

"Hey, Kelly," Ortíz said. "*¿Cómo te va?*"

Even in wraps, Kelly's hands were heavy. His shoulders smarted. Ortíz was dressed casually, but still in a neat jacket and slacks. He seemed wrong for the gym, where even the occasional promoter came in looking like a street laborer. Here the older men were like Urvano: simple, dedicated and poor. Ortíz wore a gold watch.

Ortíz stepped up and mimed a body punch. "Looking good, Kelly. You lost some weight. About one sixty, huh?"

Kelly nodded. Beyond Ortíz he was aware of Urvano watching. "Less," he said.

"That's good. Real good. Nice to see you working so hard."

"Yeah, well, I—"

"Listen, Kelly, I heard you were looking for me. I got somewhere to be, but if you have some time…?"

"Now?"

Ortíz tapped his gold watch. "*Ahora.*"

Around the gym a few fighters went back to the workouts. Trainers turned their backs on Ortíz. Kelly knew they were shutting him out, too.

"All right," Kelly said. "Give me a minute to clean up."

"Don't take too long."

Kelly used the shower, cold even though the day was hot, changed into clean sweats and met Ortíz outside. He passed Urvano without saying anything. When he came back there would be plenty to say.

He found Ortíz outside beside an idling pick-up. The bed was loaded with plastic cat crates lashed down with bright green and red bungee cords. In each crate was a resting cock, bright feathered and healthy.

"All right," Ortíz said. "Let's get going. There's no room up front. Ride in the back."

The pick-up was big, shiny and black with a double-long cab for a back seat and reversed double-doors. When Ortíz opened one, Kelly saw big men in tight-fitting black T-shirts inside, all of them heavy with muscle. One looked at Kelly from behind wraparound Gargoyles. Freezer-cold air conditioning spilled from the open door.

"Kelly, you coming, man?"

"Yeah, sure."

He tossed his gym bag in the back and used the running board to climb in. The bed of the truck was rubberized and clean. Kelly found a spot beside the cat crates and settled in. Ortíz shut himself up front and the truck pulled out.

They drove almost an hour until they reached a long, low building on the far side of Ciudad Juárez. Kelly had never been there, but he recognized what it was: a *palenque* where fighting cocks did battle. It was not a *turista* spot, and the neighborhood was rotting into the desert flats where broad sprawls of *colonias* held sway.

Ortíz got out and so did the men. Kelly saw one of them wore a gun open on his hip. The air smelled of dust and when the wind shifted the odor of open sewage pits carried from the south. Kelly had grit in his hair.

"All right," Ortíz said. "Come on, Kelly. Let's go inside, have a *cerveza*, all right?"

They left the men to unload the cocks in their plastic cat crates. Ortíz led the way. Inside the shift to fluorescent lighting left Kelly blind until his eyes adjusted, and then he saw the unpainted concrete walls festooned with grafitti and posters, the terraced benches around the fighting pit and, on the far side, a lively beer bar crowded with men. The terraces were almost empty, but already there were cocks fighting.

"You ever come to the *palenque*, Kelly?" Ortíz asked.

"No," Kelly said.

"*This* is fighting," Ortíz said. "You know I love the boxing, but there is nothing better than this. Even when *los perros* fight… it's not the same."

Kelly smelled blood, but in the bar there was too much smoke, beer and the odor of bodies and the whiff of blood vanished. Ortíz paused to talk here and there, but never for long. Kelly waited, and soon they were at the bar itself. Ortíz got two bottles of Tecate and presented one to Kelly.

"*Salud, dinero, amor y tiempo para disfrutarlo todo*," Ortíz told Kelly, and it was bottoms up. This was the first beer Kelly had tasted in over a month. Ortíz wiped his mouth with the back of his hand. "I have six cocks fighting today. Good animals, the best money can buy."

Kelly nodded. It was possible to see from the bar the head of the judges in the fighting pit, but not the battle itself, though occasionally a feather flew loose, or there was the sudden, visible flurry of dark wings.

"I like the pure fighting, you know?"

"That's what you said."

"How much fighting are you doing these days, Kelly?"

Kelly shrugged. "Not much. I've been training."

"And you look *muy bueno*, Kelly. Better than ever. Listen, my friend, I know you like to fight and that you want to earn some money, so maybe you want to hear about this. I have some clients that like the pure fighting. Not boxing, but traditional. You know what I mean?"

"Not really."

"Bare hands. Like they used to do it in the old days."

The beer didn't taste right to Kelly. A bowl of lime slices was close at hand. Kelly took one and sucked the juice. He shook his head. "There's no sanction for fighting like that," he said.

Ortíz spread his hands wide. Around them, men were filing out of the bar area and down to the terraces. Kelly saw one of the men from the truck down by the pit talking to one of the judges. "You think everything that happens has to have paperwork? This is a good time, Kelly. Lots of money. You can even get your dick wet; lots of girls at these things. Pretty girls. Young girls."

"I got a girl."

"Yeah, you got a ballbusting *puta*," Ortíz said. He made a face. "Some people, they think maybe *she's* the one with the cock, you know?"

Kelly pushed the limes away sharply. "Don't talk about Paloma like that."

"Nothing personal."

"Okay, then let's talk about business. I want to fight. Real fights."

"I got nothing like that."

"You can get something."

"How? There's nobody backing you, Kelly."

"You are."

"Sure, sure. I mean who gave you all those fights when you came to Juárez? *Me*. I watched out for you, kept you in the ring."

"I know. That's why I wanted to talk to you."

"About a real fight."

"That's what I said."

Ortíz finished his beer and signaled the bartender for another. "You're reliable, Kelly. I don't care about what happened in the past. This is now."

Kelly took a deep breath. He felt light headed, but it couldn't have been just the beer. "I'd like to see about getting into some sanctioned matches. I don't have to fight under my name. We can work something out, get me in under the radar. Little fights, you know? Four-rounders to start. I don't care who you put me up against."

Ortíz's beer came. He turned from Kelly and rolled the cold

bottle between his hands. His expression was pensive. He glanced sidelong at Kelly. "I'm not sure what you're asking me, Kelly."

"We're talking about a real fight."

"And I'm telling you I don't got nothing like that for you. I got something better."

"I'm not fighting nobody bare-knuckles," Kelly said. "A *real fight*, okay?"

"What do you think I'm saying, Kelly? I'm talking about real fighting without all those gloves and all that *huevadas*. You don't need to get some paper from some *burócrata* behind a desk."

Kelly thought about taking another drink, but the taste for it was gone. "No, I'm telling you that's not my thing. I'm not that kind of fighter. I want to *box*. It's not like I don't appreciate what all you've done. I mean… that's why I'm talkin' to you now. I know you can get me in the ring legit."

The bar area was almost empty now. The bartender took Kelly's bottle away. Ortíz was quiet for a long time. Another cockfight started and the spectators cheered.

"I want to get back up there," Kelly said finally.

Ortíz shook his head slowly. He half-smiled, took a swig and then laughed out loud. "I don't know what the fuck you're talking about, Kelly. You look all right; did you get hit in the head? Maybe that's it."

"I'm just saying—"

Ortíz waved Kelly silent. "I hear what you're saying."

"So—"

"Don't you get it? Nobody wants to see some washed-up *bolillo* in the ring with decent fighters. You get paid to *bleed*. You ain't any kind of contender. This is *it*, okay? Nobody in Juárez would touch a fucking junkie gringo but me."

"I'm not a junkie."

"Whatever you say, Kelly. You think I don't know those marks on you? Huh?"

Kelly crossed his arms unconsciously. He was short of breath. Kelly forced himself to inhale and exhale.

Ortíz went on: "I always gave you what you could get. This is what you get."

"I can do better than that," Kelly returned.

"Who says? Is it that fucking Urvano feeding you this shit? That *puto* doesn't know nothing I don't know, Kelly. Where was he when you wanted to fight back when? Huh? *Huh?* You tell me!"

Kelly wanted to be angry. Ortíz advanced on him with his hands waving. He spilled his beer. The few men left near the bar moved away fast. Kelly backed off. "I'm clean and I'm not playing," Kelly said. "I know you done right by me before. We have respect."

"'Respect'? When you got respect for *me* then you do me a favor after all the favors I've done for you, *naco*. Where do you think I get the money to pay you? You think I'm some kind of asshole you can take for a ride, like those fucking *turistas* you and that *zurramato* Estéban peddle dope to?"

"That's got nothin' to do with nothin'," Kelly protested.

Ortíz ignored Kelly as if he hadn't said a word. "You stupid *fuck*. Talk about respect to *me*? This is *my* country, *pendejo*, this is *my* city. You want to talk your white bullshit to me? Is that it?"

"I get it," Kelly said. "All right? Fuck it. I don't need anything from you."

He left the bar. Ortíz kept close behind. "Don't you turn your back on me, *cabrón!* You don't got nothing in Juárez without me. You think Urvano can get you into real fights? They'll find out all about where you been, what you done."

"You don't know what I did."

"Fucking *bolillo!*"

Kelly saw the way out and picked up the pace. One of the big men from the truck stepped in his way. The man still wore his Gargoyles. He was tall and wide and hard as cement beneath his black T-shirt. A tattoo of *La Virgen de Guadalupe* stood out in blue and red on his forearm. "Out of the way," Kelly told him.

The big man didn't move. Ortíz caught up. "Let him out," he told the man. "He can *walk* back to his fucking hole in the wall. I should have Lalo run your white ass over."

Enough. Kelly whirled on Ortíz and the smaller man took a step back. He still held his bottle, but by the neck like a weapon. "Goddammit, you little son of a bitch," Kelly said. "You want to fight with me? I don't give a shit how many guys you got with you, I'll tear you a new asshole!"

Kelly felt Lalo move behind him. Ortíz put his hand up. "No," he said.

"You find somebody else to bleed for you," Kelly told Ortíz. "I'm out."

He left the arena and exited into the hot, clean sunlight. He skirted around the big pick-up and headed up the dust-heavy street. Ortíz didn't follow, nor Lalo or any of the other men from the truck. Kelly was alone.

PART TWO

Sospechoso

ONE

On the day after he slept late instead of getting up for roadwork. He ate a healthy breakfast, but his heart wasn't in it and he went to a *taquería* for something greasy. There he ate until his stomach started to feel all wrong and before he walked half a mile he puked his guts out against the side of a building. He wandered after that, not sure where to go or what to do. He didn't like what he was feeling, which was angry and sad and lost all at once.

It occurred to him to call on Paloma, but he didn't. Nor did he make the trip to Urvano's gym. A part of him felt like he should work out harder than before and prove something, but another part urged Kelly to simply be. He bought a liter-sized bottle of cheap beer and sat on the edge of an overpass watching buses go by. When he finished the bottle, he dropped it over the side into a concrete-lined ditch and smiled at the sound of shattering glass.

He misspent the time until well after noon. When he got back to his apartment he was suddenly tired and took a nap for nearly three hours. He was aware of raised voices outside, a man and a woman squabbling and plainly audible through the open window, but they didn't wake him; instead he dreamed about arguing with Paloma until she turned her back on him and disappeared.

Kelly woke up sweating and smelling like beer. He showered and put on fresh clothes, but then he just sat on the couch in his living room staring at the blank television. "Fuck you," he said to no one, though maybe he was talking to Ortíz. He gave the TV a middle finger.

The walk back from the *palenque* was long, even with a bus hop along the way, and Kelly was aware now of how his feet hurt. He foraged aspirin from the bathroom, chewed two and waited half an hour for them to kick in. A half-hour after that Kelly still felt the ache. He forced himself to be still for another hour because he knew he shouldn't go out the door to do what was on his mind.

He went back to a little *norteño* bar and found the woman with perfect white dentures again, tucked away in her little corner under the Christmas lights. Aside from the bartender, they were alone; shift change was still an hour away. The woman looked at Kelly suspiciously when he sat down across from her; she didn't remember him, or maybe she just didn't recognize Kelly when his face was healed.

"What do you got?" Kelly asked her.

"*No sé de lo que usted está hablando,*" the woman said, and she made to get up.

Kelly reached across the table. He put his hand on her forearm. "Hey," he said. "I thought you said you liked *boxeadores.*"

The woman paused. She looked Kelly over again. Seeing her up close and without a film of exhaustion, Kelly realized she was older than he thought before. Maybe she was close to fifty, the extra weight she carried pushing out the deep lines that formed on the faces of lean, worked-raw mothers in the city. He still didn't find her attractive.

"Why don't you say you were that white boy?" the woman asked finally.

"How many white boys you see in here?"

The woman shrugged and settled back into her seat. She smiled her denture smile again. "You want to get more *hierba*? You don't look so beat today."

"I'm not fightin' today," Kelly said.

"Maybe you come around for something else?"

"What else you got?" Kelly asked.

"Come back and see."

She took him to the ladies' room and got on her knees. Kelly let her take his cock out. She jerked it and sucked it and though it took a while to get hard, she still managed to make it happen. Kelly turned her around and took down her pants. The woman grabbed the sides of the sink and Kelly fucked her without looking at her flabby ass, the flesh stitched with dark spiderweb veins. She didn't ask for a condom and he didn't use one. He came inside her and when he backed off she dripped on the dingy floor.

"Again," the woman said. "You can put it my ass if you want."

"No, thanks."

Kelly was the first one out of the restroom. He went to the bar and drank two beers in a row. The bartender gave Kelly a look he couldn't read, but whatever the man was thinking it couldn't be any worse than what swirled around the drain in Kelly's mind. He heard the ladies' room door creak, but he didn't look over; he felt the woman watching him. It seemed like forever before Kelly could go to her.

"You want some hard-on medicine?" the woman asked Kelly when he sat down again. "A young *boxeador* like you should be able to fuck longer than that."

"I got pain," Kelly said.

"Okay. I'll fix you up."

She gave Kelly something wrapped tightly in plastic film. Kelly put it in his pocket without looking at it. The thing weighed almost nothing; in the back of his mind Kelly could calculate a packet like that down to the milligram, or damned close. He felt hot and he was sticky under his arms.

He offered the woman money. She waved it away. "Not today," she said.

"I'm gonna go," Kelly replied.

"Next time I give you something to keep your *aparato* working," the woman told Kelly. "You don't last long enough, white boy."

"Maybe it's your fat ass I don't like."

"*¡Bolillo!*"

"Like I ain't never heard that before." Kelly turned his back on the woman. She said something else, something about how he had a little white prick, but Kelly wasn't listening. The woman was still yelling when he hit the street. By then Kelly's mind was somewhere else completely.

TWO

HE SMOKED THE FIRST BATCH OF the stuff because it was low-grade heroin that wasn't worth fucking up a syringe to shoot. The whole time he argued with himself about it, but he knew his conscience was just going through the motions; after a while even the best herb couldn't do what the cheapest brown could.

Smoking *motivosa* outside was one thing, but Kelly knew to keep this indoors. He closed the windows and put down the blinds and in the still air the smoke was like acid fumes in his eyes. When the heaviness came and all the nerves went out of his body and all he could do was lie on his back in the bedroom and stare at the insides of his eyelids, Kelly realized that it was impossible to remember this kind of high; every time it was all new and just as wonderful.

Going back to the woman in the *norteño* bar wasn't an option, but there were other places to get what he wanted. He stayed clear of anyone he recognized, any of the faces that surrounded Estéban, because even though he was on the other side now and falling away, he still had some pride.

The phone rang, but he didn't answer it. No one came to the door, which was just as well because after a while if Kelly didn't have to leave the house for anything he chose to walk around in a pair of underpants. The same underpants every day, and nothing else. The itching didn't bother him because it was gone the moment he tapped a vein.

The *farmacias* gave him what he needed for his works and

Mexican strangers provided the rest. Kelly knew he didn't have the money to go on like this forever, or even for very long, but it was all temporary, anyway; he needed to get over Ortíz and the *palenque* and when that happened he would get back to doing what he was doing before. All the good things were still there... just delayed.

Kelly slept a lot and when he was awake he was tired. A dose of *chinaloa* put him into a limbo where there was no time or place and no need for worry. Once Kelly woke up in a puddle of cold urine. The sheets and the mattress were soaked through. He stripped off the sheets, piled them in the corner, and put a towel over the wet patch. It didn't occur to him to take off his soiled underpants, and by the time he remembered he was already headed back down the rabbit hole and it didn't matter anymore.

His refrigerator emptied out, though he was barely aware of eating. He lived with a stranger who was only home when he was out. Things would move or get broken or just disappear and Kelly had no memory of how or why. This would bother him when he was straight again, but not right now. Just a few days more and he would be ready to start fresh. How many days it had already been, he wasn't sure.

Kelly wandered into the living room. He knew it was morning because the sun was coming up behind the GM *maquiladora*. Something beeped at him. He was bleary and the room was unfocused. He smelled musk and rot and his mouth tasted foul. A red light blinked on his answering machine. Kelly watched it and the machine beeped and he put things together.

Messages reeled off, but they were less interesting than the beep and the blinking light. Kelly rummaged in the refrigerator for something to eat. He found only half a stick of butter, so he sucked it like an ice pop. Paloma talked to him through the little speaker. Hearing her voice made him feel angry, but whether at her or at himself, Kelly didn't know, and not knowing made him angrier.

"Bullshit fuck," Kelly told his empty apartment. He had a mouthful of butter. His stomach rolled over.

Walking from room to room was a trial. Kelly was exhausted already. He slumped onto the couch, the last of the butter softening in his hand while Paloma kept talking and *talking* and wouldn't shut up. This wasn't forever and Kelly didn't need her riding his ass to quit. Anyway, there was using and there was *addicted* and he knew the difference between them. Was he talking out loud?

Kelly threw the butter away. It splattered on the glass of the back door. "*Shut up!*" he yelled, and Paloma's voice went silent.

He curled up on the couch. Down in the pit of his stomach where the sickness curdled, Kelly felt lonely. The quiet was too quiet for him now, and his mind was too clear. His works were in the bedroom, but getting there was a marathon Kelly wasn't prepared to run. He would sleep here for a little while and then he would go there. And this would be the last of it before he stopped, because he was too close to the line.

"Paloma, just shut up," Kelly said. "I'm okay."

THREE

Estéban called while Kelly slept:

Hey, man, where the fuck are you? Listen, you need to call me, all right? I don't know what your deal is, but if you and Paloma decided to run off together... that shit's not right. You got everybody worried, okay? You get this, you tell Paloma to call me.

And don't you do nothing stupid like getting married, okay? Just call. Okay, just call me wherever. Okay.

FOUR

CHINALOA WAS SUPPOSED TO TAKE away pain, but it was a cheat because the pain didn't disappear. Instead it was all put on hold, kept in a secret place, and when there was no room for the pipe or the needle anymore, *chinaloa* gave it all back because *chinaloa* was a bitch that couldn't stand to be jilted.

Kelly hurt behind the eyes and deeply into his skull. His stomach was a knot and he heaved over and over again even though there was nothing in there except something clear and acidic and nasty. His shoulders hurt and his knees hurt and anything that could swell or bend or stab him with shards of broken glass came alive and punished him.

Even smells assaulted him. Kelly hated the odor of his body. He showered six times in a row and scrubbed himself until his skin was raw, but the rot-stink wouldn't go away. It was the dope working its way out of his blood and through his flesh and seeping into the air he breathed. He could not brush his teeth often enough.

The worst was not being able to think straight. He couldn't ask himself *why* and he couldn't remember anyway. Hot screws were jammed into the base of his skull and he could not speak or dream or even move. When he slept now he slept for relief, because only then could he earn some distance from withdrawal. He was dying.

But no, he wasn't dying. Dying was easier than detox. He knew this already, had been in this hell already and told himself he would never go back, but he had and he was and it would end when it was damned good and ready and not a day or a minute or an hour before. Kelly *wished* he were dying; that much he could hold onto.

Footsteps on the landing outside his apartment were thunderous. When the work-whistle sounded at the *maquiladora* across the way, it broke Kelly's skull in half. He dreaded a knock on the door because it would tear him apart and he would have to scream. A scream *would* kill him.

No one knocked. Even the phone didn't ring anymore. Kelly knew when he got his thirst back that he was going to live. He drank one glass of water after another until his stomach bloated. He pissed like a river through a broken dam. The hurt faded. He put on clothes and even went outside to sit by the heavy bag.

Finally he could eat, *had* to eat, but he got nothing from the store except rice and corn tortillas in the hope that he could keep them down. He ate and threw up again, but the second time he did keep it down and the time after that, too. Once he finished a bowl of rice and he wept with the bowl clutched between his hands so tightly that his flesh blanched white.

He shaved his face and left bloody nicks behind because he did not want to look at himself in the mirror. His weight was down, but not healthily. His clothes were loose on his frame.

The apartment was filthy. Nothing was picked up and nothing was put away, so the floor was strewn with wrappers and empty plates and everywhere a bottle or a can could be perched it had been done. Opening the windows wide let the smell out, but the mess remained.

He listened to his phone messages again. Once he had to pause and he cried with his hands over his face. He cried because he was ashamed and he was ashamed for crying. It took an hour to get through to the end.

Estéban answered the home phone. It was before noon, but he was awake. "It's me," Kelly told him. "I want to talk to Paloma."

"Paloma? Hey, what the fuck? I been trying to get you for a

month, cabrón! I come by your place, I call you on the phone…
don't be playing that shit with me now. Where's Paloma?"

"I didn't… you didn't come by here," Kelly said.

"The hell I didn't! I banged on your door for a fucking hour.
Where's my fucking sister, *pinche?*"

Kelly put his hand on the kitchen counter. He felt off, like the
floor was shifted, and he wanted to sit down. "She's not here. She…
she called me a few times."

"When?"

"I don't know."

Kelly heard Estéban breathing on the other end of the line,
taking shuddery breaths. Kelly felt cold. "This is not funny," Estéban
said at last. "You tell me where she is."

"I don't know. I swear to God, I don't know. Listen… I fucked
up, man. She called me—"

"She was *worried about you*, bro! We all were. I heard some shit
and I don't believe it: something about you buying horse. Somebody
tells me that, I say they're full of shit because you don't touch that
no more. Paloma says she'll go see you and then nothing. Tell me
what you said to her."

"I didn't say—" Kelly began.

"Did you hit her? If you fucking hit her and she ran off, *cabrón*,
I will put a knife in you. *¿Entienda?* I will stick you in the fucking
ground, bro. I will fuck you up."

Kelly's temples throbbed and he rubbed them. Estéban ranted
in his ear. He was dizzy and the floor canted more and more. If
Estéban would just shut up, he could think, but Estéban wouldn't
and the torrent covered Kelly over.

"Hey, are you still there?"

He was on the floor by the phone with the receiver still pressed
to his ear. "I think I blacked out," Kelly said.

"I'm coming over there."

"No. I'll come to you," Kelly said, but Estéban had already hung
up. He put the phone away and tried to clear up. Two big plastic

trash bags were full in ten minutes. Kelly threw out his old sheets. The bedroom still reeked of ammonia. The mattress showed a brown-stained outline of where Kelly's unwashed body slept and sweated and dreamed *chinaloa* dreams. It was ruined; Kelly would have to get rid of it.

When Estéban came he pounded on the door. Kelly opened up and Estéban bulled past. "Paloma? ¿Paloma, *está aquí*?"

"She's not here," Kelly said.

Estéban checked the apartment. He came back to the living room and Kelly saw that he'd lost weight, too. Dark grooves cut in beneath his eyes and his hair was unkempt. He hadn't shaved in a few days. His clothes were rumpled as if he had slept in them. Estéban looked as if he was about to cry. "Where is she, man? Just tell me where she went. I promise I won't do nothing to you if it's your fault. You broke up with her, she broke up with you… it don't matter."

"She's not here," Kelly repeated.

"What the fuck do you *mean* she's not here?!?" Estéban smacked the phone off its receiver. He kicked the front of the refrigerator and left a dent. Kelly's few dishes were by the sink, gathered unwashed. Estéban swept them onto the floor. "What did you fucking do to her? Where the fuck did you *go?*"

Kelly stood by the door. It was still open, and he hadn't moved even to push it shut. He felt rooted. The shattering dishes didn't make him flinch. He was aware of his pulse rushing in his ears. "She didn't come here."

"You said *I* didn't come here!"

"I didn't hear you," Kelly said. His throat hurt and his voice pitched higher. "I was high, man. I got messed up. If she came… I didn't hear her."

"*¡Mierda!*"

Estéban kicked the refrigerator again and the door popped open. Kelly's stack of plastic-wrapped tortillas was there half finished. The rest was empty, stained yellow by the little light, and forlorn.

When Estéban came at him, Kelly didn't try to get out of the way. Estéban grabbed Kelly by the front of his shirt. His expression was twisted, frantic, and now he did cry. The whites of his eyes were bloodshot. "She said she was going to *see* you!"

"I didn't hear her," Kelly wanted to say, but he only whispered.

"What the fuck, Kelly? What the *fuck?*" Estéban shook Kelly and the tears came freely. "Why won't you tell me where she went? Just tell me where she went, Kelly, so I can go get her."

"I don't know where she went," Kelly said.

Estéban didn't let go; he buried his face against Kelly's chest and sobbed. Kelly put his hands on Estéban and they clung to each other. Kelly shook all over as he cried and a part of him was ill at ease when his tears fell into Estéban's hair, but there was no time for that.

"I want to bring her back home," Estéban said.

"I know," Kelly said because it was all he could say. "I know."

FIVE

THE MATTRESS STANK SO BADLY THAT Kelly couldn't stand to sleep on it. He put a pile of gym clothes on the floor of the bedroom and used his training gloves for a pillow. Estéban crashed on the couch. They shared Kelly's tortillas and rice for dinner and made little conversation. When Kelly fell asleep that night, he heard Estéban weeping quietly to himself.

In the morning they would go to the police. That much they decided on. They would get cleaned up and dress right and when they made their report they would be taken seriously. Estéban had a wad of American bills; he would pass a couple hundred bucks to the man in charge. That, too, would be taken seriously.

Kelly had dreams. Maybe they were of Paloma and maybe they were nightmares, but he remembered nothing about them. He slept longer than he intended, and when he stirred he heard Estéban moving around in the front room. "Why didn't you wake me up?" Kelly called. He went to the bathroom and washed and dressed in the clean, button-up shirt with a collar that he saved for Sunday meals with Paloma.

He owned no fancy shoes or slacks, so had to wear sneakers with jeans, but it would be enough. He went to the front room. "Bathroom's open," he said. "You want to hurry up and—"

"Estéban isn't here," Rafael Sevilla said. He sat on the couch where Kelly and Estéban shared their quiet, simple dinner the night before. "He's down with the locals. Says his sister's disappeared. He's not so dressed up like you, Kelly."

"What the hell are you doing in here?"

"The door was wide open."

The door was open still and the glare was bright. Kelly had his shoes in his hand and he felt stupid standing in front of Sevilla in his Sunday shirt, his skin still damp from the shower and Estéban long gone. "When did he go?" Kelly asked.

"I don't know, but they called me a couple of hours ago. I tell the locals who I'm interested in and they pass word on to me. Same with you. That's how I know when you're in the shit again, Kelly. And you've been in the shit, haven't you?"

Kelly didn't look Sevilla in the face. He went to the kitchen, though there was nothing there to keep him. He had only one unbroken glass for water and he used it. "I fucked up," he said.

"I know. But that's the kind of fuck-up you can't afford, Kelly. I told you before: I turn a blind eye to the *hierba*, but not the other. I thought you were smarter than that."

"I guess not," Kelly said with his back to Sevilla.

"No. But all you addicts are stupid when it comes to *heroína*, eh?"

"I'm *not* an addict. I fucked up. That doesn't make me a junkie."

"Then look me in the eye when I'm talking to you, Kelly."

"I'm not some kid you can boss around."

Sevilla had a quiet voice, but it had strength. Kelly heard it before and he heard it now. Sevilla said: "A *man* could look me in the eye."

Kelly turned. He looked at his feet and then the counter, the phone, the sliding glass door at the back of the apartment and finally to Sevilla. The old cop sat utterly still. His eyes seemed sadder and the lines around them deeper. Just looking at Sevilla made Kelly feel tired, as though there was an unwelcome weight shared between them.

"I slipped," Kelly said. "It wasn't what I wanted. I got right again."

"Until the next time."

"No. There's no next time."

"If you were with Paloma I'd believe it, Kelly," Sevilla said. "But she's not around. Where did she go?"

"I don't know."

"What did Estéban tell you?"

"Nothing. He said... he said she went to check up on me and, hell, I don't know." Kelly's eyes burned and he rubbed them. He didn't want to cry in front of Sevilla. That would be too much.

"Who sells Estéban his heroin?"

"Oh, for Christ's fucking sake!" Kelly shouted. "The man's sister is *gone*, all right? She's just... just fucking *gone* and I don't give a *shit* who gives Estéban what and what for! Now why don't you just get the fuck out of my place?!?"

Sevilla didn't move, but his expression settled into something hard. He wore a suit, but like all of them it wasn't pressed and had the impression of age. Sevilla took the handkerchief from his breast pocket and held it out to Kelly. "You want to wipe your snotty nose?"

"What the hell are you talking about?" Kelly demanded, but he touched his nose with the back of his hand unconsciously.

"I mean if you're going to be a spoiled little boy—"

"I'm not anybody's—" Kelly began.

Sevilla cut him off: "*¡Parate!* Right now I talk and you listen. And listen closely, Kelly, because I don't want to lose my temper with you. *You* don't want me to lose my temper with you."

Kelly closed his mouth. Sevilla rose from the couch and walked the room the way he did: a slow circuit that never paused long, but missed nothing. He lingered at the sliding glass door and touched the thick splatter of dried butter leavings. When he looked back to Kelly, his eyes were dark and no longer sad.

"She's been gone ten days," Sevilla said. "I know because I asked around. You were gone, too — crawled up into your fucking needle — but Estéban was also missing. Did he tell you that? Did he say he was out of town?"

"No."

"I didn't think so."

Kelly waited for Sevilla to say more, but instead Sevilla looked out toward the *maquiladora* beyond Kelly's balcony. He was quiet for a long time, until Kelly couldn't stay silent anymore. "Where was he?"

"Somewhere," Sevilla said. He put his back to the view and fished a pack of cigarettes out of an inside pocket. "I could make a guess, but I don't have real answers. That's because I don't know *names*. Names like who supplies Estéban with heroin."

"Goddammit, I told you I *don't know*."

Sevilla knocked one cigarette from the pack, perched it in the corner of his mouth and lit it. He inhaled deeply and exhaled through his nose. He came away from the sliding glass doors and closer to Kelly. He used the cigarette as a pointer. "Then let me tell you what's happened. Estéban and his good friends you don't know, maybe they aren't such good friends after all. Maybe Estéban makes too much money, or maybe he doesn't make enough. Someone gets angry or he gets angry, but the end result is the same: Paloma goes for a ride and until everyone's happy again and made friends again she stays away."

Kelly shook his head. "No," he said.

"No? Maybe she doesn't come back at all. Maybe she's dead already."

"No, that's not what happened."

"I don't know what happened, Kelly," Sevilla said. He moved closer and left fading streamers of smoke in his wake. "I don't know because I don't have *names*. With names I can get faces and places and times. *Then* I can know."

Kelly felt flushed, breathless, and put his hand on the counter by the sink. A shard of broken plate pressed against his palm. "She's not dead. No dealer took her."

"You know that for certain, do you, Kelly?"

"I know it."

Sevilla was close enough to touch. The smell of cigarette was all around Kelly, and the aroma of his aftershave. Kelly wanted to push Sevilla back, but he was afraid he might fall; he was lightheaded and the smoke didn't help. "You *don't* know, Kelly. You *can't* know. But we can… if you help me."

"I don't know what I can do for you," Kelly said. He closed his eyes. He felt nauseous.

"Help me cut through Estéban's bullshit. What he tells the locals I don't care; we both know these men, these *distribuidores de la heroína*… they're bad men. You're not a bad man, Kelly; a woman like Paloma would never love a bad man."

"Get away from me." Kelly shoved Sevilla. The cop stumbled and his cigarette hit the floor. Kelly staggered backward and got tangled in his own sockfeet. He toppled onto his rear. When he looked up Sevilla had his hand on his gun and his face was flushed red.

"Don't be *stupid*, Kelly! I want to find her, too. You think I don't want to? After all the good she's done? You don't know how many people owe her, Kelly. You'll never know."

"Get the fuck out of here," Kelly said. His eyes stung and he blinked away tears. "You just… you just get the fuck out of here now."

"If I leave here now, Kelly, you'll get no help," Sevilla said.

"I don't want your help. I want you to leave."

Sevilla sighed. The high color drained from his face and he let his hand move away from his pistol. He crushed the fallen cigarette into the vinyl tile with the tip of his shoe. When he went to the door he paused as if to say one last thing, but Kelly wouldn't look at him and finally Sevilla just left. Kelly put his face in his hands and all the words and pictures and ideas and fears and hopes whirled around behind his eyelids until they could only come out in more tears.

He felt it again: shame, warm and hot as blood. He smelled that blood, too, and it was then Kelly realized his palm was cut after all.

SIX

ESTÉBAN DIDN'T COME BACK THAT morning. Kelly waited into the afternoon and watched shadows slide with the sun until he couldn't stay still anymore. He left the apartment and made for the bus stop. He turned his head from the pink telephone pole when he passed it, though his mind framed the image on its own: *Justicia para Paloma*.

It took hours to reach the familiar street, the leaning building and the office with the pink door, or so it felt to Kelly. Every stop, turn and delay on the bus route was agony. Everyone moved too slowly. Those who talked on the bus were too loud. The sun was too bright and it was too hot in his plastic seat.

Kelly felt unshackled when he stepped onto the sidewalk. He walked quickly, and then ran, but his stamina was gone and he gassed before he got halfway there. Even so he took the steps to the second floor two at a time. At the last moment he was afraid the office would be closed, but the door was open and Kelly heard a typewriter from inside.

He expected Ella, but it was another woman, one he didn't recognize. She was older, like most of Mujeres Sin Voces. When Kelly came in, she made a sour face as if he smelled.

"Excuse me," Kelly said. If he'd worn a cap, he would have taken it off. "*Estoy buscando* Ella. *Mi nombre es* Kelly."

"Ella Arellano?" the woman asked.

"*Sí.*"

"Señorita Arellano *no está aquí.*"

Kelly hesitated. The flyers in the office drew his eye, demanding *justicia, justicia, justicia* like every time before, but the faces were different because he saw them now. He came no farther than the doorway; he didn't dare enter the room and be surrounded by all those faces.

"*¿Señor?* I say she no here."

He had to stop looking at them, but they would not stop looking at him. Kelly dragged his eyes back to the woman. "Yeah. Where… um, where is she? It's about Paloma."

The woman crossed herself. "*Estamos esperando noticias.*"

"I know," Kelly said. "I've been… away for a while. I want some news, too. Can you tell me where I can find Ella? They worked together a lot here. *¿Por favor?*"

The woman was silent, and Kelly felt the hesitation coming from her mixed with fear. Ciudad Juárez was a city of fear, and Kelly was white and a stranger to be feared most of all.

"*¿Por favor?*" Kelly asked again.

Kelly needed another bus, this one headed into the porous boundary between Ciudad Juárez and the sun-bleached wild beyond. Where streetlights and paving ended, the *colonias* sprang up. In the States this would be where the suburbs grew — endless, identical blocks of perfect green lawns and interlocking streets with themed names and an ever-vigilant homeowners' association — but here the broken landscape was thick with shanties built from scrap wood and corrugated aluminum.

Throughways were decided by default, sometimes wide enough for the few cars there were and other times barely enough for two to walk abreast. Chicken wire and scraps of old cabinetry and cinderblocks and discarded shipping pallets were the building materials. A window was a hole in the wall. When the wind shifted the stench of raw sewage was overpowering.

There was nothing here but dirt, sand and a few water-starved trees. And people.

The only solid constructions were the bus shelters on the battered-down gravel road. The people of the *colonias* fed the buses and were disgorged by them, day and night in a steady shift-cycle from the *maquiladoras*. A worker from a *colonia* could ride to work three hours one way before the sun came up and get home after sundown. Kelly rode out of the city on a bus loaded with women in uniforms stitched with their names and the name of their *maquiladora*. None of them wanted to look at him and he obliged by staring out the window as Juárez went away.

He got off where he'd been told to and stood squinting in the harsh afternoon sun. Some of the women got off with him, while others boarded. Conversation stopped around him. Kelly was alien: white and male with money in his pocket. The only white people who came to the *colonias* were do-gooders or crooks, and Kelly didn't carry a Bible. The bus left him in dust and diesel fumes and only when he was alone did he set off toward the *colonia* sprawl.

Not all the *colonias* were like this one. Some were almost like real neighborhoods and the workers who lived there built solid homes and even managed to get services like water and sewerage. In twenty years they might be absorbed by the city and become poor but proper parts of the whole. Ella's *colonia* was not one of those.

The people here put up no signs, but the handmade structures were individual enough that a stranger could navigate by landmarks if he could remember them. The homes were swept up out of the desert from scrap, held together by rusty nails and staples and ropes and baling wire. Kelly looked for a green plastic garbage can cut and unfolded and used as part of a wall. When he found that, he could orient himself, or so he had been told.

The *colonia* was not a maze because mazes were designed with a solution. A rat could learn a maze but get lost in a *colonia* like this one, where the only constant was need and everyone fought for space. Houses here were not tall, but squat, irregularly shaped and set at imperfect angles to one another. Kelly heard music on radios and saw a black-and-white TV running on batteries inside the darkened hutch of one home. He looked for the signs of passage — a fence topped with a red ribbon, a yellow dog with a black splotch on its face, the broken-down shell of an old Buick — and kept on.

A few awkward, makeshift power lines drooped from poles and simple boards planted in the ground. Orange extension cords served instead of real cables, and sometimes not even that; in places bare wire without a trace of insulation waited for the unwary to catch hold and be electrocuted to death. Ella's *colonia* received no services, so somewhere an enterprising resident had put together a tap from the main line. A few of the larger shanties even had outdoor lights, but these were few and at night the throughways would be utterly dark except for the stars and the moon. Crime was worse here than anywhere in Juárez, and that was saying a lot. Kelly felt eyes on him always.

He passed children carrying water in plastic bottles from a communal pump. They streamed around him and moved past without a look back. Their voices and laughter made them sound like birds. He descended a steep row terraced into broad steps, but nearly lost his footing. From where he stood he saw the *colonia* spill down the hillside and beyond the farthest edge a field of pink crosses.

Ella Arellano's home had a pink cross of its own, and underneath block letters painted in the same color: *JUSTICIA.* A front window had a roughly trimmed square of screen stapled into place to keep the bugs out and old-fashioned shutters with metal hinges on the inside for when the cold came. Its front door hung awkwardly, but the shanty's face was whitewashed and mostly clean, the hard-packed dirt out front swept. Some of the homes in the *colonia* were little more than piles of scrap; the Arellanos lived with dignity.

He knocked and waited but no one answered. Kelly looked up and down the crooked throughway, expecting to see someone lingering, watching, but he was alone. He knocked again. This time he heard movement beyond the door.

Ella opened her door only enough for Kelly to catch a glimpse of her in shadow. "What do you want?" she asked in Spanish.

"I want to ask about Paloma," Kelly replied. "When did you see her?"

"I don't know nothing about it," Ella said, this time in English. The words sounded funny coming from her, or maybe it was her voice; she slurred a little. "Go away."

The gap closed. Kelly put his hand on the door. "Wait," he said. "You know she's missing? Just tell me when you saw her. Where did she go? Did she talk to anyone?"

Ella pushed, but Kelly was stronger. "*No sé cualquier cosa.* Go away!"

"Just five minutes! I need to know!"

"I tell you *go away!*"

On the other side Ella threw her weight against the door. Kelly shoved back with both hands. He bulled his way into a dim room with a dirt floor. There was room enough for a little table, a tiny wood-burning stove and a few blankets for sleeping. The shanty had a back room, too; a curtain stood half open between front and rear. Perhaps five or six people would live in this space, men and women and children alike.

Ella retreated. She wouldn't look at Kelly. "You get out! Get *out!*"

"When you tell me," Kelly said. He had to stoop inside because the roof slanted. Ella looked rumpled and her hair was unwashed. It fell in her face. At Mujeres Sin Voces she was always neat. She was not the same here.

"I didn't see her. I don't know anything."

"You're lying to me," Kelly said.

She tried to slip into the back room. Kelly grabbed her arm. Ella pulled and they ended up together on the other side of the curtain where a cast-iron bed and a few modest pieces of furniture made a private space for the man and woman of the house. A plaster statue of the Virgin of Guadalupe stood in one corner. Prayer candles in red glass burned on either side of her.

"You let go of me!"

Kelly's heart was beating hard now and his breath came fast. He took hold of Ella without thinking and he shook her hard enough to make her head rock. He saw the deep blue and purple bruising around her eye then, and her broken lip. When his hands sprang open, Ella fell back against the bed.

"What the hell is going on?" Kelly asked.

Ella covered her eye. "Why don't you leave me alone? Go back across the border."

He wanted to touch her again, gently this time, but his feet wouldn't move. The little room did not seem to have enough air. Kelly's grip opened and closed on nothing. "What's going on?" he asked again.

"Just get out."

"I can't."

"I don't want you here!" Ella shouted at him. Her hand came away from her face and Kelly saw again the closed eye and the bleeding under the skin that stained her face from cheek to forehead. On the side of her mouth bloomed a dark, unhealthy bruise.

"Did you see her?" Kelly asked.

"*Get out!*"

"Did you *see* her?"

Ella came at him with spread hands. Kelly let her push him backward through the curtained doorway and into the front room. His heel hit the leg of a little chair and he stumbled. Ella cried, but only from her open eye. "Why don't you leave me alone?"

Her nose ran and Ella wiped it with the back of her wrist. She shuddered when she breathed. Again Kelly wanted to touch her, but he knew he shouldn't. Ella turned her back on him. When her knees buckled, she sank to the floor slowly like a dead leaf and sobbed there.

"Did you see them take her?" Kelly whispered. Ella didn't answer.

She choked on sobs, kneeling and bent in her rumpled dress. Like a child she rocked back and forth and she hugged herself with her arms.

Kelly took a chair and settled into it. He was conscious of his weight, as if everything inside of him was turned to scrap iron and pulling him toward the center of the Earth. Ella's home was small before, but now the walls closed in on him. In this place there was not enough light from the window and not enough space to even breathe. He imagined himself here as Ella and he imagined himself in prison. Something fell on his cheek. Kelly wiped it and saw wet on his fingers.

After a long time, Ella's tears died. Her breath stilled and hitched until finally they were silent together in the hot little room. Kelly could not bring himself to ask the question again. Neither said anything for what seemed like forever.

"I could do nothing," Ella said at last, and Kelly's stomach turned.

"*¿Dónde sucedió?*" Kelly asked.

Ella spoke without looking at Kelly. Instead she gazed at the corner, arms still around herself. Little aftershocks took hold of her when she talked; her voice caught, but it was also hollow. "At the church. With the mothers. Paloma asked me to come with her. I didn't know why. I think she knew. She wanted me to see. Do you think she knew?"

"I don't know," Kelly said. He tasted something bitter.

"When the Mass was over, they came. One of them, he used a bat on the mothers to drive them off. Paloma fought them. I tried. They beat me."

Kelly wanted to ask a question, but first his lips worked without a voice. Then it came: "Who were they?"

"Men. I didn't know them. They had a truck. A new, black truck."

Ella put her face in her hands and she cried again. Kelly was rigid in the chair, imagining the road, the church and the mothers of the missing — he had never seen these things because Paloma wouldn't allow it, wanted it to be hers and not theirs — and the moment when the men came. In his mind the men had empty faces that were somehow still angry.

"Did you call the police?" Kelly asked, but Ella didn't answer. "Did you call the police for help?"

He had to wait until the tears stopped again.

"Did you call them?"

"What good would it do? She is dead."

Kelly didn't want to ask the question, but the words came unbidden: "You saw her die?"

"No. But she is dead."

They had nothing left to say to each other and when Kelly left they didn't even exchange farewells. Ella closed the door behind Kelly. He knew he would never see her again. Paloma was the link between them, and now Paloma was gone.

Kelly wandered unmoored in the *colonia*. Before he had been seeking, but now he was lost inside himself and let the patchwork houses drift by one after the other without really seeing them. From time to time he saw the field of pink crosses. Each time it was a little closer; he gravitated toward it unconsciously. Finally he was free of the narrow confines between buildings and before those markers and he was still inside and out.

Some of the crosses bore photographs or sprays of dried flowers. Others were marked with names, painted on or spelled out in adhesive letters. Still more were simply blank. Perhaps they stood for someone or perhaps they were just a reminder: *justicia, justicia, justicia.*

The ground was rocky and only patched here and there with hardy desert grass that could grow anywhere. No one allowed the crosses to be overgrown, though. Kelly took a step without thinking and then another and then he roved among the crosses as he wandered in the *colonia*, without direction or purpose.

Justicia para Sangrario.

Justicia para Chita.

Justicia para Miguela.

Justicia para Noelia.

He stood before a blank cross. "*Justicia para* Paloma," Kelly said aloud. He fell on his knees and for the first time in five years he prayed. It was a prayer without words. Instead he offered God everything that stirred inside — his anger and fear and sorrow and remorse — and sealed it with an *amen*. The sun glared overhead, a furious eye. Kelly sweated and cried and the mingled water fell into the dry earth. "*Justicia para* Paloma."

If God listened, he did not answer. Not even a breeze stirred the field of crosses. Kelly wiped his face with the palms of his hands. When he pushed himself back to his feet, slate-colored dirt clung to him. He wished for a knife for carving or a marker so he could put Paloma's name on the empty cross, but he had neither.

She is dead, Ella said.

She is dead. Dead.

"She is dead," Kelly tried, but the words felt wrong in his mouth. He dusted his hands, but the dust was like mud and it stuck to him like clumps. Instead he made fists and ground the dirt inside them.

Now the crosses themselves watched him. He walked fast to get away, through the field and back toward the bright stretch of worn-down dirt that was the road back to the city. Once he brushed one of the crosses. A sun-bleached piece of tape gave way and a whitened photograph fell facedown onto the ground. Kelly knelt to pick it up, but suddenly he didn't want to touch it, because he *knew* that on other side he would see Paloma's face regardless of whose picture it was. He left it there.

The bus could not come fast enough. He stood in the shade of a covered bench, apart from the girls and young women in their *maquiladora* uniforms. Kelly didn't look any of them in the eye. They were all watching him, whispering to one another about him, angry with him because he was not there when the men came for Paloma and they drove the mothers of the missing away with baseball bats. Ella Arellano was there, but Kelly was not; he was inside a needle and swimming in *chinaloa*, and if Paloma called for him he was beyond hearing it.

A rushing sound of blood in his ears became the roar of a diesel bus engine. Kelly overpaid his fare. He stood instead of sitting and he felt like a zombie. The moving air through the open windows of the bus was not enough to cool him and he was bathed in sweat that reeked of shame. All of the women could smell it. Even the bus driver looked at him with disgust.

He left well before his stop and wandered the streets. He drank a soda he didn't taste, ate a taco that settled in his stomach like shot. Everywhere people glared at him because they *knew*. A part of Kelly knew it was insane, but Ciudad Juárez was insane. Drug dealers had firefights in the streets and it was insane. Women were dying and it was insane. Paloma was dead and it was insane. Kelly was alive and it was insane.

It was insane.

SEVEN

"**H**AVE I EVER TOLD YOU ABOUT my daughter?" Sevilla asked.

Kelly opened his eyes. He was mostly in the shade, but his legs were out in the sun and he leaned against a bare concrete wall in a narrow alley. A bus roared past on a street six feet away, churning dust and diesel smoke in its wake. Kelly's head throbbed. He looked at his forearms automatically. The old scars were there, but no new marks.

When he moved, an empty tequila bottle toppled onto its side. Now Kelly recognized the taste in his mouth and the ugly pain behind his eyes that snaked back into his brain. He didn't remember getting to this place or even the drinking, but it wasn't a small bottle, either.

Getting to his feet was all right; Kelly used the wall for a brace. He straightened his shirt and ran a hand over his head. His hair was getting long and it felt greasy and gritty. Out on the sidewalk he recognized the street. Walking home would only be a matter of minutes. His wallet was still in his pocket and his watch was on his wrist. He couldn't have been out overnight, Kelly thought, though it seemed like morning all over again.

When he reached his block he took the long way around so he wouldn't have to walk past the pink telephone pole and the forest of flyers on it. He knew he wouldn't see Paloma's face there among the others, not yet, but he imagined it being there and that was bad enough. Going by, he might see a girl who looked similar enough to play tricks on his mind and Paloma would be there and he would have no choice but to imagine terrible things.

He went up the steps to his apartment and let himself in. It was hot. He opened the windows. A work-whistle sounded at the *maquiladora* across the way. Kelly saw the way the sun fell on the plain concrete blocks of the factory and knew it *was* morning. He had passed the night in an alley sucking on the neck of a tequila bottle as the city and the *turistas* and the hours marched by blindly. Kelly felt shame.

A memory of Sevilla played at the edge of his mind while Kelly fixed himself breakfast. It was a dream, not the man himself, that Kelly remembered. They were in the alley passing the bottle like *vagos* with a taste for the cheapest stuff they could afford, though Sevilla wore a suit. What they talked about, Kelly couldn't recall, but he did remember Sevilla and his wallet and a photograph.

"Have I ever told you about my daughter?"

Kelly ate without tasting anything that passed his lips. It was always this way now. He was aware of the chewing, the swallowing and then the sense of fullness in the belly that told him to stop, but it was all purely mechanical. Once he enjoyed food, especially when he was with Paloma or when he was cutting weight and couldn't afford an ounce of bad fat to tip the scale. The dish and the fork went in the sink. He rinsed them and dried them and put them away.

Sitting on the couch was intolerable, even with the television on. Later, as the evening light turned yellow and red, he changed to sweats and a T-shirt and wrapped his hands. This was a meditation for him, the wrapping, and he found he could disconnect from everything while he did it. Wrapping was his rosary — the thumb, the wrist, the knuckles and between the fingers. Tighter and tighter, but not *too* tight, and his mind was empty.

He punched the heavy bag and ignored the buzz and bite of mosquitoes drawn by the odor of his sweat. The *maquiladora* came alive when the night came, festooned with white lights and spotted with the glow of windows transformed from daytime black. Kelly's shoulders started to burn—he was throwing arm punches, not bringing them in from the hip—and his lungs felt shallow. Where had he gone, that Kelly at the *palenque*? For that matter, where was the Kelly that never touched a needle, and whose favorite pastime outside the gym and the ring was a cold beer on the tailgate of an old pickup truck?

An answer drifted to the surface: that Kelly was as dead as Paloma.

"Motherfucker," Kelly spat. He slugged the heavy bag once more and stepped away breathing hard. The trance was gone, the meditation of the hand-wrapping and the stillness in its wake. He could not think of Paloma and stay in the peaceful place, but now he could think of no one else.

He put his hands on the balcony rail and squeezed. He kept his eyes shut and tried to follow the splashes of light on the inside of his lids.

"Have I ever told you about my daughter?"

"No," Kelly said aloud to the Sevilla of his dreams. When he opened his eyes it was all there: the city, the *maquiladora*, the lights and the sky turned sick orange by all of it, but Paloma was a smaller part of it. He didn't cry. Part of him was proud of this, another angry; didn't Paloma deserve his tears? Ella Arellano cried for Paloma. Even Estéban cried for her, and he cried for no one.

Kelly unspooled his wraps. He stood under the shower for an hour in the dark, heedless of the cost. In his imagination he walked a field of pink crosses and every one of them had the name of someone he knew.

He considered calling Estéban. What Ella told Kelly, Estéban would want to know. But with his skin still wet from the shower, his muscles spent, his mouth finally cleansed of the taste of sour old tequila, Kelly did not want to talk about it. Besides, where Kelly went Estéban had surely gone, too. It would make sense. Estéban didn't need Kelly telling him what he already knew.

Sevilla's card was on the kitchen counter with other litter from the mailbox and Kelly's pockets. Kelly waited a while before he dialed, but when he finally did there was no answer. He tried a second time. Before he called a third time, Kelly stopped himself; he had nothing to tell Sevilla anyway. But maybe Kelly simply wanted to learn about Sevilla's daughter, or if he had one at all.

This time when he turned on the TV he was able to find some distraction for a while. He found himself looking at the clock too much and before midnight he switched off the television and all the lights and went to bed.

Sleep didn't come right away because Kelly couldn't close his eyes. Whenever he did, Paloma was there, so he had to will himself unconscious while staring at the ceiling. It made no difference, because when he drifted off Paloma came to join him in bed and he held her close to him and wept silently against the back of her neck and told her he loved her. Like always, she never told him she loved him back.

"Have I ever told you about my daughter?" Sevilla asked them. He was by the bed in his suit, smoking a cigarette in the dark.

Kelly yelled at Sevilla to get the hell out so he could be alone with Paloma, but when they were alone again Paloma said, "You should have let him tell you."

"I don't care," Kelly replied. "I don't care about anyone else but you."

EIGHT

KELLY KNEW IT WAS SEVILLA knocking just from the sound of it. He stirred from sleep at the rap of knuckles on the door, less sure whether he was awake or still dreaming, but Paloma wasn't with him and she would have been if it was a dream. Putting his hands over his face didn't keep out light from the window. Sevilla knocked again, more insistent this time, and Kelly heard his voice: "Kelly? Open the door, Kelly."

"Go away," Kelly said, too quietly for anyone to hear. He clambered out of bed, pulled on sweats from the day before and made his way to the door. He unlatched the chain and turned the lock. He could almost feel Sevilla on the other side.

Sevilla had two armed policemen with him, one on either side. They were dressed in dark blue and black, armored and wearing plastic tactical helmets that looked like the kind skateboarders wore. Goggles covered their eyes. Between them, Sevilla looked smaller than usual, more rumpled than was customary for him. The bags beneath his eyes were heavier still.

"Kelly," Sevilla said.

"What the hell?" Kelly replied.

The armed and armored police bulled past Sevilla and into the apartment. One stiff-armed Kelly and he stumbled backward. More cops came in pairs behind them: two more, four more... six. Suddenly there was shouting and the crash of things being knocked over, being broken, being trodden underfoot. Kelly grabbed the arm of the closest cop and the policeman's partner clipped Kelly on the side of the head with the butt of his automatic weapon. Being struck made Kelly reel.

His hip connected with the edge of the couch. Two cops — maybe the same ones, maybe two more — charged into Kelly as one and lifted him bodily over the couch frame. They slammed him to the cushions. One put his knee on Kelly's chest. More shouting followed, and the sound of shattering dishes in the sink.

Kelly wanted to yell at them, but the pressure of the knee kept his lungs from expanding. Kelly wriggled beneath the policeman. His hand flopped against the top of the coffee table, seeking purchase and finding none. The cop didn't even look down at him. The urge to punch came and went; Kelly was not so far gone.

Sevilla appeared. He showed handcuffs to the big policeman. The pressure went away. Kelly sucked air hard enough to choke. The cop moved off. Sevilla helped Kelly sit up. "Put your hands behind your back," Sevilla said.

"What the... what the hell?" Kelly asked again.

"Damn it, Kelly, put your hands behind your back or I can't help you."

Any other time Sevilla might have pushed him, Kelly would have been too hard to give. Now Sevilla turned Kelly, hooked one wrist in steel and then another. Cops in body armor were everywhere, opening everything, destroying what they found. The floor was littered in bits and fragments of broken things. Kelly saw a policeman rifling through his refrigerator and just tossing what he found onto the floor. More were in his bedroom, some with knives. They shredded the mattress he shared with Paloma.

"Now get up," Sevilla told Kelly. His words were low, urgent and delivered right to Kelly's ear, as if they could not afford to attract the attention of anyone around them. The police moved like a whirlwind and left nothing untouched. "Look at the floor. Don't look anyone in the eyes."

Kelly still felt the cop's knee on his sternum. He let Sevilla get him to his feet and steer him toward the door. There were questions, a hundred questions, but he didn't ask them.

Sevilla pointed Kelly toward the door. "I'm taking him out," he said. "*¿Entiende?* Outside."

One of the cops stopped what he was doing. Perhaps he was one of those first two through the door with Sevilla, but Kelly couldn't be sure because he did as Sevilla commanded; his eyes were on the floor. "The captain said for you to wait."

"I'm going to put him in the car. La Bestia can complain to me if he wants," Sevilla said. He pushed Kelly forward, one hand on a forearm, another latched to Kelly's waistband. He held Kelly closely, and once Kelly felt the hard shape of his weapon between them. "Move it, Kelly. No bullshit."

They negotiated the door as still more cops came in. The sun blazed white outside. Kelly tried to raise his hand against the light, but his wrists were cinched behind him. He closed his eyes until he was nearly blind. Sevilla watched the way for both of them.

"Steps," Sevilla said in Kelly's ear. They went down. Murmured Spanish and moving shadows made Kelly look up. His neighbors watched from landings and balconies. He didn't know their names or even most of their faces, but Kelly was ashamed nonetheless. His cheeks burned. Staring at his feet didn't help now.

Police vehicles crowded the street such that even the pink telephone pole was invisible. In five years Kelly had never seen so many police in one place, even when the *federales* came to town in their hundreds to fight the *narco* cartels. Vans and trucks jockeyed for position on the street with cars, all with revolving lights and all lit. The largest truck was marked *Unidad Especializada*. Stateside they would call that SWAT.

"Here," Sevilla said. His car was nestled among all the others, a simple vehicle without armor or gun ports or official seals. He steered Kelly to the back seat, held Kelly's neck when he got in and then closed the door. Kelly let himself slump forward across the seat. His heart raced, but he felt drained, not invigorated. He was vaguely aware of Sevilla getting behind the wheel or turning over the engine. Kelly felt the air-conditioning start.

"She's not here," Kelly said at last.

Sevilla turned around in the driver's seat. Kelly saw Sevilla was flushed, perspiring hard, the veins in his temples showing. "What?" Sevilla asked.

"If they want Paloma," Kelly said. "She's not here. I talked to—"

Sevilla cut him off: "Shut up, Kelly. Listen to me now and say nothing, you understand? If you want to live through the day, you don't speak unless you are spoken to. If you can't answer a question *yes* or *no*, keep your mouth shut."

"I know—" Kelly started.

"*¡Tú no sabes cualquier cosa!* You don't know anything at all, Kelly. No, don't sit up; just stay down like that. I'll tell you again: you have nothing to say to these men that you won't tell me first. This is the only favor I will do for you, Kelly. Don't waste it."

Armed police passed Sevilla's car. They didn't stop to look through the windows. Kelly felt the cool air wicking away nervous perspiration. His wrists were hurting in the handcuffs. Old vinyl seat covers stuck to his exposed skin. "I don't understand."

"Paloma," Sevilla said.

"She's gone," Kelly said. "They took her. I talked to one of the girls at the place… Ella. She said there were men that took her."

Sevilla glanced over his shoulder. When he looked back, he shook his head. "You should have come to me, Kelly. You should have done what I asked you to do. Why did you have to be so goddamned stubborn? How many times did I offer you a way out?"

Salt-sweat got into Kelly's eyes and stung them. He squinted and blinked and rubbed his face against the seat. "I don't understand," he said again. "I told you everything I knew. I was going to call you. We could find her."

"Don't you understand, Kelly?" Sevilla asked. "She's already been found."

A cop rapped on the driver's side window. Sevilla turned away from Kelly. Everything he said to the cop fell into empty space. She was found. Not alive, not dead, only *found*. She could be anything.

Kelly trembled. He couldn't breathe deeply and he felt more sweat in his eyes, but it wasn't sweat; this time it was fresh tears. When he turned on his back, his arms were pinned beneath him and the cuffs dug into his flesh. "I want to see her," Kelly said.

"Shut up," Sevilla said. He spoke again to the policeman and the cop said something back. They were talking in gibberish.

"I said I want to see her!"

"Kelly, I told you to shut up!"

The back door of Sevilla's car swung wide. Cool air rushed out and hot air swarmed over Kelly. The cop wasn't at the front window anymore, but here. He wore a lighter version of the body armor, what the police called a stab vest. His arms were bare, long and ropy with muscle. He blocked out the sun.

The cop dragged Kelly from the back of the car by his ankles. Sevilla shouted, but Kelly only heard the thud of his skull against the lower doorframe and then the asphalt outside. He caught a boot to the ribs that he couldn't block or twist away from. He sensed a descending fist before it crashed into his face.

Sevilla threw himself on the cop and they struggled over Kelly like titans mantled by the sun. The cop pushed Sevilla off and there followed more kicks, more punches. Kelly's skull rebounded on the pavement. He saw flashes of new light that didn't come from the sky. Unconsciousness came like exhausted sleep. One blow after another raised the blanket and there was only darkness underneath, warm and safe and free of pain, where even the sensation of knuckles on flesh became distant.

Kelly was dimly aware of Sevilla shouting and the other cop's voice cutting through, driven behind every punch: "You want to see? You want to see something? I'll show you something, *pinche puto!* I'll kill you! I'll fucking kill you!"

Ring the damned bell, Kelly thought. *Ring the bell. This one's over... right?*

NINE

THE CEILING WAS MADE OF STEEL springs and cotton. Kelly opened one eye first and then the other, but slowly; his head felt swollen on the inside and even the flesh behind his eye sockets was sore. He felt cool concrete beneath him and sore muscles from sleep without comfort.

Kelly was on the floor. His head lay half beneath the lower of two bunks. The air smelled heavily of chlorine, as if Kelly were in the dressing room at a YMCA, underlaid with perspiration and urine. These were the fear smells, the ones that could not be blanked out by any other. Kelly reeked of them.

He moved. Sevilla's handcuffs were gone and his hands were free. Kelly rolled onto his back, touched the sore places on his sides and chest and face. His nose was prone to breakage, but this time it was only swollen.

Sitting up was hard. Kelly used the wall to help himself into a corner beside a toilet without a seat or lid. The cell was six-by-six, the cinder blocks whitewashed and chipped and riddled with graffiti. *Tú madre es puta y pendeja,* one scrawl proclaimed in letters three inches high.

Both bunks were empty. The bottom rack had a thin mattress patterned with red and white, the stripes stained and faded by years. The top rack's mattress was rolled up. Kelly could look up from his place on the floor through the wire mesh to the low ceiling. The lower bunk had no pillow, no sheets.

Men called to each other in Spanish in other cells nearby. The light in Kelly's cell came from a compact fluorescent bulb screwed into a protected socket overhead. Without a window, he couldn't know the hour. Kelly didn't remember arriving.

He managed to get onto his feet. He was still in his sweats and barefoot. It took effort to urinate and when he did Kelly spotted flecks of blood in the stream. He used the cell's little sink to rinse his mouth and scrubbed his gums and teeth with his finger. This brought more blood. Some of his teeth were loose.

Kelly walked to the bars and tried to look left and right, but the cells ran along one wall, making it impossible to see from one into the next. The air was crowded with voices and odors. The fluorescent lights made everything sallow.

Kelly had thirst he satisfied with warm water out of the tap. It seemed clean enough and it washed away the last bad taste of unconsciousness. He was too sore to pace, so he sat on the edge of the lower bunk, clasped his hands between his knees and prayed without praying that way he had in the field of pink crosses, but without knowing what to ask for.

Somewhere a heavy door opened and closed. The chatter from unseen men in other cells surged and then subsided. Kelly came to the bars of his cell and looked again. Hands with little mirrors sprouted from neighboring cells, angling toward an invisible stretch of corridor where footfalls rang. Kelly's stomach knotted.

Seeing Sevilla was not a relief. He came with another man Kelly didn't recognize, though the uniform was familiar enough. Once Kelly had to pick up Estéban from the city jail; all the men there wore the same tan shirts and slacks, shiny patent-leather shoes and a belt adorned with a billy club and a can of mace. Sevilla's face was leaden. He didn't greet Kelly and Kelly kept quiet.

The jailor came close to the bars. He took out his can of mace and motioned to the rear wall of the cell. "Move it," he said in English. Sevilla was unreadable.

Kelly backed away and the jailor opened his cell. He turned

around when he was told to turn around and put his hands behind his back as he was instructed. The jailor cuffed him and led Kelly out to where Sevilla waited. Kelly looked into Sevilla's eyes and saw nothing.

"Two," Sevilla told the jailor. He walked behind so that Kelly couldn't see him.

Out in the passageway Kelly finally saw the far end and the gleam of sunlight from a window out of sight. The jailor marched him forward and prisoners watched him pass by. Every cell was crowded with three and sometimes four men. Where there was no bunk space, prisoners had bedrolls on the meager open floor.

"Hey! Hey, gringo, go fuck yourself," someone called out, and men laughed.

A heavy steel door ahead was painted green, but rust showed in deep gouges across its surface. The jailor made Kelly rest his forehead against the door while they waited for a guard on the far side to open the locks.

The cinder blocks and the whitewash didn't change when the cells were gone. Instead of barred doors, steel portals with judas holes stood sentinel. They were stenciled with numbers. Kelly saw four of these before they reached the one marked 2.

Kelly held his breath when the jailor opened this door, but on the other side was a space akin to his cell. The bunks and the toilet and sink were missing, replaced by an ugly wooden table bolted to the floor and two chairs secured the same way across from each other. A short metal rail adorned the table on each end. The jailor cuffed Kelly's left wrist to one.

"Sit," Sevilla told Kelly. Kelly sat.

Overhead lights banished every shadow from the room. It was a square and ugly space, every pit and scrape on the walls and the table under a surgeon's lamp. Kelly saw lines on Sevilla's face that he had never seen before. When Kelly looked at his hands, he hardly recognized them.

"*Gracias*," Sevilla told the jailor. He let the man close the door and lock it. They were alone together, except for a video camera mounted high in one corner, a gray metal shoebox with a black eye.

Sevilla followed Kelly's gaze upward. He nodded slightly and then sat down on the other side of the table. A wrinkled manila folder went between them. Sevilla folded his hands over it. He said nothing.

"Who's watching us?" Kelly asked at last.

"Does it matter?"

"I guess not."

"You had your chance to talk to me alone, Kelly," Sevilla said. "You never took it. Now whenever we speak, someone else will listen in."

"Local police?"

"It's complicated," Sevilla said. "The locals made the arrest, but the state police will lead the investigation. There is a task force for these things."

"A task force?"

"Yes. And a special prosecutor. This is very serious, Kelly. You don't seem to understand how serious it is."

"I do understand."

"If you say so."

"You're in this task force?"

Sevilla shook his head. "No. I deal with drugs. I am here as a courtesy only. Because I asked to be."

Kelly found it impossible to sit comfortably with one wrist chained to the table. He found himself leaning on his trapped arm, but the angle was wrong and it made his shoulder hurt. Straightening up was no better. "Why would you ask that?"

"I have my reasons. And I want you to know I asked to be there at the arrest, as well," Sevilla said. "I wanted to make sure you were taken in without any problems. Accidents happen."

"I think they did," Kelly replied. He touched his face. When he touched his teeth with his tongue, they were definitely loose.

"No. You're still alive."

"Why would they kill me?"

Sevilla opened the folder and held it up. Kelly saw the photo inside and retched. He snapped his head to the side before a rush of sour vomit surged into his mouth. Kelly spat and shut his eyes tightly, but the image flashed on him again and he was sick a second time.

"Take it away!"

"This isn't the only one, Kelly."

"I don't want to see that!" A patch on Kelly's arm was warm and wet. His belly churned wildly. He gripped the table-rail with his left hand and his leg with the other. His eyes stayed shut. "Put it away."

Kelly didn't look again until he heard the folder whisper closed. Sevilla folded his hands over it again and Kelly shivered. Once more Sevilla's expression was dark and unreadable, his eyes lidded. He hardly seemed to breathe.

"Less than three hundred meters from your apartment," Sevilla said. "Just a little dirt on her grave."

The little room moved. Kelly held on. His nose burned with the stink of vomit. "Oh, fuck," he said.

"Partially burned," Sevilla continued. "Raped. *Las dos vias.* Her piercings were yanked out: the tongue, the nipples, the—"

"*Why the fuck are you telling me this?*"

"Because you did it, Kelly. You did these things to Paloma. Don't you remember?" Sevilla pushed the folder across the table. Kelly recoiled from it. "Look at the pictures if you don't remember. For everything you did to her, Kelly, there are a dozen men in this building who would kill you like *that*."

Sevilla snapped his fingers. Kelly flinched. He wanted his mind to be blank, but it was not blank; something fire-blackened and mutilated and chewed by animals rushed in and filled the space between thoughts until the thoughts were crowded out completely.

Kelly did not even notice when Sevilla stopped talking, or how long there was silence. The manila folder lingered on Kelly's side of the table, one corner dangling. Kelly didn't want to touch it. At last he did, and shoved it back at Sevilla. "I didn't do that."

"Did you rape her first? Or was it Estéban?"

"Shut up."

"I don't know how a brother could rape his own sister, but it's happened, Kelly. This wouldn't be the first time. Were you high? Help me understand, Kelly. Was Estéban high, too?"

"Shut your mouth, just shut your fuckin' mouth!"

"Is that why you decided to go back to the needle, Kelly? You just couldn't take it anymore? Tell me: was it easier to do those things to her after you tore her tongue apart, Kelly? She could still scream, but at least she couldn't talk right. She couldn't say your name when she begged for mercy. When you set her on fire, she was still alive."

"I'm gonna fuckin' kill you if you say another goddamned word," Kelly said. He didn't look at Sevilla when he said it; he couldn't raise his eyes from the table, from the folder, to the man on the other side.

They were quiet a while then. Kelly shivered though it wasn't cold, his bare feet flat on the concrete floor. The heat was leached from him. He could have shed more tears, but this time they didn't come no matter how much Kelly wished. Tears would cloud his vision and then, even if Sevilla opened the folder again, Kelly would see nothing.

"I would never hurt her," Kelly said finally.

"You'll have to forgive me, Kelly, but that's something they all say."

"It's *true*."

"That's something they all say, too." Sevilla stood up from the table and took the folder with him. He went to the door. "And they say something else."

"What?"

"They say *please*, Kelly. In the end they all say *please*."

"Don't leave me here."

"*Buena suerte*."

TEN

THEY KNOCKED KELLY'S LOOSE TEETH out and he choked on his own blood. With one holding him over the table, another punched Kelly in the kidneys until his back was a mass of unbroken pain.

His head went into a sack and the sack into water. A metal basin the size of a baby bathtub was as deep as the ocean. In the end, Kelly heard nothing but his heart beating in his ears, slowly and more slowly.

Men stripped off Kelly's shirt and whipped him with electric wire. Alcohol on bare meat was white-hot agony.

A fat battery and copper-toothed clamps set his flesh ablaze.

Strangled with a wire.

Burned with a lighter.

Kicked in the corner.

Why did you do it?

Where did you do it?

When did you do it?

Begin again.

ELEVEN

KELLY HEARD THEM ARGUING IN THE next room: Dennis yelled at the men from the athletic commission and they yelled back at him. The dressing-room shower smelled like chlorine and half-dead mildew and perspiration. Kelly had the hot water on, but he slumped into one corner and the spray went into another so that all he got was a drizzling spatter and lungs full of steam. He was only half undressed, but his head wasn't there and he couldn't finish the job Dennis started.

Dennis yelled about piss-tests, but the men from the athletic commission didn't need a piss test to know Kelly was unfit to fight. He was flying on a dose of heroin that should have worn off a long time ago. Or maybe he injected too late in the day. Or maybe he shouldn't have injected at all. Or… he lost the thought.

Once Kelly wouldn't have played with anything stronger than tequila for thirty days ahead of a fight, then three weeks, then two. After that, if he could play games with the piss-tests—buying clean stuff or pulling a warm-piss switcheroo—he did. Just make it to the ring clearheaded, even when that meant making it to the ring less often. Kelly had enough money that he didn't have to fight all the time, anyway.

Doors slammed and there was more yelling. Kelly plucked at his T-shirt, cemented to his skin with water. This wasn't the best high he ever had. He was confused and too many sensations were coming at him at once: the tile, the water and the noise. His favorite part about the high was lying still and listening to his blood rush, driven by a heartbeat that was so steady and so slow. But here he couldn't have that.

"I don't give a fuck," Kelly tried to say, but his tongue never worked right when he had a heavy dose in his system. He slumped over some more, felt his cheek touch the wall and rested a while.

Eventually there was quiet. Kelly may have dozed. When he opened his eyes again, shadows moved outside the shower. His hands were awkward, but he found a way to push himself and he climbed the tile wall until his feet were flat beneath him. He left the shower on behind him.

Dennis had his back to him. He packed away his things: the tape, the enswell, the swabs and little vials of 1:1000 adrenaline mixture. Before a fight Dennis always laid out his kit to check each thing. Being a cutman was serious, as serious as fighting and maybe more. Dennis' shoulders tensed when Kelly stumbled over his hi-top boxing shoes and collided with a padded bench.

"Denny," Kelly said. This he could say. His shin hurt now. He sat on the bench. "Hey, man. Denny, man."

"I got nothin' to say to you, Kelly. We're quit."

"Listen…" Kelly began, but the words were slippery. How much did he shoot? When did he shoot it? The details weren't only foggy; they were gone completely. Kelly blinked and worked his mouth as if to tease his voice out. "Listen, Denny."

Dennis turned on him. The old man's round face was red from shouting, his eyes from crying. His cheeks were blotched up. "Don't *talk* to me, Kelly! I can't stand fuckin' listening to you when you're high. Not a word. Not one more goddamned word. I said we're quit, so we're *quit*."

Kelly leaned back without knowing whether there was anything behind him to catch his fall. The wall pressed him from behind. He breathed deeply. Outside the shower the air was cooler and it stirred him a little. Cool air like that could put him to sleep. His eyelids drooped. "It was an accident."

"I could fuckin' kill you," Dennis said. He put his back to Kelly again. "How dumb do you think I am, Kelly? *How dumb?* Stub my toe, *that's* an accident. What you are… it breaks my heart."

Dennis teleported across the room, or maybe Kelly blanked for a second. All of Dennis' things were packed away and the bag gone — no, it was by the door — and Dennis was suddenly there above Kelly, blocking out the light. A corona burst around Dennis' head. Kelly's brain shuddered. He was coming down finally, really coming down.

"Denny," Kelly said.

"It ain't the money," Dennis said. His hand zoomed in and out of Kelly's vision, abruptly larger, then smaller, then gone and then back again. Kelly's eyes drifted unfocused. He was acutely aware of Dennis' skin, but the old man's eyes were impossible to see. "It's the *waste*, Kelly. Do you even know what's wastin'? *Time.* You're wastin' my *time*, Kelly. Hell, you're wastin' *your* time. You ain't gonna live forever."

"I don't want to live forever," Kelly said.

"That's good, because you won't."

Dennis was gone. Kelly stared at the light overhead. Dennis was back. Kelly felt paper pressed into his hand.

"What is this?"

"That was your life, Kelly."

A door closed. Kelly tried to read the notice from the athletic commission, but the *chinaloa* shut all that out; he saw shapes and colors and sometimes he saw the air moving, but words were a jumble.

"Denny? Denny, come back."

Kelly's fighting trunks were still laid out for him. His robe was beside them. All of Dennis' things were gone. When did he take them? Dennis was just there, right? Kelly heard him talking. The shower was on. Dennis must be in the shower. Why was he taking a shower?

"Denny, I don't know… help."

He made it from the bench to the shower. The water was on,

but Dennis wasn't there. Kelly turned back toward the room too quickly and his knees went wobbly. He sat down hard with his legs sprawled.

"Denny? Denny, I need you."

He didn't want to, but he cried. Getting up was too hard and his brain wasn't thinking right. He felt everything too much because the high was wearing off all the clean gears and sticking. Dennis gave him something... there it was on the floor: a yellow sheet of paper, a form marked with pen scribbles. Confused, confused.

"Denny, I'm sorry."

Beer helped. Kelly bought a case of Red Dog and drank one after the other in the parking lot behind the wheel of his old gray Buick. Beer killed the headache that always came after a long high, cleared up the fog and took the edge off the world. He spent time drinking, not sleeping. When he saw a cop eyeing him for loitering, he moved on.

Three times Kelly used a pay phone to call Dennis' number, but the old man wasn't home or wasn't answering. Kelly wanted to be angry, but he could muster it only for a little while and then he was sad again. There was no more of the heroin to put feelings out of his mind, and the little Mexican who sold Kelly the stuff dealt only at night.

It was too bright to drive around. Even with sunglasses on, the sun was too much for Kelly. He parked in the shade of a coin-op car wash and watched the traffic go by. He didn't know the town or the things to do, and anyway tourist hangouts weren't what he needed; Kelly didn't want people in his world right now.

The beer was all gone. Kelly dozed with the motor running so he could keep the a/c going. When the fuel light went on, he tooled for a while instead of gassing up. Maybe he was daring the car to die.

He paid cash for a full tank and used the pay phone to call Dennis again. A dozen rings went without an answer. Kelly cursed and pounded the phone with the receiver until the plastic cracked and the handset fell into two pieces. Inside the gas station Kelly bought another six-pack of something cheap. He drank one in front of the pump and cracked a second for the drive.

Eventually he had to go home, he knew, but Kelly kept circling neighborhoods he didn't know, driving down nameless streets. He was alone here. No one could see him when he was in his car.

The floorboard in front of the passenger seat was littered with empty cans. Kelly finished another and let it fall. He steered the Buick with his knees while he popped the tab on the next. On his left were a bunch of businesses all jumbled together the way bad Texas zoning let it happen, and on his right were streets with houses and trees and lawns. He saw kids on bikes or playing in sprinklers. Up ahead a railroad crossing cut the road diagonally and the lights were flashing. There was no one up ahead.

"Come on," Kelly said. He didn't see the train, but now the safety barriers dropped. He was annoyed. The brake was an imposition. Kelly balanced the beer on top of the steering wheel and goosed the accelerator. "Come on, come on."

A side street split from the main road and ran parallel to the track. Kelly saw some kids in the grass on the shoulder, idling with their bikes, watching for the train he still didn't see, seven- or eight-year-olds needing entertainment on a Saturday.

Fifty yards away and the train appeared. Kelly touched the brake and then let off. He angled for the side road. The sign said YIELD. He passed the kids at forty-five miles an hour with the clanging of the train signal filtering through the closed windows, the sound of the Buick's engine and Kelly's thoughts.

Impact came just past the turn. A bicycle transformed into a tangle of rubber and metal on impact and tumbled across the hood. A pedal struck the corner of the windshield and cracked the glass.

"Goddammit!"

Kelly heard children shrieking and the train horn blowing. He swerved and the bicycle fell away. He lost his fingertip grip on the beer can and it hit the dashboard spraying foam. The Buick skidded, the wheel alive under Kelly's hands. Kelly stomped with both feet, got the brake and the gas. The engine revved and the wheels screamed. He came to a stop across two lanes. The Buick stalled.

His crotch was soaked. Kelly smelled piss. He struggled with the door and when he got it open he tumbled onto the blacktop. The kids were in the street. The mangled bicycle was thirty feet away. The train churned past on steel wheels, heedless of it all. Kelly's eye drifted back to the children, how they gathered around and how the shrieking hadn't stopped, and how they concealed nothing.

He had never known a boy could be so full of blood. The asphalt was painted with it, deep red and almost pink intermingled. The boy was torn open so that his hipbones were visible. The other children were caught in his orbit, too frightened to come close, too shocked to flee.

Kelly's lungs were empty, or he might have screamed. He couldn't feel his arms or legs. He was still the way the dead boy was so terribly still and he could not bring himself to look away. The train kept coming, hauling car after car. Kelly heard its fading horn.

The boy's limbs were shattered, twisted up like the bicycle. One mangled hand pointed toward the sky, perched on the remains of a forearm and a crushed elbow. Shorts and T-shirt were stained darkly and the pool of blood kept expanding. Where did it all come from?

He was moving before he realized he could move. The knot of children broke apart. Some ran, some cried and others looked to Kelly. He turned his face from them. Numb hands found the open car door, helped him clamber in and turn the key. The Buick's engine hitched once before it started. Kelly swallowed his heart.

The car laid an oily trail of rubber on the road behind it. Kelly drove fifty miles without slowing or stopping, but only a hundred before he took another drink. Then he turned toward Mexico.

TWELVE

KELLY WOKE CRYING. HE STARTED on the narrow bunk mattress and felt pain everywhere he could still bear it. The rest of him was beyond hurt; when he stirred those injuries he felt suddenly and deeply sick to his stomach, but retching only made the suffering worse.

"Kelly," Sevilla said.

One of Kelly's eyes was swollen shut. He saw Sevilla outside his cell. It was so quiet and so still that for a moment Kelly wasn't sure whether he was dreaming again or whether this was real. The pain was real enough. He remembered the crushed body of the little boy in the road; that was real, too, but left behind.

"Help me," Kelly said.

"Open it up," Sevilla said.

A guard moved into Kelly's vision. A key was put to the lock and the door was opened. Kelly needed the guard and Sevilla to get to his feet. Something warm and wet flowed down Kelly's leg: he couldn't stop himself from pissing. *"Eso es repugnante,"* the guard said, but he didn't let go.

When they marched Kelly past the other cells there was silence. The men behind bars simply watched. Kelly walked dragging his right foot; he couldn't make it work right and he was too far gone to care about impressions. The end of the cell block seemed a dozen miles away. When they reached the door, the guard didn't bother commanding Kelly to lean against the wall; he had no energy to run.

They passed the steel doors with their plain numbers and judas holes. Kelly had an arm across Sevilla's shoulders. He clutched at the material of Sevilla's suit and his grip was weak, terribly weak. "Please," Kelly said. He hated the sound of his own voice.

Kelly held his breath as they approached Room 2, and then they went by. He prayed they would pass them all, but Sevilla and the guard stopped at Room 4. Another lock and another key and now Sevilla helped Kelly alone into another space with another bolted-down table and another pair of immobile chairs.

The guard locked them into the room alone. Sevilla put Kelly in one of the chairs and stopped to straighten his jacket and tie. Kelly let his head fall back and he saw above, tucked in the corner, another video camera watching, but this room was different: a set of cheap plastic blinds covered a window across from the table. If the blinds were opened, Kelly could look through the window from where he sat. Maybe he would see the sky, or a little open ground. Maybe he would feel real sun.

Sevilla didn't open the blinds. He sat opposite Kelly.

"I won't ask you how you feel," Sevilla said.

"I need a doctor," Kelly replied.

"I'll see what I can do."

"When?"

"Soon."

Without a clock on the wall, time in the room went on forever. The chipped surface of the table had something that looked like dried blood caked in the cracks. No matter how he sat, Kelly's body protested. He would almost rather lie on the bare concrete floor, but he didn't want to sleep because then he might dream of the little boy on his bicycle and the crowd of children around him. Or worse, he would dream of Paloma the way she was in Sevilla's photos.

"They asked me to talk to you one more time," Sevilla said. "I need for you to listen."

"I didn't kill her."

Sevilla had no reply. He brought out a pack of Benson & Hedges, took a cigarette for himself and left the pack on the table. Kelly didn't touch it. He watched Sevilla light and drag and exhale toward the ceiling. The sound of shouting carried through the walls.

Kelly's head throbbed. He closed his eye and saw patterns in the dark.

"Have I ever told you about my daughter?" Sevilla asked.

Kelly didn't open his eye. "No."

"I know every father thinks so, but she was beautiful. The most beautiful girl in all of Mexico. Too beautiful for this world. And my granddaughter... oh, you should have seen her, Kelly. Something so lovely would break your heart."

More shouting. Kelly thought he recognized a voice, but his ears hurt as much as the rest of him. He put his hands on the table. The room swayed around him and his stomach protested. Kelly wondered whether his eardrums were damaged. A boxer who burst an eardrum couldn't fight; balance is everything.

"All we want is the truth, Kelly," Sevilla said at last.

"I didn't kill her."

"Kelly, look at me."

Kelly opened his eye and he saw Sevilla wreathed in smoke. The man was haggard, sweating. Something thumped hard against the wall behind Sevilla and the blinds jumped. "I did not kill her," Kelly repeated.

"Paloma didn't kill *herself*, Kelly. And the men in charge... the man they see is a drug addict working with a known *narcotraficante*. They know about the heroin, Kelly. They know about Estéban and Paloma and how the money came. They know you can't go back to the States. All of this they know, and yet now they must take your word for something so serious? Think about it, Kelly. Think about it and save your life."

"What will you do?"

"Whatever I can do."

"That's not enough."

"That's all you get," Sevilla said, and for an instant Kelly saw Ortíz in Sevilla's place, and smelled beer and limes.

"Goddammit."

"All these years, Kelly, I've been watching you, talking to you… but we were never friends. I always liked you, or maybe I just felt sorry for you."

"Fuck you."

Sevilla dismissed Kelly with a wave of his cigarette. "And then you had Paloma. Of course, she was a drug dealer's sister and I know when she went with Estéban to visit their 'cousin' in Mazatlán they were really making contact with Estéban's supplier. What, you didn't know this? I'm surprised at you, Kelly."

Kelly wanted to spit on the table, but his mouth was dry and tasted of blood. "I don't believe a goddamned word of it," he said.

"Believe it or don't believe it," Sevilla replied. "It's true. I had no illusions about her or her brother, but her work — her *real* work, Kelly, not the other things – that was real. I told you before: you wouldn't believe how much good she did."

"I don't want to talk about her anymore," Kelly said.

"You need to tell me who did this to her, Kelly."

"I can't."

"Because you're still keeping secrets."

"Because I don't know."

Sevilla stubbed his cigarette out on the table and tossed the butt into the corner. The weight beneath his eyes seemed to deepen. When he shook his head, Kelly thought Sevilla might weep.

"They come to me and they say here is the body, here are the terrible things that have been done and here are the men closest to her. In Juárez, you know, we are always looking for *el extranjero*, the monster we have never seen before who will do us harm, but we hurt ourselves so well, Kelly, we don't need strangers. We are a city of dead women. We feed on our own."

"I didn't—" Kelly began.

"Okay," Sevilla said. He put a hand up for silence. "Okay."

Sevilla rose from the table. He came around and offered his arm. Kelly used the old cop like a crutch and they walked together to the covered window. Sevilla drew the blinds up. On the other side wasn't sun or open space, but another room like this one.

Kelly recognized both policemen on the far side of the glass. One was young, maybe only twenty-five, soft in the middle and already beginning to lose his hair. The other was older, stronger and wore his mustache and graying hair like a military man. The older cop used his fists a lot. His name was Captain Garcia. The younger sometimes asked questions, though now he was silent.

Estéban sat between them with both hands cuffed to the table. Kelly saw the washbasin and the head-sack discarded in a corner. The table was washed in water turned pink with oozing blood. Estéban's face was a welter of swelling and bruises. His lips were split a half-dozen times. He was stripped to the waist and his chest was badly marked.

"Wake up, asshole!" Captain Garcia shouted. He took Estéban by the scruff of the neck and pointed toward the window. Kelly saw Estéban's eyes flickering, alive, and then he realized the window was just that, and not a two-way mirror. Kelly put his hand on the glass. "There's your fucking friend, *puto!* What's he going to do for you? *¡Nada!*"

"If you didn't do it, then tell me who did," Sevilla said in Kelly's ear.

"I don't know," Kelly said.

"Enrique, go get it," the older cop told the younger.

"You're small fish, Kelly. I always told you that. Why did they kill her, Kelly? Give me names and it can be *them* in here instead of you."

Kelly's good eye stung with salt tears. "I don't know," he said. The younger cop, Enrique, disappeared from sight. When he returned, he gave something to Captain Garcia. Kelly saw it when Enrique stepped away: a cut-down baseball bat wrapped in masking tape and stained by dirt and old blood. Estéban saw it, too; Kelly recognized fear, but Estéban didn't plead.

"Don't do this," Kelly said instead.

"*We* aren't doing this," Sevilla replied. "*You're* doing this."

"Hold his goddamned hand," the older cop told Enrique.

Kelly struck the window. The policemen ignored him. He tried to push away from Sevilla, but he was too weak and his uncooperative leg refused to hold his weight. Kelly sprawled against the glass and only Sevilla kept him from falling.

Enrique pinned Estéban's right hand.

"You want to say something now?" Garcia asked.

"*Chinga tu madre,*" Estéban replied.

Captain Garcia raised the bat and Enrique looked away. Kelly could not.

One blow smashed three fingers and left them bent in different directions. Estéban screamed. Kelly felt it through the window, shaking the glass, or perhaps it was Kelly's voice, because Kelly didn't know himself anymore. The bat came down again and again and once more after that until there was torn flesh and pieces of shattered bone sticking out. Estéban's pinky was mush, oozing blood and pink meat and flecks of white.

"Stop it! Stop it, goddammit, *stop!*"

"*Make* it stop, Kelly! Tell me who did it. If it wasn't you, then who was it? Tell me, Kelly! I'm begging you, just talk."

Kelly's stomach turned over. He broke from Sevilla and toppled onto the floor spitting up bile and water and coral-colored foam. Kelly lunged for the closed door on all fours. He still heard the shrieking and the steady, crunching blows of the bat like a butcher at work.

Sevilla grabbed Kelly by the shirt and half-hauled him from the floor. Kelly swung wildly, felt his knuckles connect and then he was at the door. There was no handle on his side to grab. He pounded his fists against the metal. "Stéban! *Stéban!* Paloma, I'm so sorry. *Lo siento, lo siento, lo siento.*"

Kelly heard Sevilla yelling and the door suddenly bucked. He could not stand. The floor reached up for him. Two guards pushed in through the half-open door and then all Kelly saw and felt were clubs and boots and pain until everything went away.

THIRTEEN

HE AWOKE WITH SOMEONE FLICKING warm water on his face. His left eye still wouldn't open. Concrete pressed against his wounds because Kelly was on the floor of his cell and not the bunk. He saw a thin, dark man in a white T-shirt and work pants with a metal bowl and dripping fingers. The T-shirt had a big, black peace symbol printed on it.

The man saw Kelly was awake. He smiled thinly and cast more water on him.

"It's all right," Kelly said.

The man showered more water from his fingertips. Kelly's shirt was soaked.

"Cut it out!"

The man shrugged. He put the bowl aside and reclined on Kelly's bunk. His build was lean, almost like a hungry dog, but he wasn't weak. A boxer read a man's body in the ring and out, saw emotion and skill tied up together in muscle and bone. This man was not afraid of anyone.

Kelly managed to sit up. He looked at his hands. They weren't smashed. Seeing his fingers, he saw Estéban's and heard the sound of them breaking beneath the bat. The memory made Kelly feel sick again. He was out of breath from the effort of moving even a little.

"¿Cómo le llaman?" Kelly asked the man on his bunk.

The man didn't look at Kelly. "Gaspar," he said.

"I'm Kelly."

Gaspar shrugged again. He studied the underside of the upper bunk with his thin arms folded behind his head. Kelly saw the man was barefoot; his slip-on shoes were set neatly by the door of the cell.

"I don't think I can get to the top bunk," Kelly said. "*Estoy lastimado.*"

"Everybody gets hurt in here eventually," Gaspar said. He spared Kelly a look out of the corner of his eye. "You want to sleep off the floor, you climb, *cabrón.*"

Heat rose to Kelly's face. He wanted to stand, grab, kick, punch, but just thinking about it made him feel exhausted. Instead he did nothing. "Whatever," he said finally.

"Whatever," Gaspar repeated. He closed his eyes and Kelly watched the man's chest rise and fall in instant slumber beneath the peace symbol.

Kelly lay down on the concrete again. He listened to the voices calling back and forth between cells and the crash of metal on metal. His body was exhausted, but he was beyond easy sleep. Being unconscious was not the same as rest. Every part of him ached inside and out and the pain clung tightly to the memory of Estéban and the room and the bat.

Gaspar stirred awake. He sat on the edge of the bunk again and took up the metal bowl. For a moment he seemed to consider showering Kelly with water again, but then he simply drank. He offered Kelly the leftover.

"Thanks," Kelly said. He managed to rise on one arm, take a drink and keep it down.

"What the fuck are you doing in here?" Gaspar asked.

Kelly shook his head. "You don't want to know."

"They say I raped a girl," Gaspar said. "I say that *puta*, she took my money, I get what I paid for. You can't call that forcing her."

"I guess not," Kelly said, and he lay back on the concrete.

Gaspar watched Kelly for a while. His face was narrow and

he had a long nose broken in two places. Finally he rose from the bunk and offered Kelly his hand. "Get up off the floor. You're going to get sick lying there like that."

His joints were on fire and his muscles shrieked, but with Gaspar's help Kelly got to the bunk. He couldn't lift his bad leg; Gaspar picked it up for him. When they were done, the wiry man turned down the bedding on the top bunk and clambered up. Kelly saw the shape of him on the springs overhead.

Gaspar's voice floated down: "El Cereso is not a good place for a white boy."

"I know," Kelly said.

"Whatever they want you to say, you should say it."

Kelly heard the thump and crunch of wood and bone. "I can't," he said.

"What, you think you are some kind of tough *hombre*? Believe me: you aren't so tough as you think."

This time Kelly only nodded. The lumps in the bedroll were like knives in his flesh. He closed his eye and willed himself to sleep without dreams or memory. The babble of a dozen conversations happening all at once — shouted and whispered — turned into the drizzle of raindrops on a windowsill.

Somehow Kelly knew it was nighttime when he came around again. The fluorescent lights were the same, and he saw the outline of Gaspar on the top bunk as if the man hadn't moved an inch. The quality of talk outside the cell had changed. A guard wandered past the barred door and paused to look at Gaspar's shoes before moving on.

Rest made Kelly stronger and he was able to rise on his own. He used the toilet and ignored the blood that ran thick in his urine. The upper bunk creaked and when Kelly turned around, he saw Gaspar watching him. "How do I look?" Kelly asked, but he couldn't smile.

"You look dead already," Gaspar answered. Before Kelly had

seen only boredom in the man's eyes, but now there was the wet shimmer of fear. This, too, Kelly recognized from the ring and from his own mirror on mornings he would rather not recall.

He tried to push it away. "Did I miss food?" Kelly asked.

"No."

"Good. I'm hungry," Kelly said, and he was. He did not remember the last meal he was able to eat and keep down, but now the craving for something in his belly was strong and growing stronger. Food would put power back into his muscles again. He didn't like the way his foot continued to drag, or the way his calf felt strange and half numb when he touched it.

He sat but didn't lie down again. The same guard passed his cell again, and this time the man looked at Kelly. When their eyes met, the guard turned his head away and hurried on.

Gaspar descended from his bunk and crouched on the floor with his back against the wall. "They can see it, too," he said.

"What?" Kelly asked.

"When they come back for you, I get the bottom bunk again," Gaspar replied.

Kelly watched the cell door. The guard didn't reappear. "They won't kill me," he said.

"No," Gaspar said. "They don't kill nobody in here. People just die."

"I'm not going to say what they want me to say."

"Then you are more stupid than you look."

Gaspar fell silent and Kelly turned his eye on the man. He looked at Gaspar's shirt and his clean work pants and his bare feet. Gaspar had heavy calluses on his toes, especially his big toe, and the faded lines of old scars. He had scars on his hands, too.

"Are you a cop, or are you just working for the cops?" Kelly asked.

Stretching made Gaspar look like a rangy stray cat. "Nobody asks questions like that in here," he said at last.

"I'm asking."

"I don't got an answer for you," Gaspar said, and then he looked away.

Kelly smiled to himself. "You tell them whatever you want to tell them. Get what's coming to you."

"Did you kill that girl?"

The smile died. "She wasn't a girl. She was a woman."

"Did you kill her?"

"No."

"You know I got to ask. It's nothing personal."

"I didn't kill her," Kelly said. "And I'm not saying otherwise to anybody. You tell them that. Tell them that and see what they do."

FOURTEEN

GASPAR CALLED FOR A GUARD AND after a while one came. He left without saying goodbye to Kelly. That was fine. Another jailor brought food that Kelly ate with his bare hands, chewed with loosened teeth and barely tasted. He shoved the tray back out through the bars when he was finished and someone picked it up.

Only when he was alone did Kelly feel fatigue pressing down on him again. He lay on the bunk and slept and this time when he woke the lights were almost all shut off and the cellblock was utterly still. The cell itself was inked in darkness.

It hurt to move, but he sat on the side of the bunk and removed his shoes. He put them side by side, neatly, the way Gaspar had done. His bare feet picked up the slight vibration of the living structure; hundreds of moving bodies translated through the concrete to something Kelly could feel, like trembling. One foot felt more than the other. A part of Kelly realized his injured leg would never function properly again, and strangely knowing that didn't bother him so much.

"I'm sorry for everything," Kelly whispered aloud. His voice was scratchy and it hurt to speak. Once more he didn't recognize himself. "I've been an idiot. I'm sorry."

Kelly put his hand on his knee as though he were touching the head of that poor dead boy in the street, or Paloma in her sleep. His fingers trembled. He was crying again.

"I didn't think about it… everything. I know that's not enough, but it's all I got. And I'm not gonna be the one who fucks things up anymore. I promise. I'll make it right somehow. If God'll let me, I'll make it right."

He used the bunk to help himself stand, and from the bunk to the wall. He forced himself to walk the six feet from front to rear three times before collapsing into the bunk again, his flesh soaked in perspiration. His heartbeat surged and fluttered.

A locked door opened and heels rang on cement. The inmates didn't stir. The jailors patrolled the block hourly, sometimes alone and sometimes in pairs, the sound of their passing like a great ticking clock. Kelly panted on his bunk. He waited for the shadow to pass in the half-lit passageway beyond the cell door.

The man came to his cell and stopped. Kelly recognized the older cop's frame — broad shoulders, big head and thick neck — by shadows alone. The cop said nothing, but Kelly heard him breathing.

"I didn't do it," Kelly said, but the words faltered. He tried again. "I didn't do it."

Keys jingled and the cop opened the cell. He didn't close the door behind him, but Kelly couldn't run even if he wanted to; he was dying on the inside, broken up and going nowhere. When the cop stood over the bunks he seemed ten feet tall and Kelly only a child.

"I… I won't say I did it."

Other figures gathered at the door of the cell. They were also quiet and the cellblock refused to take a breath. Kelly knew if he called for help he might as well be alone; the policeman wasn't there and the others weren't there and every cell was completely empty because the prison was deserted.

"Fuck you if I say I did it."

Kelly didn't see the bat, but of course the cop must have had it all along. Wood connected with his flesh and Kelly felt meat and bone give away. His jaw was broken, his mouth filled with fresh blood. Pain had color and texture. Kelly put his hand up and had his wrist shattered. He turned to put his back to the worst of it, but the cop dragged him out of the bunk and onto the floor of the cell where kicks and blows followed one after another until Kelly couldn't tell them apart.

He waited for the bell to ring, but the referee never noticed when time came and passed. Kelly grabbed for the ropes and someone stepped on his fingers. The roar of the crowd was the rush of his blood in his ears. *¡Délo a la madre! ¡Délo a la madre!*

How would Denny get the bleeding to stop? There wasn't enough time between rounds to bring down all this swelling. He was broken and the ref should have stepped in, but they were letting it go on and on. Ring lights beat down and faces outside the ropes were twisted and shadowed. Paloma was there. Estéban was there. The little boy was there with his shattered bicycle beside him. And Denny in the corner shouting for one more round, *Kelly, you can make it one more round?*

On his back he saw Captain Garcia with his cut-down baseball bat dripping with crimson and spattered with it himself, but bringing the weapon up and down again and again and again bringing hurt so deep that it didn't even register anymore.

A prayer was a bubble of blood on busted lips. Begging was a murmur. When Kelly reached up, he raised the same mangled hand as a crushed child on the street as the train thundered by. And then all he heard was music, and Eliseo Robles singing for Ramón Ayala and the Brave Ones of the North as if from far away:

> *Un rinconcito en el cielo*
> *Juntos, unidos los dos*
> *Y cuando caiga la noche*
> *Te daré mi amor...*

PART THREE

Padre

ONE

WHEN RAFAEL TÉODULO SEVILLA Adán was young he chose beer and tequila as his poisons. These things were cheap and readily available and they got the job done, which was all a man could ask for. Over time Sevilla developed a taste for blended whiskies, especially Johnnie Walker, and now it was all he chose for himself.

Drinking was something he did alone, not in a bar. And because Sevilla did not drink at home, he did it in the only place he felt comfortable: behind the wheel of his car, parked outside his front gate.

Little houses were crowded up against one another here, but shielded by whitewashed concrete walls, wrought-iron gates and burglar bars. If Ciudad Juárez had any constant at all, it was those bars, always whispering nowhere was safe, nowhere, nowhere.

The sun went down, but the heat lingered. Sevilla sat in the darkened car with a bottle of Johnnie Walker between his legs, swigging directly from the neck when the urge struck him. Tonight it was Red Label because he hadn't enough cash for Black Label. The flavor was good enough, and the end result the same.

Sevilla did not drink in the house because his wife forbade it. Smoking and drinking were things to be done *elsewhere*, not even in the tiny courtyard outside the house, where Sevilla could touch both walls with his extended fingertips. Liliana didn't begrudge anyone their vices, not even her husband, but she could set a line against them beginning at her front gate.

It was time to smoke. Sevilla put down his window and lit a cigarette. He flicked the ashes into the street. When drunk, Sevilla was fascinated by the shifting pattern of burning tobacco at the end of a smoke. His legs had long slipped into a comfortable lack of sensation, as if his body were falling asleep apart from his mind. He let his head lay back against the rest. His eyes slid shut and forgot about the cigarette until the ash nipped at his fingers.

Sevilla cast the butt out the window. Lights were on and he heard music and voices. His house was black and silent. A young woman in a *maquila* uniform walked past Sevilla's car down the middle of the cracked road and Sevilla's heart ached. Another pull on the bottle of Johnnie Walker put things in better order.

He watched the woman in his rear-view mirror until she vanished out of sight. No one bothered her, or so much as called to her. Sevilla wondered where she lived; he didn't remember seeing her before. That was the problem with Juárez: the faces were always changing.

Sitting no longer appealed to him. Sevilla swished the last of Señor Walker around at the bottom of the bottle and then poured it out the open window. He got out carefully and locked the vehicle up. Thieves wouldn't bother Sevilla's car; even teenage joyriders passing through got the word that this was a policeman's house. Graffiti marked the garden walls and even the garbage cans of his neighbors, but none marred Sevilla's. This, along with a badge and a gun, was a privilege.

He was gentle with the squeaking front gate even though there was no one at home. At the door he fumbled with his keys in the dark and caught a whiff of himself in the process: he smelled of drink and sweat and stale smoke. Once he got the lock open he let himself into the still shadows inside.

"*Hola*," Sevilla called softly, and shut the door behind him. He set two locks and the chain, though these too were unnecessary. A standing lamp near the entrance when switched on cast dim yellow light across a crowded front room. Sevilla put his keys in a bowl by the door and realized he still carried the empty bottle of Johnnie Walker. He tucked it into his jacket and felt ashamed.

The furniture was simple, plain and comfortable. Liliana decorated with hand-sewn throws and pillows and a great painting of Jesus dominated one wall. Christ pointed to his Sacred Heart. Sevilla touched his chest unconsciously when he passed.

Another wall was devoted to family photographs new and old. Frames brushed against frames, black and white with color in a sunburst radiating from a picture of Sevilla and Liliana on their wedding day. Sevilla wore his uncle's best suit on loan and Liliana her mother's wedding dress. They were outside, but though the sun shone in the photo it rained later on and the reception was driven indoors.

Sevilla disposed of the empty whisky bottle in the kitchen and put a few pieces of newspaper on top of it. The squat, rounded refrigerator was the same one he and Liliana bought with their wedding money. The freezer had to be defrosted manually, but it still kept food cold. Sevilla found a bottle of Jarritos to wash away the lingering taste of Señor Walker.

His home had two bedrooms. More family photos decorated the short hallway that divided the house. These were mostly of his daughter Ana in her growing years, though a few showed Ana and her daughter Ofelia. Once Sevilla and Liliana hoped to fill the hallway with pictures of all their children and grandchildren, but one wall was empty and the other only partly filled.

Sevilla undressed in the bathroom and took a shower. He did not like the look of his reflection — the deep redness of his eyes, the heaviness of his cheeks — but he shaved and put on cologne and hoped for better the next day. Briefly he thought of Kelly, but forced from his mind the image of Kelly in his cell. "*Mañana*," Sevilla said aloud.

He put on pajamas, a tatty robe and slippers and went to his daughter's room. Originally the space belonged to Liliana and him, but when Ofelia came without a father the decision was made to give up the room to the child and her mother. The bed was small and neat, Ofelia's crib beside it. A changing table was still stocked with cotton diapers, pins and ointments. Once Señora Alvarez, who cleaned up, asked whether Sevilla wanted it all taken out, given away, but Sevilla said *no*, though he could not explain why.

"*Hola, hija,*" Sevilla told the empty room. "*Hola, nieta.*"

He sat on the bed. A picture of Ana with Ofelia rested on the endtable. Sevilla allowed himself to hold it, but not to look at the image directly: a young woman and a baby at the Parque Central in autumn. Ana's smile had a crooked tooth in front.

Sevilla didn't cry because there were no tears anymore. He simply sat with a weight pressed on his heart until the whisky threatened to put him to sleep. When he could barely keep his eyes open any longer, he put the photograph away and went back to the room he once shared with his wife and went to bed.

He slept, but it was not a good sleep, though at least the dreams were only half formed and he remembered none of the details whenever he woke, however briefly, during the night.

TWO

THE TELEPHONE RANG IN THE morning after coffee. Sevilla stood in the kitchen wearing rumpled pajamas with the early sun showing through the bars on the back windows. The house smelled of the fresh brew, but not of home.

"¿Bueno?"

"The American is dead."

Sevilla felt heat and pain in his ear. "What?"

"Kelly Courter is dead," said the man on the other end.

"What? When? Who is this?"

The line buzzed. Sevilla missed the cradle with the receiver and spilled his coffee at the same time. He cursed and got it right, but his hands shook while his mind turned.

"I'll clean it up," he said to no one, and then made a new call.

THREE

Sevilla drove to the Hospital General, a plain hunk of functional building peppered with windows. He showed his identification to the attendant at the parking lot and parked in a space marked for a doctor. In his time Sevilla had spent hours upon hours at the Hospital General, enduring its crowded waiting rooms and cracked plastic chairs and the smell of death, urine, blood and cigarettes.

It was no different at this early hour, though perhaps there were fewer people than usual. Sevilla saw an old man in a wheelchair, already hooked up to fluids and his leg elevated. People slept sitting up, leaning against one another. A television droned quietly near the ceiling of one corner, the color out of sync and the signal diffuse.

The counter had cracked sliding windows to protect the staff and as Sevilla approached a nurse opened one. They had no computers here. At the Hospital General they used clipboards and awkwardly photocopied forms for everything. Her workspace was crowded with paper. Sevilla showed his identification again. "I'm looking for a patient: Kelly Courter."

"When did he check in?"

"I don't know. Sometime last night."

The woman was young, no more than twenty, and something about her made Sevilla's heart ache. She sorted through her many layers of documents. The skin creased between her eyebrows, but when she looked up it was gone. "I'm sorry to say he is in *Cuidado Intensivo*."

"Which way is that?"

"Through those doors. Down the hall. You'll see the signs."

"*Gracias, señorita.*"

Sevilla passed through double doors into a broad, greenly lit hall. He followed the signs until he saw the first uniformed policeman, and then another and another. A knot of six stood guard around the entrance to the emergency room, talking to each other or idly watching a television fixed on a stand.

The cops snapped to when Sevilla came closer, then relaxed when he showed his badge and ID. He was one of them. "Where is he?" Sevilla asked them. "The American."

"In there. But he's unconscious. The doctors say—"

"I'll find out," Sevilla interrupted. "*Con permiso.*"

He pushed through them and through the door. The room beyond was larger than he expected, with space for three beds though two were empty. Kelly lay twisted in the nearest bed. No television chattered here; the steady beep of a heart monitor kept the quiet at bay. A respirator hissed in concert and in the far corner a woman in a coal-colored pantsuit spoke quietly into a cell phone.

Kelly's face was obscured by an enormous mass of gauze and the respirator hose snaked out of a nest of transparent tape that let the color of bruises and blood show through. Both of his arms were bound in casts from upper arm to fingertips. His lower legs bulged beneath the light blanket, cuffed in inflatable sheaths that breathed on their own, squeezing away clots that might form and kill the lungs or brain.

"Damn you, Kelly," Sevilla said under his breath.

Sevilla wanted to go to Kelly's bedside, but he waited for the woman on the phone. She raised a finger to him while she talked and Sevilla nodded. The conversation lasted another minute. When the woman closed the phone, she crossed the room and shook Sevilla's hand. "Rafael Sevilla? It's good to meet you. I'm Adriana Quintero. With the FEDCM."

"I know you," Sevilla said. Quintero had a firm grip. He saw that her nails were manicured and painted a subtle shade of seashell pink. She smelled faintly of good perfume and her hair was perfect. "I've seen you on the television."

Quintero smiled briefly. The cell phone went into her pocket. When she looked at Kelly, the smile was gone. "They told me you helped secure his confession."

Sevilla didn't want to look directly at Kelly. "If he confessed, he didn't do it to me."

"No? Captain Garcia said—"

"Someone called me this morning," Sevilla said. "The man... the caller told me Kelly was dead. When did he come here?"

Something flickered behind Quintero's eyes when she looked at Sevilla, and then it was gone. "He was found in his cell during rounds at three o'clock. Why would someone call you? Did you recognize the voice?"

"How did it happen?"

"He was attacked by another prisoner."

Sevilla shook his head. "That's impossible. He was in his cell alone."

"It's very crowded at El Cereso. He was placed with a prisoner awaiting trial on drug charges. He was a nonviolent offender; no one could know he would attack like this."

"Where is this prisoner now?"

"In solitary."

"I'd like to talk to him."

Quintero waved the words away with her hand. She was poised in person just as she was on television. The FEDCM was the Special Task Force for the Investigation of Crimes against Women. Whenever a *feminicidio* occurred, someone from the FEDCM was on television to make a statement or a comment with the offices of the Procuraduría behind them. The faces changed over the years, but the message was always the same, waved away with a hand.

"There's no need for that," Quintero said. "Captain Garcia and his people will handle it."

Sevilla winced. "And what about Estéban Salazar?"

"Who?"

"The other suspect," Sevilla said. "He's the dead woman's brother. Paloma Salazar is the victim."

Quintero turned toward Kelly and Sevilla couldn't see her face. "I'll have to check on that."

Sevilla wanted to take the woman by the arm, but he didn't. He kept his voice low. "*Señora*, I don't mean any disrespect, but I think I should—"

"Let's go outside," Quintero cut in. She favored Sevilla with a smile. "Have you had any breakfast? I'll buy you some."

They left Kelly and passed through the cops outside the door. Quintero led the way out through the emergency room. A baby cried and a young man waited patiently on a vinyl-upholstered chair with his bloody hand wrapped tightly in gauze.

Out in the sun, Quintero lit a cigarette with a disposable lighter. She offered Sevilla one. He took it. Quintero's brand was Marlboro Lite. Sevilla lit it with his own lighter and for a long moment they stood in silence breathing nicotine and smoke.

"You're a narcotics investigator, yes?" Quintero asked at last.

"That's right."

"How long have you been doing that?"

"Nearly thirty years."

"That's impressive, *señor*."

"Thank you," Sevilla said.

Quintero flicked her cigarette away half finished. She turned to face Sevilla and her expression was stolid. "I'm forty-three," she said, "so I don't have your experience, but I've worked for the office of the Procuraduría for eleven years. I'm good at my job. That is why I'm here, doing this: because it's important work that can't be made a mess of."

"I understand," Sevilla said, though he did not. He wanted to read Quintero, but he couldn't; nothing moved behind her eyes anymore. "It's only—"

"This American man, Courter, you knew him well?"

"Perhaps not as well as I thought. But, yes, I knew him."

"Then you should be glad you were allowed to be a part of the investigation at all. We've had to deal with these *feminicidios* for almost twenty years. It's a shame. It's an embarrassment. They mock Ciudad Juárez all over the world because we can't stop this. It was almost a relief when the cartels started killing each other; it took the pressure off."

Sevilla took a long drag on the Marlboro, but he no longer had a taste for it. He let the cigarette fall to the pavement and ground the coal beneath his toe. "You don't have to tell me these things, Señora Quintero," he said.

"Kelly Courter was a fighter and a drug user and a drug *dealer*. Isn't that right?"

"Yes, that's right," Sevilla said. He wanted to spit the bad taste from his mouth.

"Then you see where this is going," Quintero replied. "The victim's brother was a drug dealer, as well. You know how these *narcotraficantes* are, how crazy they can get when they use their own stuff. They're running riot all along the border. Maybe we don't know why they killed Paloma Salazar, but we'll find out."

Sevilla dragged his foot across the broken cigarette and smeared the ash on the sidewalk. "Not from Kelly," he said.

"What?"

"I said, 'Not from Kelly,'" Sevilla repeated. "I was told a confession was paramount, but now he can confess to no one. And why would Estéban do such a thing to his own sister? These things... they make no sense."

"It wouldn't be the first time," Quintero said.

"No, but—"

"It's a terrible thing, what happened to Señor Courter," Quintero continued, "but it's done now. We can only work with what we have, and there's evidence—convincing evidence—pointing to these men for the crime. If it doesn't make sense, it's because none of this makes sense. Ciudad Juárez doesn't hate its women."

"Why was Kelly removed from the jail?"

Quintero smiled a little but it was quickly gone. "That was a decision I made. The jail's infirmary isn't capable of dealing with a man in Courter's condition."

"Why not just let him die?"

"Like I said: I want him as an example. And he's American."

"The other," Sevilla said quietly.

"What?"

"Nothing."

"And who knows how many other murders he's responsible for. We're taking statements from witnesses who attest to strange behavior on Courter's part. Behavior that might lead to additional convictions."

"What witnesses are these?"

"Reliable ones."

Sevilla frowned. "I'd like to see Estéban Salazar taken from the general population in El Cereso and placed under protective custody. If it's examples you want, you can't have anything like this happen again."

"I find it unlikely that lightning will strike twice."

"All the same, it would make me more comfortable."

"I'll do it if the opportunity presents itself."

Sevilla stared at his feet. He crossed the line of ash with his toe. *Justicia*, said an echo in the back of his mind. When he looked sidelong at Adriana Quintero, he saw she had her cell phone in her hands, texting with her thumbs. Somewhere close by an ambulance's siren whooped once and then went silent.

Quintero put her phone away. "You are a very dedicated police officer," she told Sevilla. "We need that, now more than ever. If you want our office to keep you informed of what's happening with this case…?"

"Yes. Yes, I'd like that. Can I contact you directly?"

"It would be better if I gave my assistant your number," Quintero said. "The way things go, I would miss your message and I don't want that."

"All right," Sevilla said. "Here is my card."

Quintero vanished the card into a pocket of her jacket.

"I should go. I'm sorry about the breakfast. Perhaps some other time," Quintero said. She turned to leave.

"Of course. I understand. And *señora?*"

Sevilla caught a faint trace of something passing over Quintero's face when she stopped, but she smiled and it went away. "Is there something else?"

"Paloma Salazar was a good woman. She worked hard for the dead women of Juárez. That this happened… it's not right. We owe her the very best for her sacrifice."

"I assure you she will get nothing less."

"I will take your word for it," Sevilla replied.

"Goodbye," Quintero said.

"Goodbye, *señora.*"

Sevilla watched Quintero go. When the doors to the emergency room closed behind her, Sevilla walked the pavement to the parking garage, letting the morning sun penetrate him where he was cold inside. He found his car where he left it, but a scrap of paper under the wiper was new.

He expected a nasty note from a doctor angry at the lost space. Instead, the note read, *They tried to kill the American.*

Sevilla crushed the paper in his hand. He looked left and right, but the garage was still, and even the sound of engines was absent. When he unfolded the note, the words were the same; he was not mistaken.

It occurred to him to use his phone, but he didn't know who he could call. Quintero was with Kelly and before that she had been with him. The police outside Kelly's door had all been there when he left, but what about afterward, while Sevilla and Quintero were outside?

This time he folded the note and put it away inside his jacket. He unlocked the car and got behind the wheel, but didn't put his keys in the ignition. For a long while he sat. He pulled the hood release and got out again.

The engine looked normal. Sevilla lowered himself onto one knee and peered beneath the frame. He felt foolish, but his mind raced ahead of him and he checked the concrete for fluid that might have leaked from a severed line. There was nothing.

He started the car and let it idle for a full minute before putting it into gear and backing out of the space. His eye strayed to the spot beneath the wiper where the note was lodged. He forced himself to feel for strangeness when he depressed the brake, but there was none. His paranoia was embarrassing; out on the street he felt his face reddening though there was no one around to know what he was thinking.

Work and his office were both south, but Sevilla turned east. He fell in behind an American tour bus and into the clogged-heart rhythm of morning traffic through downtown. Already in his imagination he mounted the steps to Kelly's apartment and got inside. He would begin in the bedroom and work his way out to the front room and the kitchen. Searching the whole apartment would take less than an hour because it was small and Sevilla knew what to do. The drive there would take longer.

Sevilla drummed his fingers on the steering wheel. He opened the windows and let the polluted morning air fill the car. He did not play the radio.

FOUR

HE DIDN'T HAVE TO THINK ABOUT the way to Kelly's apartment; he'd driven it many times over the years for his unexpected visits. Not to roust Kelly, but to talk and put a little pressure on, chat by chat. Droplets of water could cut through a boulder, and so it was when it came to cultivating informants. Sevilla hoped Kelly would give one day, because a man like Estéban would never succumb. He was too far inside, while Kelly was always going to be on the outside no matter what else he might aspire to.

Sevilla only had to look at the neighborhood where Kelly settled to know something about him. This place, with its flat-roofed and unremarkable blocks of apartments and little businesses catering to the working poor, was far better than many around Juárez. A neighborhood like this spoke of hope and hanging on to a modest sort of success that the desolation of the *colonias* had abandoned long ago. Kelly could have gone headfirst into the sewage that streamed constantly from the clubs and bars and brothels, but he chose here instead.

The street was still when Sevilla parked and even the traffic sounds of the city seemed distant when he got out. He did not feel eyes on him because there were no eyes to feel; people minded their own business in a neighborhood like this one. And when there was nothing to hide, strangers weren't a worry.

He mounted the steps one at a time. He felt heavy, and not just because temperatures were on the rise. When he got to Kelly's door there would be no one home, and what was left behind was the terrible scene in El Cereso. What he did, Sevilla did for Kelly's good, but that did not make the burden any lighter.

In America the police might have sealed Kelly's door with bright yellow tape, but there were no such markers here. Sevilla paused by the railing and looked north. It was possible to see Texas from this spot, though the demarcation between Ciudad Juárez and El Paso was not a prominent one. From this perspective it all seemed washed together along the banks of the Rio Grande in the wake of a flood, with only luck determining who came to rest in the land of opportunity and who was left in Mexico.

Sevilla had a key for Kelly's apartment. Sevilla paid the apartment manager for it with the idea that he could slip in for a search from time to time. This was how he knew Kelly was clean — except for the *motivosa*, of course — and how he came to know Kelly better through the evidence Kelly left when he felt no one was paying attention.

Inside, the police had turned Kelly's home into a scattered mess. Even the few dishes were broken as the cabinets were cleared, dismantled and searched. Sevilla paused in the door, once again taken aback by the spiteful chaos, and then he went in.

He didn't think to find anything the other police had missed. For all the disdainful talk of the cops across the river, cops in Ciudad Juárez knew how to go about their business. Or at least they could dismantle a suspect's apartment without leaving any secret behind. Sevilla wanted... he wasn't certain what he wanted. He simply wanted to be here.

Sevilla drifted from the front room to the bedroom and back again. Out on the rear balcony the heavy bag was unhooked from its spot, dashed to the concrete and slashed open. Stuffing and sawdust drifted from its corpse.

The remains of a sofa cushion were still enough to pad a seat, so Sevilla made himself comfortable where he had done so many times before. He lit a cigarette and looked at his reflection in the cracked face of Kelly's broken television. It wasn't here, that essence of Kelly, and being here did not help Sevilla understand.

A shoe scuffed on the doorstep and Sevilla looked over. "What are you doing here?" he asked.

Enrique Palencia lingered in the open doorway as if unsure whether to enter or turn away. He was a young man, seeming younger still despite the little goatee he tended into neat life. With Sevilla watching, Enrique put one foot over the threshold before drawing it back. He had guilt on his face.

"Well, come in if you're coming in," Sevilla said. He looked for somewhere to stub out his cigarette, but the sidetable was overturned and the ashtray was gone. Enrique came in and closed the door behind him. Suddenly the front room was very dark.

"I don't want to disturb you," Enrique said.

"You aren't disturbing me. How did you know I was here? Did that *pendejo* Garcia send you?"

"Captain Garcia doesn't know where I am. I took the day off."

Enrique stood awkwardly by the door. Sevilla watched him until the heat of the cigarette nibbled at his fingertips. He put the butt out on the sole of his shoe. Enrique Palencia looked as though he had slept in his clothes not one night, but maybe two.

"You know, I can put up with almost all of it," Sevilla told Enrique at last. "The things we do... I've done worse in my time. And I helped when old cops, wise cops, did terrible things to get at the truth. I've smelled the blood. I've had it on my hands. Now it's your turn."

The young cop didn't answer. He moved into the kitchenette, crunching over broken glass and shattered dinnerware. He looked in the refrigerator where even the shelves were yanked loose. When he chanced a look in Sevilla's direction, he never met his eyes.

Finally there was nothing else to inspect. Enrique stood with his hands awkwardly as his sides. Only then did he look Sevilla in the face. He was sweating. "I didn't do that to him," he said. "But I know who did."

"*I* know who did," Sevilla replied. "Oscar Garcia doesn't believe anything he's told if he hasn't broken a bone to hear it."

Enrique Palencia was silent.

"You were the one who called me," Sevilla said.

"Yes."

"You left the note."

"Yes."

"Do you want to tell me why?"

"I couldn't stand it anymore."

"You stood beside Garcia," Sevilla said. "You didn't tell him *no*. You didn't tell him *stop*. How many times has it been?"

"You said yourself you've done the same," Enrique returned.

"That was a long time ago."

"Time doesn't change anything."

To this Sevilla could only nod.

Enrique was quiet a while. "It was too much."

"It is too much," Sevilla agreed. "Thank you. Now come and sit down."

Sevilla waited while Enrique salvaged another half-shredded couch cushion. They sat at opposite ends of the little divan. Sevilla put another cigarette between his lips and offered Enrique one. Sevilla saw Enrique's hands shake when he lit up.

They passed the time smoking without talking and after a while Enrique's hands steadied. "It wasn't enough to turn Estéban Salazar into a cripple, but he had to do the same to Kelly?" Sevilla asked then.

"No," Enrique said. "He didn't have any questions. That was why I couldn't go with him. He made fun of me, but I wouldn't do that."

"He went to kill him," Sevilla said. "Just like that? Of his own accord?"

"I don't know. He went away for his dinner break and didn't come back for a long time. I thought he'd gone home, but then he called and said he wanted me to stay late. He showed up after shift change.

He told me what he was going to do. 'If he won't talk, he won't talk,' he said. 'What does it matter when we know he did it?'"

Sevilla considered using his shoe to stub out his cigarette again. He ground the butt into the carpet instead. It would have to be replaced anyway. Enrique sat with his own butt cradled in two hands across his knees, slumped forward and staring into the rising smoke as if memory were there. He said nothing else.

"Why tell me these things?" Sevilla asked.

Enrique stirred. He dropped his butt on the floor reluctantly, crushed it with hesitation. He spoke to his empty hands. "Captain Garcia said the American was your friend."

Sevilla didn't correct him. He was unsure what Kelly was to him. Once he'd told Kelly he respected him and that was true. Now Kelly was…

"You think that makes a difference?" Sevilla said. "All cops have friends. We don't tell tales on each other."

"I'm not telling tales!" Enrique returned. He looked up sharply and his back went tense. Sevilla saw anger and hurt in the young cop's eyes. "This is what happened!"

"I believe you. Calm down," Sevilla said, and he put his hands up. "But people will wonder why you come to me, friend or no friend. Ask Garcia and he'll tell you that I deal with *narcos* and junkies, not killers. Why not go to Señora Quintero? Take it to the Procuraduría. Someone might even give you a medal for your honesty. But I doubt it."

"This is a waste of time."

Enrique moved to rise. Sevilla stopped him with a hand. "I didn't say it was a waste of time. I only want to know why you care. Why you came to me."

The tension fled from Enrique and he slumped back into the ruined couch. He put his hand over his eyes and breathed deeply and for a moment Sevilla thought that *now* he cried, but when the hand came away the young cop's eyes were dry.

"Why did you come to me?" Sevilla asked again.

"I thought... I don't know. I thought you would understand."

"About Garcia."

"About all of it. I didn't join the police force to beat confessions out of innocent people. Because I don't believe they did it. The American and Salazar. I don't believe it."

Sevilla nodded slowly. "And you think you and I, we can find out the truth when everyone else can't?"

"I don't know. Do you think so?"

Sevilla spread his hands. "You aren't the only one without answers."

"The way Garcia talks about you, I know he is jealous of you. He says they let you do your work without interfering. He says we could do so much more if the higher-ups simply got out of our way."

"And let you get on with torturing people?"

Enrique looked at his shoes. "Yes."

"Nobody with a conscience should be forced to work with La Bestia. You should count yourself lucky you still have one. He could have torn it out of you and ground it up. Then you wouldn't have come to me, except maybe as a tool. A spy."

"I'm not a spy."

"Why should I believe you?"

"I've already told you enough that there could be charges against Garcia. People turn a blind eye, but that's only because no one speaks up. I could say something. Like you said, I was there."

"Do you think anyone would believe you?"

"I wouldn't know until I tried."

"The mere fact that you would even think to put yourself through that says you're either a fool or a romantic. Why should I burden myself with either?"

"You'll need help."

"What sort of help?" Sevilla asked.

"You are on the outside. I'm on the inside. You want a spy? I can be that for you."

"To what benefit to yourself? There's no glory here."

"There's no glory in beating a man's head in, either."

"It's possible no one will even care," Sevilla said. "You know how it is on the streets of Juárez these days. People are dying everywhere. Even the police aren't safe. One more woman dies, this is nothing new."

"What are you saying?"

"That is a very good question."

"This is right," Enrique said. "I want to do what's right."

"Now I *know* you're a romantic. You might be useful, after all."

FIVE

"Kelly kept a notebook, a spiral *cuaderno* with a red cover. I've seen it here before, by the telephone," Sevilla told Enrique. "It must have been collected. We'll want to have a look at it."

Enrique nosed around the shattered kitchenette, poking into cabinets with broken doors and occasionally lifting some ruined dinnerware with his toe to peer beneath. Sevilla felt the tension radiating from the young man, saw it in the way his shoulders hunched even when he played at being nonchalant. Enrique would have made a terrible boxer; he allowed too much of his mind to show in his body.

"You'll need to get it," Sevilla said.

"What's in it?" Enrique asked.

"Kelly kept his life in that notebook: his accounts, his telephone numbers, his appointments. I have some things copied, but nothing so recent as could help us now. I want to see what he wrote during the time when Paloma died."

For a moment Enrique disappeared into the bedroom. When he reemerged, he shook his head. "I've never heard of a drug addict who kept records before. No records that make sense, anyway."

Sevilla rose from the couch. He felt his expression sour despite himself and he turned his face from Enrique. He did not want to show his mind, too. "If you think Kelly is just some American junkie, then why bother with him at all? Let them say he did it with Estéban and it all goes away. What's one more dead woman on the pile? It's not like there's not a hundred other things to worry about."

"That's not what I meant."

"Understand this, then: I know Kelly. I spent a long time watching him, grooming him. The people who put this in motion against him, they saw him as a foreigner, a stranger. Foreigners have no one who knows them for who they are. These people, they didn't expect someone like me. They thought Kelly was easy to make look guilty."

"He was."

Sevilla shook his head. "For some."

"Even you," Enrique insisted.

"At first," Sevilla said, "but that was because I only listened with my head, and not my heart. What kind of men are we if we forget our hearts?"

SIX

SEVILLA WAITED TEN MINUTES AFTER Enrique was gone before leaving Kelly's apartment. He went to his car and fished under the seat until his hand settled on the paper-wrapped neck of another bottle of Johnnie Walker. The temptation for a drink, even this early in the day, was strong, but Sevilla knew one swallow would lead to another and another until he was too spent even to drive.

The bottle went back where it came from. Two bottles in two days would be too much to excuse. Many men his age lived inside a glass of alcohol, their wits dulling as they aged into dust. Sevilla had never wanted to be such a man, not now and not before, and so the whisky would stay where it was for at least another day. Perhaps he'd forget about it and it would be a week before his thirst reminded him of what would make it all better.

He drove and while he drove he thought about Enrique Palencia.

Mostly Sevilla knew Enrique from Captain Garcia's shadow. When state police worked with city police on drug-related matters there were often bodies involved. The *narcos* of the south honed their bloody-mindedness in Mexico City, the *narcos* of the west in Tijuana. Murder, not only drugs, was their major export. This they sold to their countrymen as eagerly as they dispensed to the Americans. Garcia was the sort of policeman Ciudad Juárez valued today: one whose expertise lay not in teasing apart layers of an investigation but in rendering them up in pieces.

Enrique lacked the hardness and flatness of Garcia, but these things would come in time. Juárez was a hard wind off the desert. Heat and sand and sheer force cut stone and sliced away the soft parts of a man until there was nothing left but sharp edges and an underlying brittleness that an unexpected blow could shatter. Garcia was expert with such blows.

Sevilla stopped at a light and watched a cluster of school-age girls dash across the walk from one curb to the next. A woman, maybe a teacher, followed them. Some carried boxes for lunch and the sight of these made Sevilla hungry. Eating was better than drinking himself into a stupor in the front seat of his car.

He drove a while longer, tracing a path that was half familiar from his time with Kelly and from the years before. In the early days when he was still getting to know Kelly, Sevilla walked the pavement well behind the man, observing but never from too close. Kelly had a wandering spirit and he was not afraid to go where the other Americans never went. At first this was because he was still in the grip of an addiction, but eventually because he had a taste for the city and its people. Sevilla thought Kelly might have made a good cop if things were very different.

Storefronts Sevilla recognized began to populate the streets. He knew a restaurant that served a hearty lunch for very little, a workingman's place, and he navigated there without having to watch the street signs. Unconsciously he put his hand on the seat beside him, half-expecting to feel human warmth, but there was no one with him. This was not *their* drive anymore, but *his* drive.

He ate chicken and rice and tortillas in the shade of a faded orange awning. People passed his table close enough to touch and conversation bubbled up from the seats around him. From time to time Sevilla's attention wandered to the offices across the street, the little dentist's and the open door on the second floor.

Enrique would be back at the central station by now. It might take an hour or more for him to find Kelly's notebook even if the rest went smoothly. Likely they wouldn't meet again until tonight, and even then they would have to be careful who saw them and what they were doing. Much as Sevilla would have to be careful when he finished his meal and crossed the street.

He left coins on the table for the young woman who cleaned up, wiped his mouth on his handkerchief and went back out into the sun. The weather took no holiday and offered no respite. Sevilla wilted in his suit. The temptation was always there to switch to something lighter, breezier, but the suit was important to him.

A suit was Sevilla's armor. Like his badge and identification, it was also a shield. When people saw a man in a suit, they reacted differently, behaved differently and sometimes told more than they wanted to tell by virtue of their discomfiture. Even when the temperature climbed to over a hundred, Sevilla wore a suit because after all this time he couldn't do his work without it.

Crossing the street, Sevilla reached the switchbacked steps and climbed them one at a time. The sun felt like a weight across his shoulders. This place had a familiar smell about it that prompted unwelcome memories. He shoved them aside, and by the time he reached the door of Mujeres Sin Voces he was composed fully.

The sound of hunt-and-peck typing came from inside. Sevilla rapped on the door frame and then peered through. A slight breeze followed him through the doorway and stirred the flyers on the walls. The woman at the desk stopped her work. For a moment Sevilla saw Paloma Salazar's face. This was where they first met.

"Police," Sevilla said, and showed the woman his identification. "Sevilla. What is your name?"

"Adela de la Garza," the woman replied. "I'm sorry... is something the matter?"

"Something is always the matter," Sevilla said, and he made a gesture that vaguely encompassed the wall of flyers, all the faces and the cries for *justicia*. "I'm here because of Paloma."

Adela crossed herself and then put her hands in her lap. She nodded. "We heard the news."

"It couldn't have happened to a finer woman," said Sevilla.

"Are you the investigator? The one in charge?"

"No, I'm not. Paloma's case is with the city police. But I consult with them."

"They say it was her lover, that American. He came here, you know."

Sevilla took a small pad from his jacket pocket and flipped back the cover. He wrote left-handed with a pencil. "Did he? This is Kelly Courter? The American who boxed?"

"*Sí*, that's the one. He came here after she was gone." Adela's expression curdled and she made a spitting gesture. "He pretended to know nothing! But now we know the truth about him."

"You asked him about her?" Sevilla inquired.

"No. He asked me about Paloma. Where she went, how long it had been. What kind of a man doesn't know these things? Is it true he was a *drogadicto*? It makes sense to me. And Paloma's brother…"

Sevilla held up a hand for quiet. "I can't tell you very much about the case. It's not allowed. Where did you get all of this information?"

"From the policeman who came yesterday."

"A policeman came here?"

Adela nodded. "That is why I was confused. He only came yesterday. How could anything have changed so soon? He told me about what happened."

"What was this policeman's name?"

The woman thought for a moment. Sevilla tried to remember whether he'd seen her before, even once in all the time he had come here with his wife, but Adela's face didn't come to him. "Jiménez," she told Sevilla at last. "Yes, I think that's it."

"Jiménez?"

"Yes."

"What was his first name?"

"Cornelio, I think."

"Did he show you identification?"

"Yes."

"Was it city or state police?"

"I can't tell the difference. I do clerical work here; I don't speak to police. Not like Paloma did. Or Ella."

Sevilla thought to ask Adela more questions, but there was no point. Paloma he knew and Ella Arellano, as well. There were two or three others he could recall by their faces if not their names. Marina? He wasn't sure. "What did he want to know?"

"He wanted to ask about the American. He was lucky I was the one here; I remembered everything the American asked. And to think I sent him after Ella! I even gave him directions! What did he want to do to her, I wonder?"

Sevilla scribbled as quickly as he could. "He? You mean Kelly wanted to see Señorita Arellano?"

"I told you: he pretended he didn't know where Paloma was. I sent him to Ella. I felt so stupid when the policeman told me everything."

"You had no way to know," Sevilla said automatically. His thoughts were turning.

"I should have known. Anyone who could do such a thing… you can tell from their eyes."

"If only that were true. Señora, what else did you tell this policeman? Did he ask to see Ella, too?"

"Yes. I gave him the same directions."

Sevilla flipped his notepad to a new page. Tension crawled in his back, made the muscles around his spine ache. He wished for another little breeze to flush the heat out of the office; it was as hot in here as it was in the full sun. "Can you give them to me?" he asked finally. "In case I can't get a hold of this Jiménez. It would be a great favor."

"Of course," Adela said. She talked and Sevilla wrote and in the end Sevilla left his card with the woman and stepped out of the stifling little space with relief. The streets had grown still in the after-lunch quietude. When he reached the sidewalk he saw a CLOSED sign in the dentist's window.

Normally he would also sleep in a still, shaded place where the troubles of the day so far could be shed, but Sevilla went to his car quickly. He rolled the windows down and invisible clouds of intense heat flowed out of the cabin. He sweated afresh beneath the layers of suit and shirt. The engine idled until the air conditioner was strong enough to take over. With the windows up and cool air circulating, Sevilla pored over his notes.

Cornelio Jiménez left no card. If it had been Garcia or even Enrique on the doorstep of Mujeres Sin Voces then Sevilla would have no reason to doubt the man or his appearance. The tension in his back climbed higher and settled between his shoulder blades to clench the nerves there.

He dialed Adriana Quintero's number and got her voice mail instead of her assistant.

"*Señora*," Sevilla said, "this is Rafael Sevilla. I wanted to ask you about one of your investigators, Cornelio Jiménez. Could you give me his number? I wanted to ask him a few questions. It would be a favor to me. *Gracias*. Goodbye."

Almost no one walked the streets. The city was drained of bodies at this hour. Only the *maquiladoras* worked around the clock without pause. There were no quiet and shaded spots there.

He wanted to call Enrique, but it was too soon. His thoughts turned still further and pushed toward the *colonias* and Ella Arellano. There the people would be sleeping, as well.

"Damn it."

Sevilla smacked the steering wheel with his palm. He put the car in gear and drove away.

SEVEN

O<small>NCE</small> E<small>NRIQUE'S</small> <small>POLICE</small> <small>STATION</small> had seemed just another government building in a simple collection of such buildings near the office of the Procuraduría. White brick and windows tinted against the sun and barred entryways saying NO ENTRANCE and a glass-and-metal box the size of a phone booth where a single policeman stood on duty, checking identification and manually operating the electric lock.

When the Sinaloa cartel came to the city, the landscape changed. At both ends of the block heavy, x-shaped sculptures made of steel crossbeams blocked traffic into a single lane. Barbed wire obstructed the sidewalks. Instead of a lone cop, a handful of armed federal police controlled the flow of people back and forth through the barricades. Still more guarded Enrique's building, two of them from a parked jeep mounted with a heavy machine gun.

Already there was word of still more men and equipment headed to the city, more guns and more vehicles. Two days before, Enrique saw an armored personnel carrier patrolling the area around the Procuraduría. Government buildings were secured against assault within and without; uniformed officers with automatic rifles walked the halls, chatted with the local police, made themselves comfortable as if they would be there for a hundred years.

Enrique parked in a lot ringed by chain-link fencing and barbed wire a block away. Three others waited for the white van that shuttled them to and from the main building. An armored *federale* occupied the passenger seat, the window down though the air conditioning was on, the barrel of his rifle pointed out through the open frame and into the sky.

He didn't recognize the men with him and they didn't speak. Enrique knew they tensed as he did each time the van passed another vehicle moving slowly. The Sinaloa cartel and their enemies, Los Zetas, used drive-by tactics and overwhelming firepower. The van was not armored; bullets could pass through the metal skin as easily as through a sheet of corrugated aluminum. In May two years before, the Sinaloa gunned down the chief of police.

The van made a too-sharp stop in front of the building. All four got out and went in different directions. Enrique paused a moment with the sun directly overhead. A federal policeman sat in the metal-and-glass booth. The butt of his rifle rested by his boot. He nodded at Enrique and made a motion toward the door.

"Yes," Enrique said. The lock buzzed and he went inside.

Inside there were normal sounds, the only real survivor of the drug wars. Telephones rang and there was talking and bursts of laughter. Enrique didn't like being here anymore. A look out the windows in any direction revealed the city at siege, the city the *turistas* didn't see and didn't care to. When the Gulf Cartel and the gangs and the Sinaloa clashed it was Mexican blood that flowed. In the west, in Baja, tourists were sometimes shot, sometimes kidnapped, but here it was still a domestic war; *el Paso del Norte* was too valuable to jeopardize.

Enrique climbed the stairs to the second floor. Here was the open bullpen, desks crowded together in clutches of three or four under harsh fluorescent lighting. The air had the smell of men working and coffee and dust.

First he checked his desk. He kept his space neat. His desk calendar was carefully marked with appointments, times and people. The logo of the Policía Municipal bounced around the screen of his computer. A few messages on pink slips of paper were stuffed beneath his keyboard. He could wait to answer those.

Captain Garcia kept an office at the edge of the bullpen, away from Enrique. Normally an assistant would have an adjoining space and enjoy a small part of his master's cachet, but Garcia kept Enrique among the rest to watch and listen and report. Enrique didn't tell Garcia most of what he heard about the man they called La Bestia.

Thinking of Garcia made Enrique glance toward the man's workspace. The blinds on the office windows were open, the desk was empty. Garcia had a computer he rarely used for anything except playing games and wandering the internet. His filing cabinets were empty. His messages were routed through Enrique and he hadn't bothered setting up his own voice mail. There was no need for any of these things because La Bestia was not an investigator. La Bestia enforced.

He left the bullpen. A few men said hello, but most kept clear of him. This was the only benefit of being close to Garcia.

In the basement the ceilings were lower and the cool air drier. Exposed veins of wire and pipe snaked along the walls and overhead. Occasionally an air compressor roared and pumped cool to some section of the great structure. It was not like being in the heart of the building, but in its guts.

Evidence stood behind a barricade of mesh steel. No soldier stood guard here. Two women in uniform kept watch over ten interconnected rooms of metal shelving installed floor to ceiling in tight rows. Los Tigres del Norte played quietly on a radio, the accordion jumping through "La Puerta Negra." The heavy-framed metal door was secured with two locks. An opening above the check-counter was no more than two feet wide.

"*Buenas tardes,*" Enrique told one of the women. One was young, the other old. It was always women down here, away from the sun and blood and gunshots of the street. In America women worked the streets alongside the men. Not so here.

"*Buenas tardes,*" the old woman replied. She came to the counter.

"I need something," Enrique said. He filled out a slip and passed it through the barrier. "For Captain Garcia. I don't know the item number, but this is the case. It's a red notebook. It should be the only thing like it."

The old woman examined the paper. Her face was expressionless. "All right," she said at last, and passed it to the young woman. "It will be a few minutes."

"I can wait," Enrique said.

They had no words for each other. Enrique caught himself pacing in the open space beneath a hanging rack of exposed fluorescent bulbs and stopped. On the radio the Tigres gave way to Conjunto Primavera and the Chihuahuense band accompanying Tony Meléndez while he sang about his first time in love. Enrique did not care for *norteño* and never had.

When the young woman returned she had the red notebook in a marked plastic bag. Somewhere nearby a fan kicked into motion and clattered loudly enough to drown out the radio. Enrique signed Garcia's name in the log. He had to speak up to be heard. "*Gracias, señoras.*"

He felt the women watching him as he went. He resisted clutching the bag to his chest and looking back. At the stairs he put the notebook inside his jacket. It was too large to fit into a pocket, but it lay against his body. His shirt was damp with perspiration.

At the lobby he peered out of the stairwell before emerging. The building was quietening. Men were out to lunch, gone home or to a local gathering place where policemen could take the *comida corrida* with other policemen and a soldier at the door for safety. The shuttle van back to the parking lot came every fifteen minutes. Enrique checked his watch.

He didn't want to wait out in the sun, but huddling in the stairwell was no good, either. He crossed the lobby and went into the men's room, found a stall and sat down on the toilet without pulling down his pants. It was shadowed in the stall. The notebook felt like a secret thing when he brought it out, stripped it free of the plastic bag and dipped inside.

The *cuaderno* was a cheap, spiral-bound thing with a battered cover. Shredded-edged worms of paper crowded the spiral binding from pages torn out and discarded. The first half was names and addresses and telephone numbers, none of which Enrique recognized. A thin divider of brown paper marked the section the American used for his appointments.

Kelly Courter had a child's kind of writing with big loops and letters that were not always the same size or shape. He wrote in English, but Enrique knew the language well enough to interpret this word or that. In the final third of the notebook he found a letter to the victim, half written, and dated more than a month before the crime. He saw no hatred there or the kind of anger that would leave a violated corpse half burned in a fallow field.

Enrique checked his watch. He had five more minutes to wait.

He paged through the notebook again. Paper stuck to his fingers and he realized his hands sweated despite the air-conditioned cool. He imagined Captain Garcia bulling into the restroom, cracking the stall open with a single blow. Enrique would be trapped between flimsy metal walls and the beating would come. He had seen many of these.

Now his hands trembled and that was enough. Enrique stuffed the plastic bag in his pants pocket and secreted the notebook into his jacket again. He stood and flushed the toilet automatically. Doing so made him feel stupid. He unlocked the stall and peeked out, but no one had come into the restroom behind him.

The van pulled up at the same time Enrique left the building. He and a half-dozen other cops piled into three rows of bench seats. "Turn up the air," said one. Another agreed. The driver complied, but the fresh cool escaped from the open passenger window around the barrel of their guardian's rifle.

The man beside Enrique nudged him. "I know you: aren't you Garcia's boy?"

Enrique didn't recognize the man. He was heavyset, older and maybe his face might be familiar, but not now. Enrique nodded. "I'm assigned to him, yes."

"La Bestia," said the first cop who spoke. "Fuck."

"You don't look stupid enough to be his apprentice," said another.

"That's true," said the older cop. His eye appraised and Enrique turned away to look out the window. "You seem more like the kind to crack a book instead of a head."

The other cops laughed. The van moved. Enrique watched the entrance as they turned around in the street and doubled back. Garcia did not emerge from the smoked-glass doors. The soldiers didn't even watch them go; their attention was elsewhere.

The policemen kept talking heedless of Enrique's silence. "You know," said one, "La Bestia is so stupid, he tried to drown a fish."

"Do they have you read his assignments to him?" the older cop asked Enrique. "Or do they give him reports with pictures on them?"

Enrique shook his head. The notebook clung to the material of his shirt. He was sweating again.

"At least he can break those *narco* bastards," said the first cop. The laughter stilled and there was assent all around. "If stupid is what it takes, then so be it."

The older cop grunted. He nudged Enrique. "Don't take the joking too hard, *amigo*. Everyone is just jealous. They made the book for us, not for Garcia. We should all have such a free hand."

"It's all right," Enrique managed. He saw the parking lot ahead, the high fences and the curling masses of barbed wire shining in the sun. A drop of perspiration dripped into his eye. It burned and he wiped at it with his cuff.

"I heard he made a woman-killer confess," said the older cop.

"Yes," Enrique lied. He wanted to get out of the van even though it was in motion. The roof seemed too low, the doors pushed inward too far. He wished he was closer to the soldier and the open window.

"Good, good. We can joke, but he's done a good thing. *Feminicidios.*"

"You can tell him the jokes if you want," said one of the policemen. "He won't get them anyway."

The men laughed, but the humor was faded. Enrique made a weak smile. He was glad when the van stopped and he could step out onto the hot asphalt and get away from them. The older cop said goodbye, but Enrique moved away without saying anything. He felt breathless, the notebook pressing until he couldn't draw in enough air. Inside his car he ripped the notebook out of his jacket and cast it onto the passenger seat. He put his hands on the hot metal of the roof and ignored the pain. He sucked in great lungfuls of air and the edges of his vision glowed with heat and hyperventilation.

When the moment passed, he got into his car and turned over the engine. He fastened his seatbelt and cinched it tightly. He closed his eyes until the glowing faded. He opened them again. His hands were on the wheel, the air conditioner humming while the engine idled. When he looked left and when he looked right he expected to see Garcia there, but he was alone.

EIGHT

THEY MET AT THE BACK DOOR OF
Sevilla's home well after sundown. Sevilla knew he smelled of
whisky, but there was nothing to be done about it. Enrique didn't
seem to notice, or at least he pretended he didn't.

"Come in," Sevilla said. "Did you close the gate?"

"Yes."

"Good. If you don't close the back gate, dogs get into the yard
and shit all over."

Sevilla offered Enrique something cool to drink and they went
through the motions of a normal visit. Enrique's jacket went on a
hook by the door and he sat on the couch with his back resting on
the quilt Liliana made the first year she and Sevilla were married.
Sevilla took the chair. His notepad was on the endtable.

"May I?" Sevilla asked, and he took the *cuaderno* from
Enrique.

"It's yours," Enrique said.

They sat in silence while Sevilla checked each page against his
notepad. The process was long. Sevilla felt Enrique's eyes flicking
here and there around the room, sensed his anxiety from the way
he crossed and uncrossed his legs.

When he was done, Sevilla closed the notebook. He put it on the
couch beside Enrique. "How long is it until you go back to work?"

"Tomorrow," Enrique said.

"You can get the notebook back then?"

"Of course."

"And then there's more," Sevilla said. He saw darkness pass Enrique's face. "I need you to check on Estéban. He's in the system, moving around. Even Señora Quintero doesn't know where he is, or she pretends not to. We need him in one place where he can be checked on."

Enrique shook his head. "I don't have that kind of authority. If I interfere with his transport, word will get back to Captain Garcia. He'll ask questions I can't answer."

"Then at least find out where they put him," Sevilla insisted. He lapsed back in the chair and pushed his eyes with his thumb and forefinger. The whisky did not quiet his nerves like it was meant to. He felt tired, but not calm enough to sleep. He had a headache. "He's the last one who can still talk."

"Why don't you do something?"

"I'm not involved anymore," Sevilla replied. "La Bestia doesn't need me anymore. It was Kelly who knew me, Kelly who might have listened."

Silence fell over the living room. The ticking of a clock by the window was the only sound. Even the street outside the front window, past the bars and containing wall, was quiet.

"You have a nice home," Enrique said after a long time. "Where is Señora Sevilla?"

Sevilla uncovered his eyes. His vision was blurred. He blinked once, twice and again until it passed. The room was clean and ordered just so. The neatness of it made his heart ache. Perhaps it didn't show on his face. "My wife passed away," he said simply. "It's been two years now."

"I'm sorry."

"Thank you. This house was hers to keep, to decorate… everything here is hers. I was barely here enough to make it mine. That quilt, that clock… all hers."

"You have children?"

The headache stabbed at Sevilla. Another drink would take the point off the dagger, but he would not drink in the house nor drink in front of Enrique. He got up instead and went to the window. Outside it was blackness. If he turned off the lights and sat in the dark, orange-white light would filter in from the street, his eyes would grow used to it and it would be like a new room revealed to him in shadows.

"My daughter is also passed away," Sevilla replied.

"How did it happen?"

"Make a few calls," Sevilla said too sharply. "Don't ask after Estéban right away or you'll make Garcia suspicious. He's stupid, but he's not that stupid."

"If he does ask, I'll say I'm making up a report for Señora Quintero," Enrique said. "There's one due. I don't have to mention you at all, or anything else. He relies on me."

Sevilla turned from the window. There was a time he would not have stood with his back to the night, but he didn't consider such things much anymore. Talking put strength back into his voice and thinking pushed the headache back. "What do you get from him?"

"I'm sorry?"

"He relies on you. He's stupid and he's cruel. He needs someone like you. What do you need from him?"

Enrique looked away. Another silence descended. "They promised me a promotion," he said finally. "Two years with him would be like five in the rotation. There's extra pay."

"The Devil always pays well," Sevilla said.

He went to the kitchen and found orange juice in the refrigerator. He poured himself a tall glass. He let the drink sweat against his fingers before he drank. The juice was gone in three swallows. Cold spread through his sinuses and for a moment he felt no pain from the drink at all.

"If you had questions about me, the notebook should have answered them," Enrique said. He stood in the doorway as if he might flee at a harsh word. Sevilla felt a sudden urge to hurl his glass at the young cop, but it was not Enrique he was angry with. "I told you about the American. I gave that to you."

Sevilla rinsed his glass in the sink. He let hot water run over his hands and he wrung his fingers. "It's hard to trust," he said.

"What more can I do for you?" Enrique asked. "The American is guilty. Salazar is guilty. Anyone will tell you that. You and I are the only ones to say no. And what for? If it's right then it's right, but we won't be rewarded."

"Are you so sure about that?"

"Yes."

Sevilla looked at Enrique again. He saw Garcia's hardness hinted at there, the hardness of a stone worn by the wind. He didn't expect it to show so early.

"I followed a lead today and found out someone has been looking for witnesses and telling lies at the same time. If they spread enough hearsay it will become the truth; people won't remember if what they say is fact or fiction."

"Then we'll show them. Isn't that what you intended?"

"Let's sit down again."

They returned to the living room. This time Enrique stood while Sevilla sat.

"There are names in Kelly's notebook. I'll go to them. I'll ask the questions that need to be asked. When I need you, I'll call on you, but go back to your life. These are… confusing times. Maybe nothing we do will make a difference. The wheels are already turning."

"That's not what you said before. You said this mattered."

"Of *course* it matters!" Sevilla shot back. "But there's a difference between knowing it and doing something about it. My fire, it comes and goes. In the daylight it all seems so easy, but here in the night I'm not so certain of myself."

"Who will you talk to?" Enrique asked.

"There's a girl who spent much time with Paloma Salazar.

They're looking for her. Not La Bestia, but someone like him. She's a woman and she's poor. They'll find some way to push her that doesn't involve truncheons. Maybe I'll be able to push back. Maybe it's already too late."

"I don't understand you."

"I'm *drunk!*" Sevilla exclaimed. "I'm old and drunk and this—" he took up the red notebook and shook it angrily "— this isn't enough! I thought it would have some breakthrough in it that I could use against what I found today, but it's bullshit! The same bullshit it always was. Goddammit, Kelly."

"How much do you drink?" Enrique asked.

"Too much. Not enough."

Enrique paced. "What the hell am I doing here? Give me the notebook."

Sevilla surrendered it without protest. His face was burning.

"You lectured me about duty and responsibility and now you can't even keep away from a drink? What if Garcia saw me with this notebook today? What kind of excuse could I give? Or should I have just sent him to you?"

When Sevilla put his hands to his eyes again, they were wet. "I'm sorry," he said. "I shouldn't have—"

"No, you shouldn't have," Enrique agreed.

"I'm not so impressive here, I suppose."

"No, you're not."

"I'm sorry."

Enrique sat heavily on the couch and disturbed the quilt. Sevilla wanted to reach out and smooth the wrinkles, but he stayed where he was. "You should be sorry, but there's no time for that now. We are in it. The decision is made."

The clock ticked a hundred times before Sevilla spoke again. "We are in it," he said. "And we'll be in it until we have answers. That's what we agreed to."

"Who will you talk to? Who is this woman who knew Paloma Salazar?"

Sevilla sat back in the chair and gripped the armrests. The action steadied him. He did not have a headache anymore. "You know of Mujeres Sin Voces?"

"The women in black. I've seen them."

"Paloma was one of them. This woman, Ella Arellano, she is also one of them. I knew them both. From before."

"What? How?"

Sevilla took a deep breath. "Because my daughter is missing."

NINE

THE HEADACHE OF THE NIGHT WAS gone, but the headache of the new day pounded against the back of Sevilla's eyes and made him wish for a long sleep. He hid bloodshot whites behind sunglasses and drank water from a plastic bottle whenever his mouth suggested even a hint of going dry.

He parked a hundred yards from the *colonia*'s bus stop and watched the young women come and go in the unfettered sun. Some of the buses were from the city, but most came from the *maquiladoras* themselves. Once upon a time Ana Sevilla rode a bus like those, the lights doused before dawn or after sunset to save that little bit of power for the owners of the plants.

The regularity of them was hypnotizing, and Sevilla could have let the whole day pass with their comings and goings. Once he saw a black pick-up truck patrol along the unpaved road with two men in the king cab. They passed close to Sevilla's car and were gone.

Sevilla watched for Ella Arellano among the women and the buses but she did not appear. He would have to go in.

In his time Sevilla had seen worse *colonias*, some so close to the *maquilas* that one could throw a stone from one to the other if there wasn't a wall in the way. He had once been in a *colonia* in Baja built right along the tall hurricane fence that separated Mexico from the United States. The people there looked out their hand-cut windows at the land of opportunity.

Sevilla did not like the *colonias*: their closeness, their smells and the suspicious faces. As a uniformed policeman he knew officers who had been beaten or stabbed patrolling the *colonias* or collecting statements for some crime or the other. Not all were like those, but they were close enough and Sevilla stayed away.

His car was unmarked and he didn't display his badge, but the people of the *colonia* knew Sevilla for a policeman. Word of him would spread from one side to the other within minutes. The close little half-streets cleared and children wouldn't play where he stepped.

He knew without looking inside that Ella's home was empty. The rough-hewn door stood open and the shadows within were still. A spider had already drawn a line of silk between the handle and the jamb.

Sevilla went inside anyway. Nothing was left but the swept dirt floor. A few stray nails carried wisps of paper from pictures torn down. The legs of a table left depressions in the ground that time would fill and fade until even these were gone.

"*Mierda.*"

Lingering did nothing. He found no hidden message or even a hint of where or when the exodus occurred. Sevilla licked his lips, found them dry and drank more water.

The girl waited outside, half shaded by the close roofs of the houses to either side. She was perhaps five years old and small for her age. The print dress she wore had the delicate look of much-used hand-me-downs. She had a smudge of dirt on one cheek and a beauty mark on the other. One day she would be lovely.

Sevilla looked at the girl without speaking. She didn't flee on bare feet into the maze of the *colonia*. She had old eyes.

"*Hola,*" Sevilla said at last.

The girl raised her hand.

"Did you know the woman who lived here? Señorita Arellano?"

The girl moved one foot and Sevilla thought she might take to her heels, but she remained. She nodded.

"Do you know when she left?"

The girl shook her head. "*Adiós, señor,*" she said in a voice as high as Christmas bells. She turned and vanished without leaving a footprint to follow. Sevilla exhaled as though he had just watched a deer bolt into the trees.

TEN

THAT NIGHT HE DID NOT DRINK. He cooked pork for himself for dinner and sat alone at the kitchen table to take the meal. He had only water with lemon to wash down his food.

He was not in the mood for television or reading or music and so he sat alone in Ana's room with the picture from Parque Central in his lap as silent tears coursed down his cheeks. The drink would make the long hours better, or at least shorter, and he would tranquilize himself to sleep knowing that he could do the same again tomorrow and tomorrow and tomorrow until there were no more tomorrows to avoid.

"Where are you?" he asked Ana and Ofelia. His wife once said that God would answer if only the question came enough times, but even she grew tired of asking. Only Ella and Paloma and the women of Mujeres Sin Voces never tired. *Justicia para Ana. Justicia para Ofelia. Where are you? Where are you?*

For the first time in a long while Sevilla lay down on his daughter's bed. He cradled the photograph to him because he didn't have to look at it to know every color, every shape. He heard his wife humming a lullabye and then recognized his own voice carrying the tune.

Mira la luna
Comiendo su tuna;
Echando las cáscaras
En la laguna.

And then he slept.

ELEVEN

Sevilla called the hospital each morning and asked after Kelly. The nurses told him the same thing each time. Kelly slept and didn't wake. His heart still beat. He was not ready to die.

He avoided going to the office for more than a few minutes at a time. The security around state institutions was more impenetrable than the city's and the feeling of being trapped inside an armed camp was too much for him to bear. He did his work by telephone and promised written reports he would put in the mail when he had something new to say.

This latitude he was allowed because Sevilla came from a time before the black-clad army of federal police and the barbed wire and the ramparts of concrete and steel. His Juárez was a place of marijuana runners and petty theft and *turistas* coming south of the border to score a gram of something that would make the world go away for a little while. There was no place for Sevilla anymore, but still he remained. The young ones could chase the bad men with AK-47s and rocket launchers.

Enrique didn't call on him and left no messages. This was the way it should be.

On that morning Sevilla found the boxing gym on the third try. He did not know this corner of the city, had never had business there, and the streets were unfamiliar. He parked too far away and didn't know it so that he walked three blocks before he saw the place. The door was open against the gathering heat of the day, a fan on a stand turned outward to wick away the warmth inside.

Sevilla had never taken up gloves and boxed, though his brother had for a few years during his school days. Urvano's gym had the look and smell Sevilla remembered, riding his bicycle to be sure his brother left in enough time to sit for dinner with the family, waiting ringside as pugnacious old men with permanently broken noses and deformed ears showed Humberto the finer points of an art already dying.

Urvano was old, but not as old as Sevilla. When Sevilla saw the man, he imagined Humberto perched on the long-legged chair surveying his own domain. The man looked at Sevilla and half-raised a hand in greeting. Sevilla knew then Urvano was an honest man, because only honest men greeted a policeman so free of worry.

He displayed his identification. "Sevilla," he said.

"If you're looking for drugs, you won't find any here," Urvano said by way of a reply. "I don't allow that kind of thing here. Anyone with drugs has to leave and they can't come back."

"That's good," Sevilla said. Two men ghosted each other in the ring. Another practiced his body movements with the heavy bag. Punch, punch and weave. Punch, punch and weave. His head was always in motion. It was quieter here than Sevilla expected. "Drugs are no good for anyone."

"You can search the lockers if you want," Urvano said.

"There's no need. I wouldn't find anything."

"That's right."

"You can still help me," Sevilla said. "There was a man who trained here, I found a record of his payments. He was an American. Kelly Courter. You remember him."

The old man nodded. He smiled to himself a little, crookedly because the nerves on the left side of his face were damaged. His eye drooped as well. "Of course I remember him. He was my only white boy."

"I can't imagine too many would come here."

"Why is that? You see something here that's no good?" Urvano demanded.

"No, no, it's not that. It's just that gringos want rock music and air conditioning and running machines — you know, treadmills — to make them happy. This is too simple for them."

Urvano shrugged, but he shifted in his chair so he could regard Sevilla more directly. He was not punch-drunk and his eye was sharp. Sevilla imagined that eye assessing Kelly. "That's why there are no good white boy fighters," Urvano said finally. "A fighter isn't comfortable."

"My brother was a fighter," Sevilla said. "He fought three years. He had promise."

"What happened?"

"Our father wanted him to go to university, learn to be a doctor or a lawyer. Anything where he didn't have to work with his hands. You see, our father worked with his hands all his life. He was a carpenter. He didn't want that for us."

"What did he become?" Urvano asked.

"A pediatrician. And then he moved to Arizona in the United States."

"And you became a cop."

Sevilla shrugged. "I don't work with my hands."

Urvano smiled enough to show teeth and laughed drily. He offered his hand and Sevilla shook it. The old man pointed toward the ring. "Those two are the best ones I have, but don't tell them or they will get big heads. Jorge has heavy hands, but he still needs to keep them up. Oscar is better still. Fast. They'll both be champions just so long as they stay focused."

"Was Kelly focused?" Sevilla asked.

"I thought so. He was a little older, but not so old. He said he couldn't fight under his own name. I asked some people if that would be a problem. It could have been overcome."

"Did he say why he couldn't fight under his own name?"

"Some trouble in the States. Probably drugs."

"What makes you say that?" Sevilla asked.

Urvano's mouth twisted. "I can tell when one of my boys is into drugs. I'm better than those drug-sniffing dogs the police use."

"I thought you said no drugs were allowed."

"I can also tell when that's behind them. Or I thought I did."

They stood and watched the two young fighters in the ring. Sevilla saw in Jorge the problem Urvano mentioned. He liked to punch and he held his hands too low. Oscar's jabs came high and fast, and the defense wasn't there to repel them, but Sevilla saw the wheels turning and Jorge's stance changed and the sparring match evened. At some silent bell they separated and went to their corners.

"Do you see?" Urvano asked Sevilla and Sevilla nodded. "Kelly was like that: he could think."

"Did you know him well?" Sevilla inquired.

"No. What I know of him I saw in his workouts. On the bag. In the ring."

"I heard he had promise in the States. Before," Sevilla said.

"I believe it. It must have been the drugs that hurt him. Is he using them again?"

Sevilla considered what to say, how to share it. He frowned. "He was. He got free of them again. But these things... it's hard to fight them."

"I have his things if you want to see them," Urvano said. "His locker."

"Yes."

Urvano lowered himself from his chair. He walked with a pronounced limp, but his body was lean like a fighter's and otherwise graceful like a fighter's. Seeing Urvano made Sevilla embarrassed for the fat on his belly and around his waist. He couldn't remember the last time he'd run a mile, or even run at all. Perversely, he wanted a cigarette.

The few things Kelly left behind were no help. A towel and a bar of soap and a comb carried no hidden message or profound clue. Sevilla cursed under his breath.

"It isn't what you hoped to find," Urvano said simply.

"No, it's not. This is all there is?"

"Yes. I kept it longer than I normally would. He wasn't paid, but no one wanted the locker yet. I'm sorry."

Sevilla put his hand on Urvano's shoulder and shook his head. "There's nothing to apologize for. I saw from Kelly's books that he was paying you. It was the last thing he did before he… well, before his relapse."

"I blame that on Ortíz," Urvano said. He spat the name.

"Who?"

"Ortíz. If you were a fighter, you would know him. He's always sniffing around, making offers real managers can't match. He came for Jorge and Oscar but they were smart and told him to go to hell."

The old man headed back to his perch near the door and Sevilla followed. His notepad was already in his hand. "Ortíz," he said. "He comes from around here?"

"No," Urvano said. "I don't know where he comes from. Under a rock, maybe. He wears a suit, but the way he wears it he's just an animal in a man's clothing. A snake. If Kelly took drugs again, it was Ortíz that gave them to him, I'm sure."

Sevilla leafed through the notepad quickly. He found it — *Ortíz* — and a date. Kelly fought then. Sevilla remembered it. "This Ortíz is a boxing manager?"

"He books, he manages," Urvano drawled. He looked pained and the lines on his face deepened. "And sometimes he takes fighters to the States for bigger money. The last time I saw Kelly, I saw him with Ortíz. The son of a bitch came in here like he was welcome. He had some of his *pinche cabrones* with him in that fancy black truck they drive. Taking his cocks to the *palenque*."

At that moment eight young fighters spilled through the open front door of the gym. They were slick with sweat from running, their shorts and shirts plastered to spare bodies conditioned for the ring. Some of them called to Jorge and Oscar in the ring and all practice stopped as conversation rang from the walls.

Eyes were on Sevilla, the stranger in the gym. He ignored them. "You said he took fighting cocks to the *palenque*?"

"*Sí*. He has a hard-on for anything that fights, man or beast. I heard he used to book fights between men and dogs. What kind of trash is that? Kelly was better than him."

His pencil was missing. Sevilla searched his pockets until he found it. He scribbled on the back of a used page. "Do you know the name of the *palenque* where Ortíz's cocks fight? It would help me."

Urvano thought a while until a name came to him. Sevilla wrote it down. His fingers trembled and he nearly dropped the pencil. He felt as though there was a question he needed to ask, something he'd overlooked, but it didn't come to him. "If that Ortíz is to blame for Kelly's problem, then someone ought to cut his balls off," Urvano said.

"This is good information to have," Sevilla said. He moved toward the door. "Thank you for this. I need to go."

"You cut his balls off," Urvano insisted.

"Someone will," Sevilla replied, and he went outside.

TWELVE

Iᴛ ᴡᴀsɴ'ᴛ ᴜɴᴛɪʟ ʜᴇ'ᴅ ᴍᴀᴅᴇ ᴛʜᴇ long drive to the *palenque* that Sevilla called Enrique. The parking lot was a broad, dusty expanse of unpaved and tire-rutted dirt. A mural of two fighting cocks on the side of the building was once bright, but now sun-faded. A handful of trucks and cars were scattered around. The phone rang twice. A man that was not Enrique answered. "*¿Bueno?*"

"*Sí*, I'm trying to reach Enrique Palencia. Do I have the right number, please?"

"This is his desk. Who the fuck is this?"

Sevilla paused. He heard the man breathing on the other end of the line. "Garcia?"

"Is this Sevilla?"

His first instinct was to hang up, but he didn't. "This is Sevilla," he said instead. "I tried to call your desk first, Ramón. You weren't there."

Garcia made a sound like a cough. "That's because I'm here, you idiot," he said. "Why are you calling my boy? It's bad enough you have him looking after that *rulacho*, Estéban Salazar."

Sevilla's fingers were cold on his phone. "What do you mean?"

"I mean he's been calling all around about him. Trying to get him settled. He's turned into a regular guardian angel."

"He's part of your case. Maybe Palencia just wants to make sure you have all your witnesses."

"We don't need any witnesses. Someone ought to put a bullet in Salazar's head and call it a day."

"He confessed?"

"What do you think, Sevilla?"

Sevilla looked into his lap. His notepad was there, open to the address of the *palenque*. Before he had been excited, energized by the name of Ortíz and Urvano's words. Now he felt suddenly enervated, as if he'd been too long in the sun and the juice was sapped from him. "When did he confess?"

"Yesterday. I spoke to Señora Quintero about it this morning. She's a piece of ass."

Fucking naco, Sevilla thought, but he said, "That's good news."

"He said it was the American who started it. Came up with the plan and when to do it. Salazar just helped him. Can you believe someone who would do that to his own sister? He's like those sick bastards in the Sinaloa."

"He confessed to all of it?"

"*Sí*. No thanks to you or Enrique. The two of you would rather cuddle and kiss these sons of bitches than give them what they deserve."

A retort came to mind, but Sevilla sighed instead. "Congratulations," he said.

"Thank you. Now, you want me to have Enrique call you? You can go cry into your drinks about a few broken bones."

"No," Sevilla said. "No."

"Then fuck off back to your *narcos*," Garcia replied. "They're taking over the whole goddamned city."

The line went dead. Sevilla folded his phone and put it in his pocket. For a long time he sat still and silent.

"*¡Chingalo!*" He pounded his fist on the steering wheel. "*¡Chingalo! ¡Chingalo!*"

The moment passed. Sevilla lapsed back into silence. Without thinking he reached beneath the seat, his hand searching for a bottle wrapped in paper, but there was nothing there. He nearly cursed again and then he thought he might cry. Two men emerged from the entrance to the *palenque*, got into a rust-sided old Chevrolet and drove away. They were oblivious.

Sevilla covered his face with his hands. "Estéban, you stupid bastard," he breathed. In the same moment he knew he would have done the same thing if their places were reversed. The memory of the bat coming down on Estéban's hand was fresh.

He found his phone again and dialed another number. No one answered and the line switched to voice mail. Sevilla took a deep breath. "This is Sevilla. When you get a chance, call me. We should meet. I know about Estéban so there's no need to tell me. There's still a chance to make this right."

Afterward he held the phone in his hand, willing it to ring, but it was dead weight. He put it away. He started the car again and then turned the ignition off. The *palenque* squatted in the heat and dust, waiting for him. He thought of the shade and fans blowing cool air and a bar with iced beer and harder liquor. It wasn't so late in the day that a drink would ruin it, nor so early that he would have to hide what he'd done.

The phone didn't ring. If it rang he would not go inside and he would not drink. If it didn't ring, he would treat himself this once. He wouldn't drink so much that he couldn't drive safely. Maybe he would watch the fights. Maybe he would even bet on them and let the clock turn lazily toward evening. He could afford two or three drinks then.

Sevilla was out of the car and across the lot before he decided to go. The phone did not ring and he put it away. The entrance to the *palenque* was shady and smelled of mixed alcohol, chicken blood and straw. When he entered no one looked his way and when he ordered a blended whisky no one spoke a word of blame.

THIRTEEN

Sleeping in the back seat of his car was not so bad when the sun lay low along the horizon and the windows were open to allow a little breeze. The phone buzzed in Sevilla's pocket and then it rang. He stirred. His hand found the phone on its own.

"Sevilla," he said.

"I called three times," Enrique said.

"I've been busy," Sevilla replied.

"You sound like you've been sleeping. Where are you?"

"At a cockfighting arena. I won three wagers."

"What are you doing there?"

Sevilla struggled to sit up. His foot caught on the armrest and for a moment he felt trapped. "What difference does it make to you? Where have *you* been?"

"Estéban Salazar is back at El Cereso," Enrique said. "I've been trying to meet with him."

"Why? He already confessed, the stupid bastard."

"Confessions can be recanted."

"Only if he wants La Bestia coming to visit him in his cell the way he did with Kelly. He'll wish we had capital punishment again before it's over."

"You're drunk," Enrique said. "Goddammit."

"I was just resting my eyes. I haven't had anything to drink."

The parking lot was busier now at the end of the working day with more trucks and more cars nosing up to the *palenque*. Looking at the place made Sevilla's temples throb. He left the back seat and did his best to smooth the wrinkles in his suit jacket.

"Why do you want to meet with me if there's no point? What have you been doing?"

"I have a name," Sevilla replied. "Carlos Ortíz. Do you know it?"

"No. Should I?"

"He's a fight-fixer. Kelly knew him. They were together before Kelly took to the needle again. The old man who runs Kelly's *gimnasio del boxeo* said some things that made me think. Find out more about him."

"Where will you be?"

"Home."

FOURTEEN

HE WAS ANGRY AT HIMSELF FOR drinking and angrier still for lying about it. At least before, when Enrique had been in his home, Sevilla was honest enough to admit that he had drunk too much. That it was happening at all was bad enough. That he was hiding it was unforgivable. He felt Liliana's eyes on him.

The edges of his attention were ragged as he drove and the headlights made his eyes water. He was glad to reach the safety of his street, and when he at last killed the engine he breathed a silent prayer of thanks.

He wasn't ready to go in and face the empty house so he sat and stared out over the dashboard at the still avenue. The shootings and the killings of the Sinaloa and Gulf cartels' war hadn't ever broken the bubble around these houses. Other, older things had come to bear upon them, but the dead women of Juárez were invisible. Mujeres Sin Voces tried to change that, but the women in black could not be everywhere, standing silent vigil, forcing the *feminicidios* to the surface again.

Sevilla wasn't aware of dozing; his eyes were still open. A sharp rapping on the glass of the driver's side window made him twitch violently and a curse nearly escaped his lips. At first he didn't recognize Adela de la Garza in the shadow on the sidewalk between telephone pole and car. She wore a hooded sweater that obsured her face.

First he made to open the door, but the woman motioned for

him to stop. Sevilla wound the window down. "Señora," he said, "what are you doing here?"

Adela looked both ways down the street. No one was there and still nothing moved. "I have a message from Ella. Ella Arellano. You wanted to talk to her, yes?"

"*Sí*. Where is she? Her house—"

The woman thrust a folded piece of paper into Sevilla's hand through the window. "Go to this church on Sunday. The first service. Someone will know you. She will take you to Ella."

"Why has she gone into hiding? Was it Jiménez? Who is he working for?"

"She will tell you everything," Adela replied. "I must go."

"Wait," Sevilla said. He clambered out of the car, but Adela was already out of earshot and moving quickly. She rounded the corner and by the time Sevilla reached it she was gone.

Under the light of a lamppost Sevilla read the name of the church. He didn't recognize it. Once more he looked the way Adela had gone, but the woman did not reappear. Reluctantly he left the corner and returned to his home. It felt good to turn on the lamps and bathe the unchanged front room with golden illumination. For the first time the street outside his door had an unwelcome cast.

Again he read the name of the church, willing a picture of the place to rise in his mind's eye. Nothing. He would have to ask someone, perhaps Enrique if he was not too busy with Ortíz. With nowhere else to put the paper, Sevilla tagged it to the front of his refrigerator with a magnet.

He took a shower because the dust of the *palenque*'s lot was still on him. He tried to remember all he could about Adela de la Garza's face, the reflected light in her eyes, the hooded sweater pulled tightly around her like a shield. Of course there was fear, but it was fear with a shape and a name, not some nameless terror.

Señora Quintero never answered his phone message about Jiménez. Sevilla thought to call again, but it was too late in the evening. He passed on his nightly vigil on Ana's bed, beside Ofelia's crib, and went straight to his own room. Tomorrow he would visit Kelly at the hospital and then he would call Quintero again.

Despite the long, drunken nap of the afternoon, Sevilla fell asleep easily. He dreamed of battles and men without faces who brought their cocks to fight. One wore a suit and Sevilla knew this was Ortíz. The other dressed in the manner of a policeman and this was Jiménez. Still another had the body of La Bestia and stood guard over the others with his great fists. Though he had no eyes, he saw Sevilla watching, and though he had no mouth, he scowled.

FIFTEEN

IT TOOK THE BETTER PART OF THE morning before Enrique Palencia found Carlos Ortíz.

He made some excuses to Garcia about an appointment with the dentist and went first to the nearest athletic club he knew of, a place where there was boxing two Friday nights a month. There he spoke to the manager.

"Of course I know him," the man said. "He has the best new talent. It's his bankroll, you see. Sometimes it's hard for a fighter to find time to train. Ortíz can arrange that."

"What does he get?"

"Twenty percent of their earnings. From here that's not so much, but once he takes his fights to the States he gets much more. In Juárez the top fights pay less than the midcard in California or Texas."

Enrique made a note of this. "He goes across the border often?"

"All the time. I hear he has many apartments there. He likes to entertain. That's how he made his mark, you know: arranging parties."

"I didn't know," Enrique said.

The manager went on to tell Enrique more about Ortíz's fighters, hungry young men from the rough spots in the city, and how they were intensely loyal to him. Better yet, Ortíz was loyal to *them*, something that wasn't always the case among managers. Trainers were bound to fighters for the life of a fighter's career and sometimes even longer, but managers came and went without so much as a farewell.

"That's Ortíz's secret, you see," the manager said. "He has friends."

From the athletic club Enrique went to a restaurant where Ortíz sometimes held court and from there to a boxing gym. Here he saw some of Ortíz's fighters, lean and hard like street dogs. Some had jailhouse tattoos Enrique had seen on the arms and backs of convicts in the system, but these men worked as diligently at their training as all the others.

Ortíz's path led into the tourist districts and out again. The strip clubs and brothels were open in the day for those *turistas* enterprising enough to cross the bridge and secure a deal, but without the veneer of night to hide peeling paint and chipped wood the streets were sad, deflated somehow. Neon lights were on, hidden by the sun's glare. Even a short overcast rain would be enough to restore some mystery, but it was not coming.

Enrique didn't know any businessman who had no office and went the places Ortíz did. Everyone knew him, but outside of the fight venues they were circumspect about how. When they saw Enrique's badge their faces closed and the questions were harder to find answers for. They told him Ortíz didn't deal drugs, and this Enrique believed. Drugs in Ciudad Juárez were the province of gangs in and out of prison and the frontline troops of the cartels moving north and east. Drug dealers of the city didn't wear suits or dine at the Montana Restaurant on steak and baked potatoes. Perhaps elsewhere they did such things, but this was Mexico and the rules were different.

The clock turned past eleven before he saw the truck. More than once he was told about Ortíz's black pick-up truck, how clean and shiny it was, and the three bodyguards that came with him everywhere. The seats were leather and the fittings real, polished wood. *See how he does business?* they told Enrique. *You can trust a man who hasn't forgotten his roots. He doesn't need a fancy car.*

The truck stood sentinel outside another boxing gym, the third on Enrique's list. It was not like the others, but had the appointments of a fitness club across the border. Through broad windows on the second floor Enrique saw men jogging on treadmills and on the first floor the entrance was inviting metal and glass. Sunlight glared off white-painted walls that also read BOXEO — SALUD — CALISTENIA — NAUTILUS.

Enrique saw the outline of two of Ortíz's bodyguards through the heavily tinted windows of the pick-up's king cab. Their engine idled and the tailpipe dripped condensation as the air conditioning ran. Enrique sweltered with his windows down. Heat rose in steady waves from the asphalt. He parked in a red zone and watched.

A part of him felt silly. In his time with the police Enrique had never sat on a stakeout or prowled the streets looking for suspects. He went from the academy to administration, and though they issued him with identification and a pistol, there was a vast gulf between what he did and other cops did.

Garcia always made sure to point this out. "Don't get the idea that you're a real cop," he said. "Real cops sweat. Real cops have blood on their hands. When you have blisters on your blisters from walking all day and your voice is too tired for you to say goodnight to your wife, then you'll know."

Enrique had no wife and no blisters. But still he sat and watched and for a long time nothing happened. His eyelids drooped.

Ortíz emerged from the building. Enrique didn't know the man by sight, but there was no mistaking him: a man in a blazer and slacks, dwarfed by a long-limbed bodyguard in a dark athletic shirt. They moved to the pick-up and the bodyguard held the door for Ortíz. The man sat in the passenger seat. The guard went into the back.

They moved off and Enrique followed. His cell phone was on the seat beside him, and for a moment he considered calling Sevilla, but the truth was he had nothing to report. "I'm shadowing him," he could say, but that was all. If he was pressed to arrest the man he couldn't; sponsoring cocks was not illegal and nor was betting on them. Ask his fighters and Carlos Ortíz was a saint. Money to the managers of the athletic clubs where those fighters graced the ring bought still more praise.

The truck went north into the tourist areas and passed the Hotel Villa Manport. Suddenly Enrique knew where they were going, and when the truck glided to a stop alongside the coral-tiled façade of El Herradero Soto he saw he was right.

Everyone in Juárez knew the restaurant: the cheap, good food and the family atmosphere. The waiters brought pork skins and spicy red salsa to the table as an appetizer and their *pico de gallo* was renowned. At lunchtime a crowd formed under the sign. People talked to each other as if they were friends until a table came available. Out of the car, Ortíz smiled broadly and shook hands and then passed through the entrance without waiting.

Parking closely was out of the question. Enrique circled the block and found a lot with room. He hurried though he had no need to hurry; lunch at El Herradero was nothing to be done away with quickly.

The truck waited on the curb the way it waited at the boxing club. Enrique looked at the crowd of patrons, considering the wait and what he intended to do once he was inside. Did a real cop linger over a meal in the same dining room as his quarry? Should he just stand among the men waiting for food and look through the window? These things weren't taught to him and he hadn't learned them by experience. He knew where to file paperwork and the knowledge stung.

He was at the tail of the line when he saw Captain Garcia. The man crossed the street in front of the black pick-up. He thumped his hand on the truck's hood and made a shooting gesture at the driver. If the driver did it back, Enrique couldn't see.

There was nowhere to hide himself on the sidewalk except to hunker down below the line of heads. Enrique dropped his shoulders and slumped as if shot. He risked a look through the restaurant window and there was Ortíz in the back corner with his bodyguard at the same table. Garcia made his way across the dining room and joined them. Ortíz shook the cop's hand and motioned for him to sit.

Enrique didn't stay to see what they ate.

SIXTEEN

"**THEY DELIVER BABIES IN THIS** hospital," Sevilla told Kelly.

If he heard, Kelly gave no sign. He was still and the only sounds that came from him were really from the machines that monitored him and fed him fluids and ensured he still took breaths when he should and his heart beat when it should.

They were alone. Even the police guard had gone because Kelly showed no sign of waking. The nurses asked Sevilla to turn off his cell phone and to refrain from smoking. He asked them where he could find something to drink and they brought him a tray with a carton of juice and a carton of milk. He hadn't eaten breakfast or lunch and his stomach was empty.

When Sevilla spoke to Kelly he did so in English. This was always the way between them: to speak in English. With Juárez so close to America, so close that one block blended into the next, Sevilla did not understand why people didn't learn the language of the north. Speaking Spanish and only Spanish in Ciudad Juárez was stubborn and prideful and Sevilla was having none of that; he spoke English with Americans whenever he met them, even if that English wasn't always so perfect.

"My granddaughter wasn't born here, of course," Sevilla continued. "My wife and I, we talked about moving somewhere away from the city where we could keep a garden and maybe some goats. You can make good cheese from goat's milk."

The most livid of Kelly's bruises were fading. He was healing, but he would not wake.

"Ofelia was my granddaughter's name. Her father... we won't talk about him. The last thing he gave us was little Ofelia and it was the best he could give. I don't think he even came to visit her in the hospital. He never called Ana or wrote. For all I know he's dead. I heard he moved to Monterey, but there's no way to find out. I don't care to.

"They were alike, Kelly, my Ana and Ofelia. You could tell just from looking at Ofelia that she would grow up like her mother to be full of life and happiness. And that is saying a great deal in this city. I don't have to tell you."

Sevilla worked the waxed cardboard of the drink cartons while he spoke, teasing the seams apart and slowly flattening them. His hands felt the need to do something while his body was still. The smell of disinfectant and the quiet scraped at his nerves; he could not stand to be here for very long.

"When Ana and Ofelia disappeared, of course we were worried. A mother and daughter don't vanish. Not our Ana, anyway. That *rulacho* of a husband, that was different, and it's true I suspected he had a hand in it at first. But it wasn't so easy as that.

"That was when we met Paloma. I knew her years before you did, Kelly. She and the other women, they made flyers for Ana and Ofelia and pressured the Procuraduría for answers. It made no difference to them that I was a policeman; they wanted only to help... and bring my girls home."

He was silent a while then, just listening to the hushed functioning of the machines. Somewhere down the hall two nurses talked about another patient and then went on to complain about long hours and scheduling. Sevilla supposed such conversations were the same everywhere, even here.

"I wish you could talk to me, Kelly," Sevilla said, and then he left.

SEVENTEEN

ORTÍZ AND GARCIA ATE A LONG
lunch together and then they parted. Enrique followed Ortíz; Garcia
would go back to his office now and spend the afternoon with the
internet. Enrique burst with questions he wouldn't be able to ask.

He tried to call Sevilla, but there was no answer. The black
truck led Enrique away from the tourist centers and away from the
crowded heart of the city and even away from the *colonias* clinging
to the desert edge of Juárez. It passed westward along roads that
grew less crowded and wound among hills dotted with trees and
hardy grass. He saw tall, black-painted bars of a long steel fence
marching parallel to their route and coils of barbed wire like the
kind that guarded Juárez's civil buildings.

The more open the drive became, the farther back Enrique fell
until the truck was barely visible ahead of him. He almost didn't
notice the truck turn until he came closer and closer to where it
stopped. There was nowhere else to go; he pulled over onto the
shoulder and hoped no one would look back.

A bright white gatehouse broke the line of the steel fence, the
roof cupped and spired like a little church. An armed guard in
a uniform went to the truck's window and even from a distance
Enrique recognized Ortíz speaking to the man. A moment passed
and the ornate gate swung wide. The truck passed through. The
way was closed behind.

Enrique turned his eyes to hills. There were more trees here than
anywhere along the way and the rolling terrain was greened. Great

houses were stashed here and there among the woods, shockingly bright lawns carved out of mesquites and live oaks to go along with white pillars and many windows. There was also a long pool of grass that could only be a golfing fairway. The black pick-up vanished up the road and didn't reappear.

The gatehouse held three men with truncheons and rifles. They looked out through green-tinted windows at Enrique's car as it approached and this time two emerged when he drew to a stop before the high gates.

"*Excúseme*," Enrique said.

"Turn around," said one of the guards.

"I was wondering: what is this place?"

The guard drew his truncheon from his belt. The other one held a gun. "I won't tell you again, *pendejo*. Back up and turn around."

"I'm with the police."

Enrique showed the men his identification. The one with the truncheon stiffened. The second retreated to the gatehouse. Enrique saw the third talking on a telephone.

When the second man returned, he was no longer armed. He spoke quietly to the first and the truncheon went back in its loop. "What can I do for you?" the guard asked then.

"What is this place?"

"Los Campos," the first guard replied.

Enrique nodded. "I've heard of it. Listen: I'd like to ask you about the truck that came through here before."

"We don't talk about visitors," the second guard said. "It's not allowed."

"You don't have to tell me any secrets; I know it was Señor Ortíz," Enrique said. "I just wanted to know, does he live here?"

The guards smirked at each other. The first shook his head. "No, he's only visiting."

"May I ask who?"

"He comes to see Señor Madrigal," the first guard said, and the second elbowed him sharply. "Though I didn't tell you that."

"Your secret is safe with me," Enrique said pleasantly. "As long as you can keep a secret for me."

"What's that?"

"Don't mention I was here."

"I don't even know you," the guard replied.

"Very good," Enrique said. He put his car in reverse. "Thank you for your help, gentlemen."

He turned away from the gates of Los Campos and felt the guards' eyes on him as he pulled a u-turn in the road. They were still watching him as they shrank away in his rear-view mirror, and then both the men and the gate were gone.

Enrique did not know Los Campos specifically, but he knew of communities like it. They dotted the territory around Ciudad Juárez, well away from the unpleasantness of the city center, the crime and the violence. The big houses were owned by the men who ran the *maquiladoras* or made it in some other business. Some were ranchers whose holdings were hundreds of miles away. Others still made all their money across the border in the United States, but kept their wealth away from American tax collectors.

Ortíz was not wealthy enough to live in one of these places. This Enrique knew before he even asked. The men and women of the gated communities drove Bentleys and Mercedes and didn't share the cab of a pick-up truck with anyone. It was doubtful any of them had even so much as touched the seat of the pick-up truck, or would even come near one.

He tried calling Sevilla again, but again there was only voice mail. "Call me when you have a chance," Enrique said, and tossed the phone back on the seat beside him.

Enrique was excited, but he also felt a fool. He was full of inquiries and mismatched information and names and faces he didn't know. For hours Carlos Ortíz was a ghost to him and then suddenly he was there, dining with Captain Garcia and patrolling the city as if he were tax collector to some great lord who owned all he surveyed.

The thought gave him pause. Enrique looked toward the fence still rolling past him, marking off land no one visited and where no house was built. There were not even roads leading there to make the promise of new life. The people of Los Campos owned the space because they could own it and not for any other reason.

He wanted to call Sevilla a third time, but he would wait. Instead he drove.

EIGHTEEN

A<small>T</small> E<small>L</small> C<small>ERESO</small> <small>EVERYONE GOT A</small> little and no more: a little space, a little time, a little safety. Even those prisoners injured in one way or another got little attention, though the most serious were kept in a segregated unit of eight beds. Estéban was one of the eight, shuffled to and from the mess hall on a staggered schedule that kept the badly hurt inmates from being caught in the crush of the meal line, but still dining among the rest.

They were the walking wounded of El Cereso, with their broken bones and stitches. Estéban's cast reached from the tips of his fingers to the middle of his upper arm. He hobbled because his legs were still sore from the beatings and his joints ached from being twisted until they nearly came loose of their sockets.

Eye contact was frowned upon in any part of the jail, and the medical exceptions were doubly bound. The others knew that these men had more space, more freedom, more quiet, than all the rest. Those who had little hated those who had more and it did not enter into their minds that abundance was bought with extreme suffering.

Estéban balanced his food tray on the artificial bend of his cast arm. He couldn't hold it out the way the others did and the men behind the steam trays grumbled and cursed because this meant a smidgen of extra work. "Why don't you break your other arm already?" one of the mess workers asked and then slopped black beans on the tray. "Then some pretty nurse can come feed you."

To this and other things Estéban said nothing.

He was gone from El Cereso and the interrogation rooms and the prisoners and the guards and the police. He was gone from the city entirely. His body operated automatically, put food into itself without any guidance and did the little things to maintain itself simply because some part of Estéban's brain knew they needed doing. He was by the concrete skate ponds of Parque Xtremo, shaded by the climbing tower. He ate spicy tamales, drank beer or got high and he talked to his best friend, the gringo.

Sometimes when it was quiet and Estéban had no demands except to lie on his bunk and be alone, his talks with Kelly roved far and wide. Sometimes they were fanciful. He imagined there was a wedding in Kelly's future, and though it seemed a womanly thing to do, they talked about who would be there and where the honeymoon would be and then, when all the pageantry was over, when the children would come.

"I'll be a good uncle," Estéban said. "I'll spoil them terrible. '¡Tío Estéban, Tío Estéban! ¿Qué tú nos trajó?' And I'll give them candy and all kinds of shit. That's what uncles do."

Kelly agreed that was what uncles do. They gave knee rides and brought puppies as surprise birthday gifts. They took nephews fishing and sometimes for their first, secret beer. These were the things Estéban looked forward to doing when Kelly and Paloma were married.

In the mess hall Estéban sat with the other invalids and ate his food. He stared past the tray and past the scratched metal surface of the table and to a winding, sun-soaked road leading south toward warm water and beaches and Mazatlán. Sometimes he saw cliff divers when he got there and tourists parasailed behind speedboats among great rocks that looked like sailing ships on the high seas.

You want another beer? Kelly asked Estéban. Of course he did.

The beer was bright and refreshing and perfect. Heat waves rose from the concrete ponds of Parque Xtremo. The skaters were still at their avocation despite the heat. They lipped the ponds and turned in the air as if gravity was temporarily of no concern and then down again out of sight.

Estéban put his hand on Kelly's shoulder and squeezed it.

What's wrong?

"I wanted to make sure you were still here," Estéban said. "Sometimes... sometimes I feel like this is all a dream. I don't want to wake up, *carnal*. This is where I want to be."

They had Sunday lunch together at the house. Paloma served them while wearing her light dress that caught the sun. Today Estéban chose not to smoke afterward and the three of them sat talking in the front room within sight of their painting of Nuestra Señora de Guadalupe. Seeing it used to make Estéban uncomfortable, but he wasn't bothered by it anymore. Not now. Now it meant he was home and not somewhere dark and filthy and terrible.

Two men raised voices to each other at another table. The benches and the tables themselves were fixed to the floor and the flatware was made of flimsy plastic, so they used the trays as weapons and then their feet and fists. A pair became a quartet and then a dozen. Food splattered and was trod underfoot. Imbalances left long unaddressed were suddenly and violently corrected. Estéban saw none of this.

"I knew you were the kind of man I could count on," Estéban told Kelly in the Parque Xtremo. "I knew it from the first time, you know?"

They sat on the little couch in the front room. Paloma had *limonada* set out already. Estéban could hear her in the kitchen with the pots and the dishes.

"I'm glad you're getting married to my sister. I'm glad we're brothers. I always wanted a brother like you."

He wanted to hug Kelly, but that was too much emotion for two men. They bumped knuckles. Estéban had some of the lemonade. It tasted like beer.

"I think we should all go down to Mazatlán together," Estéban said.

Around him the invalids were up and the guards waded among warring bodies with clubs and shouts. Estéban sat sightless and deaf even as a prisoner stabbed him through the neck with a sharp piece of steel. He toppled to the floor and didn't see the blood pooling around him; only the house fading and Paloma coming from the kitchen to be with them and Kelly smiling in the sun until the sun went black.

PART FOUR

Justicia

ONE

THE CHURCH WAS CALLED IGLESIA del Anuncio, the Church of the Annunciation, and it was not the ugliest such building he had ever seen, though it was close. The neighborhood around it was crumbling into sun-scorched dust and so was the sanctuary inside and out. Frescoes were faded and even the great crucifix above the altar was chipping and flaking. When there was not money or manpower enough to tend to Christ, Sevilla mused, a church was ready to die.

He sat away from Ella Arellano though he saw her well enough. She wore black like the cluster of women around her. They assembled before the church at the appointed time. Sevilla didn't approach them, but he knew Ella was aware of his presence.

The battered old confessional was near Sevilla and during the long service his eyes were drawn to it. He hadn't been inside one since Liliana passed, and it was just as well. When he needed to confess, he confessed to her. If his sins were too much for Liliana, then no priest could hope to understand.

Out of habit he said the prayers and from memory he sang the hymns. When it was time for Communion he stayed in his pew, though he put two hundred pesos in the plate as an offering. Afterward he lit a candle for Estéban Salazar. The old church made him feel sad because it was unloved. Half the place was empty and the other half was growing irrevocably aged.

When the mass was all done, Sevilla trailed outside behind Ella and the women. Ella came to him in the narthex while the women greeted the priest in turn. She wore a veil like the others and seemed much older than Sevilla remembered her being. "Thank you," she said.

"There's no need to thank me," replied Sevilla. "I wanted to see you."

"Do you have a car?" Ella asked.

"Yes."

"Meet us. We'll go on foot."

She gave Sevilla an address and he wrote it down. He didn't know the street, but he knew he could find it.

"Who are they?" Sevilla asked of the women in black.

"They're like you," Ella said. She went back to them.

Sevilla left the church and went back to his car. He made two wrong turns finding the address, but he got there before Ella and the women in black. Sitting behind the wheel on the sleepy Sunday avenue he felt stupid and exposed, but there was no one watching him.

Eventually he saw them coming, a little processional for some cause or saint unspecified. When he left his car he saw them hesitate as a group, like a horse shied from sudden movement on the ground, but Ella calmed them. "Come inside," she told Sevilla.

The house was small and poor like the others around it. There was barely enough room for all of them, but they moved as if they had long practice doing so. Only Sevilla was out of place. He was always excusing himself and moving here and there because he was forever in the wrong spot at the wrong time.

After some time there was food and drink and the women settled. Before they talked about the things poor women talked about: families and money and the news of the neighborhood that would make no difference to anyone from the outside. This was something Sevilla was not a part of, but now they looked to him as if his next words meant everything.

"You left your home," said Sevilla to Ella.

"They're watching."

"Who?"

"The men with the black truck. The ones who took Paloma away."

Sevilla was stung coldly. He fumbled for his notepad and it seemed a long time before he had it firmly in his hands. "You saw someone take her?"

"Yes."

Ella told Sevilla the story, about the mothers of the missing, about Paloma and how the men in the black pick-up came. She showed Sevilla the last of her fading bruises. All the while the mothers listened in silence like stones bearing witness.

"Did they say names?" Sevilla asked. "Did they talk to each other?"

"No names."

"Did you see a man, he's called Ortíz." Sevilla described him, but the mothers shook their heads no.

"Three men," Ella said. "Big. Strong."

"They are cowards," said one of the mothers. "Who else but a coward can beat a woman?"

Sevilla pressed, "Have you ever seen this man I'm talking about? What about the license on the truck? Did any of you get it?"

Another one of the mothers raised her hand slightly. It was a schoolgirlish thing to do, but she was no longer young. "I've seen him."

"You have? Where?"

"Not for a long time," the woman said. "But years ago he used to come and talk to the local girls about going to parties. We knew this was just a story, that he was taking girls to the brothels, but some still went with him."

His heart beat quicker, but his hands were steady. Sevilla realized he was not thirsty for a drink. His head was clear. "How long ago was this? Did he always come alone? Tell me everything you can remember."

The woman did, but it was very little. When the subject turned back to the black pick-up truck and the big, strong men there was nothing else to add. The men struck like lightning and were gone just as quickly.

"Why didn't you go to the police?"

Ella shook her head. "We did."

"What? You did?"

"Yes. We went to the police right away and they made us give a report. All of us here told the story."

They gave Sevilla the station number. He knew it, and had even passed it on the way to the church. It was a small place with only a handful of policemen assigned to it for a neighborhood as heavily populated as any near the city center, but the poor paid little tax.

"I don't understand. *All* of you made statements on the day?"

"Yes. But the police don't listen. They never listen. Even before the drug wars they wouldn't listen to women. Women have no voices."

Sevilla sat back in the little upright chair he'd been given. He rubbed his eyes for a moment to think, to hide behind the action and let his mind catch up. When he looked again, the mothers of the missing were as sober as they had been before, though he sensed their anger.

"I saw no report," Sevilla said. "But I'm a state policeman."

"Then you can do nothing?" asked one of the mothers.

"I'm not powerless. I know a man in the city police and he can ask questions. Understand me now: with the drugs wars, everything else is pushed to the side. They have suspects and they have a confession. This isn't something anyone will want to reopen."

Ella shook her head and frowned. "Those men were not American and Paloma's brother was not one of them."

"I know that," Sevilla said. "But it is different to know something than it is to prove it."

"Then prove it," Ella said. "We are all witnesses! We saw it happen!"

Sevilla put his hand on Ella's hand and she didn't push it away.

He used his voice in the way he'd been taught a long time ago. Some things never changed. "I will find out. I promise you I will not stop asking questions. Someone must know the answers. I will find them."

"Don't promise what you can't do," Ella said.

"I'm not. This I can do. When the time comes I'll be sure you have a voice. You'll tell everyone. They will listen."

TWO

"**H**AVE YOU BEEN DRINKING?"
Enrique asked Sevilla when they were together in the living room
and sure no one was watching through the window. Sevilla pulled
the drapes. He had felt eyes all day when there were none around.
Coming home he drove around his block three times, and though
he felt foolish doing it, he could not help himself.

"Not at all," answered Sevilla truthfully.

They sat at opposite ends of a little coffee table with brightly
painted legs and a worn top made of old flooring. It was one of
Liliana's finds. Sevilla thought of it as charmingly ugly. His notes
were strewn across it now.

"There is no report," Enrique said. "I made three calls. Too many
calls. Someone will know I was asking, but I wanted to know. There
is no report."

"Those women did not lie to me, Enrique."

"I'm not saying they did. I am saying there is *no report*."

"The truck. The man. Ortíz. He's the one," Sevilla said.

Enrique sorted the pages of Sevilla's notes like cards, as if
searching for a hidden picture that would appear if only they were
placed in the right order. His brow creased and his frown threatened
to break the corners of his mouth. To Sevilla he looked like a real
policeman. "And there's Madrigal."

"Rafa Madrigal is not a criminal," Sevilla said. "I met him once
in Mexico City. It was an event for a police charity. We spoke for

several minutes. He's a rancher, he owns two *maquilas*. What would he want with someone like Ortíz?"

"That is what I asked myself. What *would* he want with someone like Ortíz. You didn't see Los Campos, but I did; men like him do not get to go inside unless they are invited. Neither you nor I could go."

"His elder son died of a drug overdose across the border in Texas, I think," Sevilla said. "He has no interest in crooks. You said it yourself: at best the man is a gambler and a boxing manager. At worst he's a pimp."

"Then why did he go there? How did he get in? Think, Señor Sevilla."

Sevilla slumped in his chair. Half-formed ideas and thoughts swirled, but one was steadily settling that he did not want to entertain and for the first time all day he wanted the drink he hadn't wanted before. "I don't know," he said.

"You *do* know."

He looked at his notes. Text was boxed and underlined and marked with arrows. He had written five pages with Ella Arellano and the mothers of the missing. Twice he drove past the little station where they made their report, both times with the same thought nagging at the back of his mind and slowly pushing itself forward.

"Ortíz could not make a police report disappear."

"No," Sevilla agreed.

"But he knows Garcia. If there's anyone with experience of making evidence vanish, he's the one."

"Captain Garcia doesn't do favors for just anyone," Enrique said. "I've been with him for two years. I'm La Bestia's servant. I would know."

"That's wrong," Sevilla said. He straightened. The thought was nearly there if only he could speak it.

"What is?"

"You're not his servant. If you were, you wouldn't be here. You wouldn't ask these questions. *That* I know for certain."

"Then you know—"

"Don't say it," Sevilla interrupted.

"Someone has to."

"You said it yourself, Enrique: neither you nor I would see the home of someone like Rafa Madrigal. And if not us, then certainly not La Bestia. Ortíz is the go-between, the cut-out. If he speaks to Garcia, no one raises an eyebrow. No one even pays attention because who cares? We have *narcos* killing *narcos* in the streets. The goddamned chief of police was murdered. What's two men having lunch together?"

"What's one missing report?" Enrique added.

When Sevilla looked at the pages of his notes again, he saw the picture and it made him tremble. He squeezed his hands into fists and let them go. The skin on the backs of his knuckles was old. He was old and he felt his age.

"What are you thinking?" Enrique asked.

"I think you will follow Ortíz again. And I will do something stupid."

THREE

THE BANK WAS THE KIND BUILT when such places were meant to be palaces, fortresses of money or cathedrals of a sort, where petitioners came with offerings of a few hundred pesos to lay the foundation of a dream. Sevilla could remember when he was twenty-two years old and had saved enough to open his account. The bank had not changed much at all.

Brass-fitted bars still enclosed the tellers, but behind this was a thick layer of bulletproof glass to protect against modern bandits. Desks where suit-wearing men rendered judgment on loans and accounts were laden with computers instead of typewriters and at some point in the intervening decades air conditioning had been installed to cool the whole edifice.

Sevilla felt sick to his stomach, and from time to time as he waited in the pre-lunch crowd of customers he thought of reconsidering and fleeing, but he didn't. When at last it was his turn, the teller raised both eyebrows at the amount on the green withdrawal slip. "Are you sure of this, *señor*?"

"Yes, I'm sure," Sevilla said, though he was not.

"Do you want this amount as a cashier's check?"

"I want it in cash. Large bills."

"Would you like to speak with a manager?"

"No."

Sevilla put the money in a briefcase and for a moment he felt like one of his *narcos*, packing thousands into neat bundles and then bricking them together until there were just rows and rows of brand-new five-hundred-peso notes.

He went to a place he found in the telephone directory, careful to put his pistol in the glove compartment of his car and lock it because this was no time for awkward questions.

Inside the shop there were dummies wearing suits, some completed and others still in a state of construction. Bolts of rich fabric nestled in hardwood cubbies and there was the smell of hot wire and cigars in the air. The tailor was a gray-bearded man a head shorter than Sevilla. He had pins stuck into a band around his left arm and wore a green visor that reminded Sevilla of the bank he'd just left.

"Good day, *señor*," the tailor said.

"*Buenas tardes*. I need a suit."

The tailor motioned with his hand to encompass the cloth, the dummies and the storefront. Behind him was a broad table with measuring sticks built into its surface. An open door to the back room revealed two sewing machines and still more fragments of suits uncompleted. "I will do my best," he said.

"The thing is," Sevilla said, "I need more than one. And I need them quickly. Within three days. The first I will need tomorrow."

"This I can do, but a rush order is more expensive." The tailor looked at Sevilla's suit, the deep wrinkles and the dulled color of what had once been nearly perfect white. He did not sniff, but Sevilla saw his contempt. "Is this the first time *señor* has had a suit tailored?"

"Is it so obvious?" Sevilla joked.

"Yes, *señor*, but no matter. Every man has a first time in a suit fitted to him. For some that time comes early and others not."

Sevilla stood with his hands out at his sides. "What do we do?"

"First *señor* makes a deposit for his suits."

FOUR

ONCE AN HOUR AND SOMETIMES more, Garcia called Enrique's phone. Each time Enrique silenced it. After a while he turned off the ringer altogether. He didn't expect a call from Sevilla and if one came he would be able to return it quickly enough. If worst came to worst, Enrique could leave a message at the Hotel Lucerna under the name Villalobos.

In poker they called this *all in*, a term Enrique learned from watching games played in Las Vegas, USA, for more money than he would ever earn in a lifetime of work. The men and sometimes women were so assured in their movements, pressing stacks of chips worth thousands of US dollars into play as if their value was nothing more than that of the clay of which they were made. He knew there must be fear behind those blank expressions, those *poker faces*, but they might as well have been ordering lunch.

At first Enrique argued with Sevilla, but the longer they argued the more it made sense. In the end they were alone because the case they pursued was already closed. The men who did it were confessed, all but convicted and, in the case of Estéban Salazar, dead. No judge need hear the case, nor jury be convened. One might come to call for Kelly Courter, but then only if he returned to the world of the living. He was suspended as everything else was suspended. This way was the only way out.

The black pick-up truck moved through traffic ahead of him and Enrique followed. Ortíz was like a policeman working a beat, patrolling endlessly and never staying in any one place too long.

He visited casinos and brothels and gymnasiums and, shark-like, moved on. Before long Enrique had his rhythm, understood the pattern of quarry and pursuer, and his hands relaxed on the wheel. He was able to think.

His phone vibrated on the seat beside him. He didn't bother to look down. Up ahead the truck made a left-hand turn. Enrique barely managed to squeak through the light.

Again the truck slowed. It was the large, shiny fitness club again. Enrique cruised gently to the curb and stilled the engine. He put down the window and let the light, heat and smells of the street come in.

FIVE

THE SUIT DIDN'T FEEL RIGHT BECAUSE it fit so well. Sevilla was used to the idiosyncrasies of his own clothes, the way they cinched and pulled where they shouldn't and where they hung comfortably loose. Without years of washing and wearing behind them, the suit also lacked the smell of well-worn clothes. He felt trussed up and foolish, but when he approached the maître d' at the Misión Guadalupe without a reservation he wasn't shooed away and that was how he knew the suit was as it should be.

"I would have called before," Sevilla told the maître d'. "But I've been so busy."

"Of course, *señor*," the maître d' replied. "We have a table we can make available for you. It will be just a few minutes. Would you care for something from the bar while you wait?"

Sevilla licked his lips unconsciously and then covered for it with a cough. "No," he said. "No, thank you. I can wait."

"Very good."

The restaurant was traditionally Mexican in its cuisine, though taken through the filter of fine dining. Light-colored walls, blond wood and marble bespoke elegance and the menu announced dishes Sevilla had eaten all his life but with variations he didn't recognize. The leather chairs in the waiting area were angular and modern looking and not welcoming when he sat down. It was as he suspected; all for show and not for use.

In the dining room three massive alabaster plinths dominated the space. Sevilla saw the bar, backlighted like some valuable statue, its expanse carved of the same stone. He was given a table near the back of the restaurant, set for one. He passed Madrigal's table along the way.

Rafa Madrigal held court at a large, round table with four other men. Three were his age, leonine faces set off by deep tans and whitening hair. The fourth was much younger, only in his twenties, but no stranger to his surroundings. The forest of crystal and silver surrounded them. The *comida corrida* was not for men like these a succession of peasant foods, but dish after dish of handcrafted excellence. As Sevilla took his seat he saw one set of plates whisked away and another laid in their place by a coterie of waiters in black pants and tight, matching T-shirts.

He was not close enough to hear what they were saying, though the conversation was continuous. Sevilla made an effort not to look too often in their direction. He forced himself to examine the menu.

When ordering he felt a fool, an ape-man pretending to be a gentleman, but his server seemed to pay no mind to his hesitation or his awkwardness. An appetizer of *quesadillas* with *huitlacoche* came to his table within minutes, and though Sevilla expected he would be too distracted to notice, the flavor was extraordinary. He tried not to think about the cost.

Of the five at Madrigal's table he recognized only the man himself. The others may have seemed vaguely familiar, but Sevilla dismissed the thought; sometimes a policeman could convince himself he knew more than he did and then make assumptions that could be crippling. Madrigal he knew. The rest he did not. He wouldn't pretend to himself or anyone else that it was otherwise.

Sevilla didn't much care for fish, but he ordered salmon anyway. Like the *quesadillas*, it was amazing. For a few moments he struggled between his plate and the men at Madrigal's table, but the salmon was gone too soon and he was left to his water glass.

Madrigal was at least two courses ahead and when Sevilla saw the servers bring coffee he knew he could wait no longer. His hands were damp. He wiped them on his napkin. When that was done, he took two deep breaths and rose from his seat. He crossed the dining room lightheaded. By the time the first head turned in his direction, Sevilla was smiling.

"*Excúseme*, gentlemen," Sevilla said. "I hate to interrupt. Rafa Madrigal? Juan Villalobos. You may not remember me, but we met once a few years ago."

All the men looked at Sevilla and he tried not to shrink under the combined strength of their gazes. Most of the faces were blank, but the young man's expression curdled. Madrigal's eyes were unreadable until the moment the corners turned up and he grinned. "In Mexico City, is that right?" he asked.

Sevilla felt clenched inside. "Yes. The policemen's charity."

"Yes, yes, I remember. You were with your wife. I'm sorry, Señor Villalobos, but I had forgotten your name. It's good to see you again."

Madrigal offered his hand and they shook. The man had a strong grip. His hair was turning prematurely white, but his handshake reminded Sevilla the man was not yet old. His face was lean and clean shaven. Though he had paid for too much for a salon treatment, Sevilla felt unkempt in his mustache and beard.

"I didn't mean to intrude," Sevilla said. "I will leave you to your meal."

He turned to go. Madrigal caught at his sleeve. "No, no, please stay. Are you still eating? Have them serve you here, if you don't mind the company."

Sevilla pretended to waver. "All right, but please don't feel you must. I only wanted to say hello."

"Nonsense, please sit."

The man signaled a waiter and Sevilla's food was transferred from his table to the empty space among the men. Sevilla was directly across from the young man whose expression still had not changed. The others were merely curious now and each greeted Sevilla kindly as they were introduced.

"And this is my son, Sebastián," Madrigal said.

"*Mucho gusto*," Sevilla said.

"*Igualmente*," the young man replied without enthusiasm.

Madrigal seemed not to notice. "When you're finished, you must try this coffee," he said to Sevilla. "It has a taste of licorice. Very good. I don't pretend to know what they put in it; I always forget when they tell me."

"You are involved with charities?" asked one of the other men. His name was Hernández.

"Yes. Particularly those to do with police and hospitals. We seem to need both very much these days." As Sevilla spoke he didn't recognize his own voice. He went on to talk about three different charities as if he was a regular contributor and he did not stammer once. He told them of his home in Mexico City, his wife's death, his retirement boredom. Food came and went. He was as smooth and flawless as the *chichilo negro* poured over the tenderloin. He was a master.

Sebastián said something Sevilla didn't hear.

"I'm sorry?"

"Why are you in Ciudad Juárez?" Sebastián asked again.

Sevilla put up his hands. "It was somewhere to go. Besides, I think the steak here was worth the trip alone."

The older men laughed, but Sebastián did not. He fell silent.

"How long will you be in the city?" Madrigal asked Sevilla.

"A week, perhaps two. I was thinking about going across the border for a while. I've never seen the Alamo."

"You'll be disappointed," Señor Hernández said. "It's in the middle of the city!"

Madrigal's coffee was long finished and the table was nearly empty. A server placed a cup and saucer before Sevilla as quickly and gently as a ghost and was gone again. For their part the other men didn't seem to notice the presence of anyone outside their own group; it was as though the room was theirs and theirs alone and everything was brought to them by magic.

"Do you play golf?" asked Madrigal.

"I don't play well, but I play."

This made the men laugh again. Madrigal waved that away. "It's no matter. If you have the time, why not come out to Los Campos for a round? Who knows the next time you will be in the city?"

Sevilla used a tiny spoon to put sugar into his coffee. He observed his hands as if from a distance. They did not shake. "That would be very kind of you, but I wouldn't want to impose."

"It's no imposition. How about Wednesday morning? I can arrange for a tee time after breakfast. You can be my guest."

Once again Sevilla made a show of considering the idea though his mind was already made up. He paused to take some of the coffee. It was as hot, strong and licorice-tasting as Madrigal promised. Sevilla hated it. "All right," he said. "You can reach me at my hotel."

"Where are you staying?"

"The Hotel Lucerna."

"Of course."

"I'll give you my private room number," Sevilla said in a voice as indifferent as he could muster. This happened every day. Men of power and influence were always his friends. A hotel like the Lucerna was the minimum of luxury. "You can call me any time."

"Then it's done."

After that they parted ways. Sevilla paid his check in cash, though the other men settled their debts with credit cards, and though he was ready to explain why he didn't carry such things there were no questions. He spoke the language of the wealthy, showed no fear. They liked the cut of his suit and the Persol sunglasses he wore outside the restaurant.

The maître d' called a cab for Sevilla. Madrigal insisted on waiting with him. One by one Sevilla said goodbye to the others as the valet brought their cars: Mercedes, BMW, Bentley. Sevilla was glad when the cab finally came and he could shake hands with Madrigal and go on his way. He did not shake with Sebastián.

SIX

ENRIQUE STOPPED AT THE OFFICE for his messages and because he felt he should at least pretend he was still working. He checked his email and made replies. It was midafternoon and most of the men were on their break. Garcia approached quietly. Enrique only noticed him when his shadow fell across the desk.

"Where the fuck have you been?"

The door to Garcia's office had been closed before. Enrique assumed Garcia was away on a long lunch that might last until the end of business. Now the door stood open. "Captain," Enrique said, but he could think of nothing else.

"I've been calling you," Garcia said. He had one cuff unbuttoned, his right sleeve rolled up. He liked to do this when he spent hours playing card games on the internet or otherwise wasting time in his office. At no time had Enrique ever seen the man fill out a report or type an email.

"I'm sorry. I've been taking care of some… family problems. My uncle is sick. I'll take care of the paperwork before I leave."

Garcia leaned across the desk until Enrique couldn't see the bank of windows beyond him. He turned Enrique's monitor and glanced at it. "Is that what you're telling everyone? That your uncle is sick?"

The thought crossed Enrique's mind that when he tailed Ortíz he hadn't watched his own mirrors or kept track of who appeared and might reappear in his wake. He hadn't checked at Ortíz's stops to see if anyone was looking out for someone looking in. Enrique smelled Garcia and these things came rushing in.

"It's the truth."

"You know I've never liked you," Garcia said. "Don't get me wrong, you're good enough to get the job done, but I know when a man's heart isn't in his work. You're a pussy."

Enrique didn't argue. He wanted to shrink back into his chair, but he made himself sit straight. Instead of looking into Garcia's eyes, he stared at the man's eyebrow. It twitched whenever Garcia spoke.

"I knew as soon as Salazar got stuck that you'd be on the phone crying for sick days. 'Oh, poor Estéban Salazar.' Am I right?"

"No," Enrique managed. His head twitched when he meant to shake it. "My uncle, he has a problem with his heart. You can check if you want."

Immediately Enrique felt stupid for saying so. If Garcia did call, he would learn that Enrique's uncle was not sick at all. But he couldn't be sure whether Garcia would call, or whether he would simply opt to escort Enrique to an interview room. He would do it. He had done it before.

"I don't have time to chase after you and wipe your ass," Garcia said. "I'm *busy*. Haven't you heard? We have *narcos* tearing the whole goddamned city apart. The Americans are complaining, businesses are moving away... it's no time to feel sorry for some sister-raping *puto*. Do you understand me?"

Enrique nodded only slightly. "Yes."

"Good. I'm glad you understand." Garcia straightened up and the sun came back to Enrique's desk. Then he swept the folders and pen cup and blotter from it with his hand. "Pick up all of that and then go check on your goddamned uncle. He better be feeling all right by tomorrow."

"Yes, sir," Enrique said.

He got down on his hands and knees and picked up his things. Garcia watched him for a little while until he was bored. Enrique didn't come away from the floor until he heard the door to Garcia's office catch. He didn't dare look, because he knew La Bestia's eye was on him through the glass.

SEVEN

"**H**OW MUCH DOES THIS COST?"
Enrique asked Sevilla from the main room of the suite.

"You don't want to know. *I* don't want to know."

After lunch with Madrigal, Sevilla went shopping. The first thing he bought was a set of titanium golf clubs. They looked as though they had never been used, but the bag was clearly secondhand. Another stop garnered a replacement that, like Sevilla's new suits, bespoke money. He practiced his swing near a long wall of floor-to-ceiling windows in the bedroom overlooking the Hotel Lucerna's lagoon-like swimming area.

Enrique joined him. "How does playing golf help?"

"I don't know," Sevilla said. "But it's an in."

"So you believe there is something wrong with Señor Madrigal?"

"I believe there is something out of place."

Children and women were playing in the pool. Sevilla's suite was on the top floor so only the vaguest details could be seen. The city sprawled out in front of them. The American consulate was close enough to be hit with a driven golf ball and the river was not far beyond it. Complimentary shuttles carried guests from the hotel to the industrial parks and the *maquilas* owned by 3M, Electrolux, Lear. The language most often heard in the hallways was English.

"You believe there is *something* wrong, but not with Señor Madrigal?"

Sevilla interrupted a swing. His shoulder felt sore already. In two days he would be on the green with Madrigal. "Why do you think I am doing this, Enrique? These clothes, this suit, these… goddamned golf clubs? *Of course* there's something wrong. Everything we learn about Ortíz tells me there is no reason for him to move in the circles of someone like Rafa Madrigal. That alone says something. But I don't know what."

Enrique opened his mouth to say something.

"*You* don't know what," Sevilla said.

Enrique paced the bedroom. Without trying to, Sevilla found himself noting all the things about the young cop that didn't fit with the place. The way he moved, the way he dressed and the simple cut of his hair. If he noticed these things, then creatures of wealth like the men at Misión Guadalupe would be attuned to them like day and night. Sevilla marveled that they hadn't seen through him, that they shared their table and their time with him.

"Have you considered what this will cost us if there's nothing to learn?" asked Sevilla. "You have Garcia pushing you, but even my superiors don't pay me to play dress-up and chase rich men around a golf course. We are committed to this, right or wrong."

"I know. I know, I know. I'm sorry."

"Don't be sorry." Sevilla practiced his swing again. He could not remember the last time he'd played the game, but some part of it was beginning to surface. "This is the answer. It must be. And I don't like the look of Madrigal's son."

"He is Madrigal's second son?"

"That's right."

"You sound sorry for Señor Madrigal."

Another swing. It felt different this time, better. "I feel sorry for any man who loses a child. Did you know his wife died last year? Cancer. Very sudden. He has no other children, no grandchildren… only Sebastián. That kind of loneliness could make a man overlook many things, even terrible things."

Everything in the suite belonged to Juan Villalobos Sanchez: the underwear in the dresser and the suits in the closet. The only thing that belonged to Rafael Sevilla was the picture of Ana and Ofelia from his daughter's bedside. He'd thought not once or twice but many times about leaving it where it belonged, but in the end it came along.

Out of the corner of his eye Sevilla saw Enrique was looking down from the windows to the pool many stories below. He didn't blame him; the view was hypnotic, the little miniature shapes swirling around an hourglass of pristine blue under a sky of the same shade. On his first morning in the suite, Sevilla sat for an hour just watching and then he cried.

Enrique broke the quiet. "I've never seen Ortíz meet with anyone in Madrigal's family."

"How can you be certain? I found a photo of Sebastián on the internet. I printed it out. Look in the office, by the computer."

The titanium driver slid easily into place among the other clubs. Sevilla let his fingers drift over their heads. This one for distance, this one for accuracy, this one for traps. When he reached for the right club he would have to do so without thinking, as if this was natural for him. He must make Madrigal believe in Juan Villalobos again.

"I don't recognize him," Enrique said when he returned.

"But now you've seen his face. Watch for him."

"You want me to follow Ortíz again? What's the point?"

The bedroom had a wet bar. Sevilla went to it and served himself seltzer with a twist of lemon. He felt Enrique watching him and smiled to himself when he came away from the bar without so much as touching the whisky.

"The point is we must know what Ortíz is doing. He's the link between the Madrigals and Kelly and from Kelly to Paloma and Estéban. This is police work, Enrique: watching and waiting. If something happens, it will happen with Ortíz."

"While you eat fine food and play games with rich people."

Sevilla sipped from his tumbler. He frowned. "Yes, that."

By some unspoken command they both drifted back to the windows and looked down upon the pool. Once Sevilla thought he might have heard a child's high-pitched squeal of delight, but he knew it was just his imagination.

EIGHT

Sevilla rented a black Lexus from an agency in the hotel. It came equipped with a GPS in the dashboard and gave him turn-by-turn directions out of the busy arena of Ciudad Juárez and into the country.

There was no place in the wilds gnawing at Juárez's edge that was beautiful. There were places that were greener than others, more populated with trees than others, but most of it was fit only for cactus and rocks and the twisted, alien mesquite tree. Sometimes the landscape exploded into strange, unexpected bloom, displaying the flowers of the purple aster and sand verbena as if daring naysayers to underestimate desert beauty again.

He found Los Campos as Enrique described it, first by its long march of iron fencing to the gate and its armed guards. The men had an earth-colored Hummer with emergency lights on the top like a police vehicle, but it had no markings. Sevilla thought he might have recognized one of the gate guards from the ranks of the city police, but the man didn't seem to recognize him in return and Sevilla let the notion pass.

They called Madrigal's security from the gate and confirmed Sevilla's entry. It was still early enough that dawn colors bled across the eastern horizon, washing the live oaks beyond in warm orange and the faintest red. Sevilla relaxed behind the wheel. He was dressed lightly for morning golf. The clubs were in the trunk.

"Good morning, *señor*," the lead guard told Sevilla when he was done on the phone. The gates slowly parted. The road beyond was perfect and black and smooth without blemish, as if the asphalt were laid just the day before. In the city there were potholes large enough to swallow whole cars. "Please drive ahead. Do you know the way?"

"Please tell me," Sevilla answered, and the guard presented him with a printed map. He marked Sevilla's route with a green marker. When the Lexus passed through, the gate swung shut behind him. Sevilla was inside.

The flawless road wound up into the hills, skirting a broad fairway festooned with jetting underground sprinklers. The sunrise caught water droplets in midair, froze them and made the sprinklers seem like trees with silver branches and white leaves. And then Sevilla was past them.

Some of the driveways of the estates within were gated themselves with more armed guards standing sentry. Kidnapping was a way of life for most of Mexico and even sometimes across the border. Children of the wealthy were the worst affected, trapped into fixed schedules to and from school, and though they were often protected by a phalanx of bodyguards, they were still taken. Sevilla remembered years before when he first heard the term "kidnapping insurance." He laughed then. He laughed at it no more.

The side road to the Madrigal home was not gated, but Sevilla saw cameras among the trees marking his progress as he wound left, right and left again up an incline to the main drive. There were no straight roads here and no unbroken curves; it was more difficult for an intruder's vehicle to get in and out that way.

The house itself was set among the trees perfectly, a green lawn spread out on three sides and marked with beds of brilliant flowers. The architect chose the chalky white stone of the surrounding hills and stately pillars for accent. As he slowed to a stop, Sevilla saw someone watching him through a broad window at the front, but by the time he was close enough to see the figure was gone.

A servant and two bodyguards emerged. One took the clubs from the trunk and the other offered to park the car. Sevilla felt almost certain it would be searched, but they wouldn't find anything; his gun was in the hotel safe and even the rental papers were kept somewhere else.

"Señor Madrigal is waiting for you," the servant told Sevilla. He wore a jacket despite the promised heat of the day. Inside it was chilly enough to be uncomfortable and Sevilla almost regretted the short pants he'd chosen for the game.

Madrigal and Sebastián waited in a sunroom off a restaurant-sized kitchen. The glass was angled to catch the worst glare of the rising sun without sparing any of the dawning light. Fruit and toast and meat were laid out on china and silver for Sevilla's delectation. Orange juice, grapefruit juice and coffee were offered. He took the coffee.

"If there's something you want that you don't see, Arturo will be happy to prepare it for you," Madrigal said. He indicated the servant, who poured Sevilla's coffee and even added the sugar to his taste.

"This is more than enough," Sevilla said.

"I always believe in a big breakfast," said Madrigal. "A big breakfast, a big lunch and just something to tide me over for the night. Some people obsess about dinner. I'm not one of those people."

"Which do you prefer, Señor Villalobos?" Sebastián asked in a tone of voice that suggested he was not interested in the answer at all.

Sevilla dipped toast in fresh egg brought by Arturo. "Breakfast suits me very well, thank you."

"My son is just learning the benefits of breakfast," Madrigal said. He cast a sidelong look at Sebastián that needed no translation. A closer look at the younger Madrigal revealed circles beneath the eyes nearly hidden by the deep tan. Sebastián turned his head away.

"That's the way it is with young people. I remember a time when I could work all night and still have energy enough to keep going until lunchtime," Sevilla said. "These days I take siesta very seriously."

"A dying tradition," said Madrigal.

Sevilla considered trying to draw Sebastián into the conversation, but it seemed it would do no good. Sebastián looked out the windows now on a perfect square of green back lawn. A long, narrow rectangle of swimming pool was set within the square, surrounded by a scattering of tables and chairs and shady trees designed for lazy afternoons whiling away the worst heat. The grass was unnaturally robust and Sevilla wondered how many thousands of pesos were spent making it look just so.

"If you'll excuse me," Sebastián said abruptly. He dropped his napkin on his plate and left the table without further word. Sevilla watched him go, and when he turned back to Madrigal he saw nothing but contempt in the man's expression.

"You have to forgive my son for being stupid," Madrigal said.

"I don't think he's stupid," Sevilla soothed. "He's—"

"He's stupid. What is that expression? 'An heir and a spare'? That's what I had, only my heir is gone and my spare is a willful disappointment to me."

"Willful?"

"Yes. As if he has nothing better to do than waste my money and my time."

Sevilla wasn't sure how to address that. He turned closer attention to his plate and his coffee. Outside on the lawn, a gardener with a broad straw peasant hat and loose-fitting white uniform used a roller to create unnaturally flawless stripes in the grass. Such a treatment might not even last an entire day, but the effect was striking.

"Do you have children, Juan?"

"No. I'm afraid my wife and I were never blessed."

Madrigal made a gesture with his hand that seemed wistful, as if he were drawing back a curtain on something. In his other hand a glass of grapefruit juice was poised, but he didn't drink from it. He spoke looking out at the grass and not at Sevilla. "Gabriel was my eldest. Manners? His were impeccable. Work ethic? He did more to monitor our business than I did."

Now Madrigal fixed Sevilla with his gaze. "It was the drugs. He was working so hard, he started using them to stay up later, do more. And then they ate him alive. By the time he went to the States, he wasn't my Gabriel anymore. He was someone else. Someone I didn't know."

"Drugs are killing Mexico," Sevilla said. He no longer had stomach for breakfast, but he couldn't think of anything to do with his hands. If he did nothing, he would look the fool, so he continued to eat as if he had the appetite of two men. He watched the glass of grapefruit juice suspended above the table in Madrigal's hand, unmoving. "All along the border. They come for the American market."

"Americans," Madrigal said. Suddenly he put the glass of juice to his mouth and drained it in one gulp. His face turned from the bitterness. "I won't say they're useless because their dollars paid for all of this, but sometimes I think they're a blight. It was one of Gabriel's American cousins who first introduced him to *cocaína*. Little weasel. From my wife's side of the family."

As quickly as the mood turned dark, there was sunshine again. Sevilla saw the lamplight come on in Madrigal's eyes. The man straightened in his seat. "I'm going to change, Juan, and then we'll play. How many strokes would you like me to give you?"

"Whatever you feel comfortable giving up. You're my host. I don't want to make demands of you."

"You see?" said Madrigal, and he pointed a finger at Sevilla. "That is what I mean. *Manners*. Men like you and me, we know what is polite and what is not. And we *try* to teach our children, but to no avail. I will return."

With that Madrigal left Sevilla with the table of food still spread before him. Sevilla put a piece of toast down and pushed the plate away from him. Arturo and two maids in uniforms came to clear up. "Señor Madrigal asks that you wait for him outside," Arturo told Sevilla. "He will only be a few minutes."

Double French doors opened out of the sunroom onto the striped green lawn. Sevilla's shoes sank deeply into the grass. He smelled water and saw droplets still suspended here and there among the blades. A sharper, chlorinated odor rose from the pool as Sevilla came nearer.

He didn't hear Sebastián approach. He saw the younger Madrigal's reflection in the pool. "You surprised me," Sevilla said.

"It'll be a little longer," Sebastián said by way of reply. The sun was higher now and lanced across the lawn. Sebastián took sunglasses from a case attached to his belt and put them on. He was dressed for the game in shorts and a collared pullover. His arms were lean and muscled so that the individual cords in his forearm stood out when he moved his fingers.

They stood together without talking for a while. Finally, Sevilla said, "I hope you know I don't take seriously the things your father says."

"Take them seriously if you like. It makes no difference to me."

"I only mean it's none of my business."

"No," Sebastián said, "it isn't any of your business. But my father doesn't have any problem insulting his own son to strangers."

"Well, I don't—"

"You don't need to explain anything," Sebastián interrupted. "You are my father's guest and I'll treat you the way I'm expected to treat you. And then you can go."

Sevilla tried to read Sebastián's face, but the man's eyes were well hidden behind dark lenses. "I didn't mean to offend you."

"Do I seem offended?"

"Frankly? Yes."

"Then perhaps I am. But as I say, it makes no difference. You'll play your round, my father will invite you to swim and stay for lunch and then you'll go back to wherever it is you come from."

"Ciudad de México."

Sebastián looked at Sevilla. His sunglasses made his face a hollow-eyed skull. "Like I say: wherever you come from."

NINE

THEY PLAYED AND SEVILLA LOST. HE was paired with a friend of Madrigal's, an older gentleman who also made his home in Los Campos. As Sebastián predicted there was swimming and drinks and a lunch as lavish as breakfast. The elder Madrigal held forth on the drug wars and the business of the *maquiladoras* and a dozen other subjects, but not once did he speak of the dead women of Juárez. Neither did he make mention of his dead son.

"When you return to Ciudad Júarez, you must visit again," Madrigal told Sevilla when they parted. "And if I find myself in Mexico City anytime soon, I may call on you."

"Yes, you must," Sevilla lied. "You have been too kind to me, Rafa."

"It was nothing, Juan. *Adiós.*"

Sebastían did not bid Sevilla farewell. He vanished after the golf game and did not reappear even for lunch. His father made no comment on his son's absence and it was just as well; the episode of the morning was still fresh in Sevilla's mind and he was glad not to have a repeat.

He felt tension slipping away from him with each mile he put between himself and Los Campos. He opened the window to let the clean country air in. Soon he would be in the thick of Juárez where the air was not as dirty as somewhere like Juan Villalobos' Mexico City, but bad enough. Enterprising youngsters and businessmen didn't ply the lanes at stoplights offering hits of pure oxygen to drivers mired in traffic, but as the city grew the promise of those days drew closer.

By the time he saw the Hotel Lucerna rising out of the buildings ahead Sevilla felt almost like himself. The golf game had been terrible, but at least he'd known the difference between one club and the next. The swim was cool and relaxing, the drinks not enough to sate a thirst built over several days. Lunch left him feeling bloated and overfull. Madrigal offered a shady place for post-meal rest, but then and now Sevilla could think only of the queen-sized bed in his suite.

He returned the car, paying the bill in cash, and arranged for someone to bring up the golf clubs. He went up on the elevator alone and emerged into a quiet hallway likewise deserted. The suite door had an electronic lock opened with a card key. When the LED above the handle showed green, Sevilla pushed his way inside.

The man yanked him through the door before it was fully open. It banged wide and then slammed shut on pressurized hinges. Sevilla felt his feet leave the floor. He fell hard then and his knee screamed with pain.

When he reached for his gun it wasn't there, but it hadn't been there for days. Sevilla was dizzily aware of two men before one kicked him in the head and opened a broad gash over his eye. He went over onto his back as if dead. The suite's front room went from light to dark and back again.

Someone grabbed a fistful of Sevilla's hair and lifted his head clear of the parquet floor in the entryway. The picture of Ana and Ofelia was shoved in his face. The glass in the frame was broken, the frame itself twisted out of true. He saw Ana smiling at him through blood.

"Who is this, old man? Your wife? Your kid?"

"Probably his whore," someone else said, and there was laughter. There were three of them, not two. Sevilla heard the crash of something breaking in the bedroom. All the furniture in the front room was overturned and the stuffing torn out. Even the area rugs had been flipped upside down.

"I—" Sevilla began.

The man smashed Sevilla in the face with the picture glass-first. Bits stung him on the cheek and lip. He was kicked in the side, in the stomach. Lunch roiled up out of him. Sevilla could see only the men's feet as they moved back and forth; he was not strong enough to look up at their faces.

"Find another family to grift," said one of the men. He stepped on Sevilla's hand.

One left. Another rummaged in the bedroom and the bathroom until it was destroyed. The third stood over Sevilla and stomped him whenever the pain tried to pass.

"Stay down there, old man," he said, and Sevilla did what he was told.

The last two conferred, but Sevilla's ears were ringing. They took turns kicking him then until there was no part of him that didn't hurt and no way to see through the curtain of red that obscured his eyes. He was barely aware of them leaving and then was aware of nothing for a long time.

TEN

He woke. "Kelly," he breathed. His teeth felt loose and he tasted salt and copper.

"It's Enrique."

Sevilla was on the flipsided rug. He saw only the ceiling, but the light had changed and he knew it was evening. His body throbbed and his kidneys ached badly enough that he knew he would piss blood when the time came. Enrique touched his face with something cold and wet and smelling of strong liquor.

"There's no alcohol in the medicine cabinet," Enrique said.

"Don't tell… the hotel," Sevilla replied.

"I haven't. You've been asleep for hours. I almost called an ambulance."

"Don't call them, either."

"What happened?"

The cut over Sevilla's eye was swollen and his vision reduced to a slash. He ran his tongue thickly over his teeth. They were all there. When he flexed his hands he knew his arms weren't broken but his knee was a white-hot coal of agony. He would have to stand to know whether he could even walk.

"Give me something to drink," Sevilla managed.

Ice jingled and whisky was poured. Sevilla knew it by scent before it touched his lips. The drink was hot and healing in his stomach and reached out for his other pains to smother them in coils of soothing warmth. He swallowed more and finished the tumbler and then sucked an ice cube until it, too, was gone.

He was ready to sit up. Enrique helped Sevilla prop himself against the ruins of a gutted sofa. Stuffing was scattered everywhere in tufts and gobbets. A slowly turning ceiling fan stirred the mess.

"Are you going to tell me what happened?"

"Have you seen the place?" Sevilla asked.

"Yes. It's all like this."

"Then it's done."

"What do you mean?"

Sevilla wanted to close his eyes and sleep again. Just the act of sitting upright drained him. But the bed would be stripped and broken, too, and sometime the housekeeper would want access and everything would be revealed. In his mind Sevilla was packing already, planning his retreat.

"The picture."

"It's here," Enrique said. He pressed it into Sevilla's hand. It was out of the frame completely now and flecked with blood Sevilla knew was his own. Tears threatened to well up. His eyes burned.

"More whisky."

"Not until we talk."

"Goddammit, Enrique, what is there to talk about? It's over. They know."

"How could they know? What happened today?"

Sevilla shook his head. The gesture made his spine hurt at the base of his skull. "I thought I had them fooled, but I must not have. It was Sebastián. He let his father keep me busy while he…"

A wave of the hand encompassed the suite. Everything was broken, even the pots of the plants, their dirt scattered.

"How could he possibly know?"

"Maybe I ate with the wrong fork," Sevilla said. He didn't laugh at his own joke and Enrique only frowned. "Damn me, I'm a fool."

Enrique let Sevilla have the bottle of single-malt whisky. He stalked the shattered rooms while Sevilla drowned the rest of his pain in spirits. Outside, the sun was going down. At the pool all the mothers and children would be out playing in the cool evening air before dinner. The windows were too far to drag himself.

"There's no way they could have known," Enrique said at last. "There's nothing here."

"Exactly," Sevilla agreed. "There's nothing here. No backstory, no paper trail, no nothing. I thought I could convince them with my word. There was no way. It was stupid."

"It *wasn't* stupid," Enrique returned. "You had no way to know."

"I knew I was too old for this kind of game," Sevilla said. "It should have been you. Sebastián might have trusted someone closer to his own age. But I thought... I don't know what I was thinking. That they would confess to me? 'Yes, I had Paloma Salazar killed. I ordered the death of her brother, her lover. I did it all.'"

The whisky was fully in Sevilla's brain now, soaking up his thoughts and pushing away worry. In a way he was clearer than before. His body was almost numb. If he drank more he would be entirely numb and unconscious on the floor. It took all his will to set the bottle aside.

"If they knew you were a policeman, why do this?"

"They didn't know; they mistook me for a confidence man. In a way, I suppose I'm lucky."

If there was anything else to say, Sevilla couldn't think of what it might be, so he merely sat and waited for the minutes to pass. It was easier with the whisky in him. How many times had he done the same thing on his own, sitting in his car with the bottle between his legs, drifting on the currents of his own languid thoughts?

"I did what you asked," Enrique said at long last. "I followed Ortíz all day. I know where he'll be on Friday: at the *palenque* with his birds. We could lean on him. He's the connection, like you said. He'll tell us what we want to know."

"He'll tell us nothing."

"How do you *know* that?"

"Because... I don't know."

Enrique helped Sevilla to his feet and into the bedroom. The men had torn the bed practically in half and gouged deep wounds in the mattress. Enrique wrestled the mattress back into place and put Sevilla there to rest. He began to pack. "Tell me everything," he instructed Sevilla. "Leave nothing out."

Sevilla did as he was told. He held the picture of Ana and Ofelia tightly, but he never crumpled it. There was no other copy. He was more grateful for this than he was for his life. The men from Madrigal could have taken both from him.

"Now I'll take you home."

ELEVEN

SEVILLA RESTED IN HIS OWN BED for a day of nearly unbroken sleep. When he woke the swelling in his eye had subsided and the pain in his knee was bearable. He was in his pajamas, though he didn't recall changing into them. Enrique put coffee on his bedstand. The man looked alien standing in his bedroom. He seemed bursting to speak; Sevilla saw it all over him.

"How long have you been here?" Sevilla asked.

"A few hours."

"Get out of my bedroom."

Looking at himself in the mirror was as shocking as Sevilla expected. A butterfly bandage held the cut over his eye closed, but his face was blotched with deep bruises. A scrape on his nostril was livid.

His body was no better, and when he urinated he did see blood. Washing himself took a long time, but four aspirin taken from a bottle in the medicine cabinet brought the worst aches under control. When he brushed his teeth, his mouth no longer tasted like blood.

Enrique was in the kitchen with coffee of his own. He had buttered toast and half a grapefruit set aside for Sevilla. They ate in silence.

"Marco Rojas, he's the cousin Madrigal spoke of?" Enrique asked at last.

"I don't know. Is he?"

"A maternal cousin, yes," Enrique said.

"How did you find that out?"

"Computers," Enrique replied. "I checked the records overnight. Gabriel Madrigal and his cousin, Marco Rojas, were both convicted of drug charges and rape in New Mexico. Madrigal overdosed on contraband heroin after three months in prison. Rojas is still there."

Sevilla put down his spoon. "Rape?"

"Yes," Enrique said. His eyes gleamed. Sevilla understood.

"You know where Marco Rojas is?"

"A place called Hiatt. A state prison. North of El Paso."

"You're already going to go," Sevilla said.

This was the thing Enrique had been waiting to say. He leaned across the table and the words came quickly: "The government has been trying to bring Rojas back for four years but his lawyers in America have been fighting for him to *stay* in a Texas prison. I looked, I know that the Rojas family is as wealthy as the Madrigals. If Marco Rojas came back to Chihuahua he would be turned loose in months, maybe weeks. It makes no sense!"

"No, it doesn't. Unless he fears Madrigal's wrath. Then there would be no release. He'd die like Estéban Salazar... or end up like Kelly."

"I can drive there in a day," Enrique continued. "No one will have to know. I arranged for two weeks of sick leave. Even Garcia won't be able to check up on me. I'll find out what's happening."

"You think the Americans will just let you visit one of their prisoners?"

"Yes."

"Why?"

"For the same reason you thought you could get close to the Madrigals."

Sevilla shook his head, but the gesture didn't bring pain. He was grateful for that. "I failed. Maybe they didn't know who I was or where I came from, but they knew I wasn't one of them. These are police. They'll ask questions."

"Then I'll answer them."

"You'll lie."

Enrique was steadfast. "I will."

"As if I could stop you," Sevilla said. He sat back in his chair and sipped his coffee. Each drink made the cut on his lip burn afresh. He made no effort to protect it.

"I'll be back before you know it," Enrique said. He got up from the table. Sevilla didn't watch him go.

TWELVE

FOR MOST OF HIS LIFE SEVILLA had not seriously contemplated the inevitability of old age. When he was in his twenties old age was an impossibility. Surely he would be dead by then, he thought, but death was itself an abstraction not worthy of real thought. Even his thirties were much the same until forty loomed and his older heroes began to pass away with greater and greater frequency.

He was always surrounded by death, especially the more time he spent working against the *narcotraficantes*. In the 1980s the *narcos* suddenly discovered that killing was a powerful tool, but not so powerful that it could be deployed in every circumstance to solve every problem. Where there had been only bushels of marijuana or stacks of packaged cocaine and heroin there were piles of spent bullet casings and blood and bodies. Car bombs were rare, for which Sevilla was thankful, because the carnage of such things was almost too much for him to withstand.

With his forties behind him he faced death each time he looked in a mirror at sagging flesh and fading muscles. Even his skin took on a different quality. The wrinkles he expected, but not the strange texture of roughness and looseness that began on the back of his hands and slowly spread elsewhere.

Now he was old, unquestionably old. All the things he knew were coming were here, from the thinning hair to the beard that was now more white than anything else. His vision was going, though he still refused glasses. When he wasn't drinking his hands were steady, but this was only one small thing to be proud of in a sea of other failures. He couldn't remember the last time he'd had an erection.

With Enrique gone he shuffled around the house in his slippers and housecoat, took naps on the couch and flipped idly through channels on the television. He lacked the energy or the focus to read, though there were many books on the stand beside his bed. He avoided going into his daughter's room though eventually he knew he must; the photograph needed to be back where it belonged.

It was evening and after a quiet meal that he finally entered. He knocked lightly on the door as if to announce his presence and slipped inside. The spot where he sat on the edge of the bed was dented, he saw.

He put the photo on the nightstand and sat. In the angled light of the lamp he saw that it was wrinkled and this made his heart ache. He wanted to press the picture, smooth it out like a piece of cloth, but the damage was done. As on his face, the lines could not be made to go away.

All day he had felt a weight on him that he thought was sadness. Alone in his daughter's room with his granddaughter's crib at hand, he understood it was anger. He felt far gone from himself, so much so that even the Madrigals did not recognize him for a cop, but as a crook, a con man. They did not see any iron in him. He was ashamed.

"I'm sorry I could never bring you home," he said to the empty room. "Maybe I didn't try hard enough. But it wasn't because I didn't care. You know I would give my life to have you home again."

Sevilla wrung his hands. The knuckles of one hand were bruised and scabbed.

"I want you to know that what I do now isn't because I've given up. Whatever anyone thinks, whatever they say, that's not the reason. It's only I don't know what to do. I'm not as smart as I believed I was."

Once there was a time he could have asked for help. He was surrounded by men like himself, men who had become authority because it was, like themselves, immortal and unchanging. Over the years they had fallen away. Some died. Some quit. The ones who remained were worn on the inside and out. They didn't speak to one another anymore and the new young men… they were not interested.

"There is nothing so worthless as an old man," Sevilla said.

He took from his pocket his pistol and put it on the bed beside him. It was the first automatic he had ever owned, a .45 given to him by an American policeman from a joint task force south of the border. He still remembered the man's name: Joe Hopkins. He was young like Enrique Palencia was young and full of the energy long missing from Sevilla's life.

"A .45 will put a man down and keep him there," Hopkins told Sevilla. "That .38 you're carrying is never going to get it done. They're carrying big guns. We have to do the same thing."

"I don't have anything to give you in return," Sevilla said to the American.

"You don't have to. Do somebody else a favor someday."

Sevilla held the pistol in both hands, feeling its weight. The metal was worn from a long time in his holster. He kept it clean and the parts maintained. The weapon held only eight rounds, but they were enough. For the thing Sevilla sometimes had in mind there was need for only one.

Tonight he wasn't thinking of ending himself, and no matter what he would not do it here in this room that waited and would forever wait for Ana and Ofelia to come home. This room was untouched, sacrosanct. Sevilla thought instead about his old .38 revolver, the one he kept in a locked box in his bedroom closet. This was the weapon Liliana brought out one night when Sevilla was away. Why she chose to kill herself in the kitchen he didn't know. A perverse thought once occurred to Sevilla that she wanted it to be easy to clean up.

Ana and Ofelia had Sevilla and Liliana to remember them. Liliana had her husband. Sevilla had no one. Perhaps Enrique would regret Sevilla's passing, but they did not know each other so well. The people in Sevilla's department knew him not at all; he was a ghost passing through their halls from investigation to investigation, the man all wished would retire but did not even though it was well past time. They sensed the mantle of death around him that didn't come just from age.

If Kelly ever woke, he might be sad to learn Sevilla was gone, but he had too many other lives to remember. Their closeness was one only Sevilla felt. He followed Kelly and learned of Kelly and eventually there was a sensation of kinship that could only come from long association, but this was something Kelly could not feel because he didn't know Sevilla was there. Maybe the nurses would tell Kelly how Sevilla called every day to check on him, or how he came to visit when no one else did. Maybe this would make a difference. Most likely it wouldn't.

The gun whispered ideas to Sevilla, but he didn't listen. He turned his mind to other things. If he had whisky he would drink it now, right here on the edge of Ana's bed, beneath the roof of Liliana's house, and would go on drinking until he could see just straight enough to put the barrel of the gun to the underside of his chin and pull the trigger.

"No," Sevilla said aloud. "I said no."

He hoped for a telephone call from Enrique to break the silence, but there was no call. Sevilla didn't know how long he stayed in Ana and Ofelia's room. Abruptly he stood and left, taking the gun with him.

Sevilla went to his bedroom and opened the closet. His old suits, his *real* suits, awaited him. He stripped naked and took a shower and scrubbed himself hard enough to make his skin tingle. He shaved his neck and cheeks until mustache and beard were only a rough square around his mouth and on his chin. He put a touch of Dr Bell's Pomada de La Campana in his hair and slicked it back. It did not make him look younger, but he felt something he could not quite identify.

His holster went into its place at his side, easily hidden by his jacket but where he could reach it quickly. He checked the magazine and the bullet in the chamber.

In his sock drawer he found a matte-black cylinder of rubberized metal. It wasn't heavy and it fit in a pocket. A flick of the wrist revealed ten inches of blackened steel.

After he settled the knot in his tie, Sevilla looked at himself in the mirror behind the bedroom door. The gun was invisible, the bulge of the impact baton something that could be keys or an oddly shaped wallet.

"I will be back late," he told the air. "Don't wait up for me."

THIRTEEN

ENRIQUE CROSSED THE BORDER early in the morning to avoid the worst of the bridge traffic. On the average day the lanes out of Mexico could be stacked a hundred deep and the Americans were slow to process the cars. There were drug-sniffing dogs and mirrors to look beneath frames and endless questions about where you were coming from and where you intended to go. It was worst for Mexicans, though it was not easy for returning natives.

Even at the hour he chose there was still a wait. When he got to the front of the line he showed his credentials to the uniformed man in the booth. This time there were no dogs, but the American broke out a long metal rod with a mirror on the end and walked around the whole perimeter of the car before asking that the trunk be opened.

Enrique answered the man's questions. It was just a ritual. Both of them knew he would go through.

Once he was free Enrique passed into El Paso. The city was still half asleep. He drove down streets of still cars and dark windows, following directions he'd printed out from the internet.

Most of the border towns in Mexico served as shadows of their American counterparts. The relationship between El Paso and Juárez was different: Juárez was bigger than El Paso. Enrique almost felt as though he was driving through a small town compared to the complex, interlocking grid of Juárez.

Eventually he found the exit for US-180 and accelerated out of the city. The highway would take him across the narrowest spoke of westernmost Texas and then up into New Mexico. The terrain was rough and flat the way it was for miles around Ciudad Juárez. There was no color except what the rising sun offered in red and orange. Once Enrique saw a jackrabbit break from the cover of a sun-blasted yucca plant. Its fur flashed white in his headlights.

It was not a long drive from Juárez to Hiatt. He could be there in a matter of six hours. To slow his progress he stopped in Las Cruces for an American breakfast of waffles, bacon, eggs and coffee. Enrique took his time over the food, but even with the delay he knew he'd be early to the prison.

Obtaining access to Marco Rojas was easier than Enrique had expected. When he called he introduced himself as a Mexican police officer and had thought he would have to go into great detail about his reasons for wanting to see the prisoner. That hadn't been the case; in five minutes he was off the telephone with a date and a time to visit. The prison promised to extend Enrique every courtesy.

He reached the town of Hiatt with ninety minutes left before his time with Rojas. There was little to the town: it sat in the middle of a broad desert, a dozen buildings or so and roads leading off to ranches hidden by distance. Everything was closed. Enrique stopped by a large rectangle of fenced-in grass that he supposed was meant to be a park and closed his eyes for a little while, trusting in the alarm on his cell phone to wake him in time.

When he had thirty minutes left he followed signs out of Hiatt proper and to the prison. He reached the first fence before he could see the buildings at all. A guard was stationed in a dusty-colored box with dirty windows, operating an electric gate. Enrique showed his identification again and explained why he was there. He was allowed through.

After a mile Enrique encountered a cluster of houses with trees planted around them and neat but dry yards. A child's swing set was stationed behind one of them, sentry in the early morning.

Finally he saw the prison itself. It was not very imposing,

consisting of long, boxy structures made out of concrete and cinder block, surrounded by triple rows of fencing and barbed wire. The yard and basketball courts were devoid of life.

He found himself a spot in a parking lot with twenty or so other cars and walked the rest of the way to the entrance. This time he showed his ID and was not waved through right away. Using a computer and an old printer, a law-enforcement visitor's pass was made for him and laminated on the spot. "You can keep it as a souvenir," the uniformed corrections officer joked. Enrique smiled.

Another corrections officer came to escort Enrique into the main building. They passed through a narrow corridor of hurricane fencing topped with barbed wire and locked securely at both ends. Enrique's pass was checked before the officer at the far side would even unlock the gate.

"It'll be a few minutes until they're ready for you," said the officer leading him. "Just wait here."

Enrique was in an area scattered with chairs and couches upholstered in deep red vinyl. There was a coffee table peppered with magazines. Enrique didn't sit down or read; he paced off the minutes while his officer went away to make some preparation.

After a quarter of an hour the officer returned. "Come on," he said.

They had to go through two electric lockdown doors before reaching a gray room with a few plastic chairs dotted around. The windows were covered with tight metal grating that cut the morning sun into little pieces.

"He'll be right in," the officer said.

Another ten minutes passed until finally a prisoner in a white jumpsuit was escorted into the room.

Enrique wasn't sure what to expect of Marco Rojas. The man was an American and so the Mexican police had no photographs or any real records concerning him. There was no family resemblance between Rojas and Rafa Madrigal, but then there wouldn't be; he was from Madrigal's wife's side of the family. He was short and blocky and full of muscles. He had a crosshatch scar on his temple, as if he'd been ground into something until the flesh peeled away.

Rojas had a waist chain and his feet were shackled. He shuffled ahead to one of the plastic chairs, led by the elbow and then urged to sit. Enrique watched Rojas watching him.

"If you need anything, just knock on the door," said the corrections officer, and then he went out of the room. A bolt was shot. They were locked in.

"You are the Marco Rojas who's cousin to Gabriel Madrigal?"

"I am."

Rojas was still looking at Enrique. When he spoke again, he spoke in Spanish: "Did they send you to bring me back to Mexico?"

"I don't have that kind of authority," Enrique said.

"Good. You're a Mexican cop, though."

"How can you tell?"

"They told me before I came in. Don't worry, I'm not a mind-reader," Rojas said, and he gave a little smile.

Enrique was still standing. He dragged one of the plastic chairs around and sat with the back facing forward so he could fold his arms in front of himself. It also made him feel a little safer, though there was no way Rojas could rush him with all the chains he wore.

"If you're not here to bring me back to Mexico, then what do you want?"

"I want to talk to you about the Madrigals," Enrique said plainly.

"What about them?"

It occurred to Enrique that he didn't know where to start. When he rehearsed his meeting with Rojas he had never gotten past the first few moments. The questions were all a jumble, each one as important as the next and finding no natural order.

Rojas made a face, as if he was impatient to be somewhere else.

"Let's start with Gabriel Madrigal."

"Okay, let's start with him."

"You were arrested for drugs and rape, is that right?"

"Yes."

"Tell me about that."

Rojas shrugged his shoulders in a slow, rolling way. "Gabriel liked to party. It runs in his family. Cocaine, heroin… girls. He liked all of that."

"There has to be more."

"Maybe. Why should I tell you?"

"Because you have to tell someone."

"Do I? I haven't told anyone anything for years. Why should I start now?"

Enrique took a slow breath, let it out. "Because I'm asking."

They were quiet a while. Enrique got the sense that Rojas was taking his measure the way convicts did in prison. Some things were the same in America as they were in Mexico.

"Gabriel liked to party," Rojas said again, and then he was silent, thinking. "It started when I came down to Juárez to visit him. He would set things up."

"Drugs?"

"Yes."

"Who supplied you?"

"Different people at first. Then Gabriel got a steady source."

"What was his name? Do you know?"

"Estéban."

"Estéban Salazar?" Enrique asked, and his heart sped.

"I don't know his last name. He was the one who started to bring in the *heroína*. Before that it was just cocaine, marijuana, that kind of stuff."

"He got you hooked."

"Not me. Gabriel. We used to get drunk and stoned and so did the girls."

"Prostitutes?"

"Not always."

"What do you mean?"

"I mean they were whores, but sometimes they had to be convinced of it."

Enrique tried to keep an expression from his face even though he felt himself twisting. There was a suggestion of something in Rojas' eyes that he didn't like, a black glittering as he remembered.

"We used to get help from a friend of Gabriel's father. His name was Ortíz, I think. Sometimes he would party with us."

"And at these parties you raped women?"

"Yes."

"How long did this go on?"

"A few months."

"How much did Estéban Salazar know about this?"

"I don't know. Enough. He stayed once or twice, but he didn't like it when things got rough. I told him not worry about it. Poor girls, who are they going to tell?"

Enrique swallowed.

"Eventually he stopped coming and he stopped selling *chinaloa* to Gabriel. That made him mad."

"What did he do?"

"He complained to Ortíz. Ortíz had the muscle to solve problems."

"But he didn't kill Estéban."

"No. Gabriel said Estéban had a sister. Even *narcos* have soft spots, you know?"

"She would be harassed?"

"Sure."

"Killed?"

"I couldn't say."

Enrique continued: "Then you went to the United States?"

"I had to get back to my business in Santa Fe. Gabriel, he had money to burn, but I had to earn a living, you know? I couldn't just party all the time."

"Gabriel came with you?"

"Not right away. Eventually."

"Did you have… parties again?"

"Why the fuck do you think I'm in here now?" Rojas said loudly.

"You were found out."

"Because Gabriel was an idiot. He was strung out half the time and didn't know left from right. He didn't have his daddy's friends no more. And things are different here. The poor girls, they go to the police. You can't get them to shut up unless you kill them… and I wouldn't do that."

"Gabriel would?"

"I don't want to talk about it."

Enrique pressed, "You know Gabriel killed women?"

"That never happened at our parties."

"When did it happen? Did he tell you he'd killed someone?"

"I said I don't want to talk about it!"

Rojas looked down at his cuffed hands, secured to the belly chain. He would not raise his eyes. Something heavy lay mantled across his shoulders. For a burly man, he suddenly seemed weak.

Enrique's mind raced. The connection between Estéban Salazar and the Madrigals was established, but Gabriel Madrigal was long dead before the murder of Paloma Salazar. The hot link was Ortíz, and Rojas had confessed that Ortíz partied with Gabriel and him more than once.

Estéban could have told Paloma. Paloma could have endangered Ortíz. And then…

"Did Carlos Ortíz ever commit a murder?" Enrique asked.

Rojas was silent.

"Just tell me this, Marco."

The quiet stretched on. Rojas did not look up. And then he nodded.

Enrique felt flushed. "He killed one of the girls at a party?"

"I saw him do it. At first I thought he was just choking her while he fucked her. But then he didn't stop. He didn't stop."

Rojas wiped an eye with the back of his hand.

"You don't get to cry," Enrique said. "You don't ever get to cry for this."

He got up from his chair and went to the door. He knocked twice and the guards came. Behind him, Marco Rojas sobbed.

"I have everything I need here."

"Wait," Rojas said suddenly.

"What?"

"There's more."

FOURTEEN

THE *PALENQUE* WAS A DIFFERENT place after dark and when the cocks were fighting. Where the dusty parking lot had been mostly empty during the day, it was packed so fully that trucks and cars were parked all along the roadside leading up to the place. Even if he had tried, Sevilla would have been hard pressed to find Ortíz's black pick-up among all these others. In the end he saw it in the space nearest the entrance, unwatched by even one of the bodyguards, who must both have been inside.

Cigarette smoke layered against the ceiling and condensed like rain clouds. Sevilla fought his way to the bar, bombarded by loud music, upraised voices and the occasional explosive reaction of the crowd around the fighting arena. He had to shout his order to the bartender.

The alcohol was good, but Sevilla allowed himself only one. After that he pushed to the highest rail overlooking the arena. The concrete seats swirled down in a vortex to the center of the action, the cocks facing each other. Men were betting with the official bookmakers and paper slips from previous fights were everywhere, even on the floor of the battleground itself. Other men were betting with bookies down in the crowd or even with the men sitting around them. Sevilla ignored this and watched faces, looking for the one he needed.

Ortíz was not as close to the fighting as Sevilla expected; he was halfway up the far side of the arena seating. The bodyguards on either side of him carved out a comfortable space so that he was not pressed flesh to flesh against other men. He wore a white suit jacket and slacks and a striped shirt of bright colors made brighter by the stark arena lighting. He didn't carry betting slips, but made a note of each fight on a pad with a pencil.

Hot breath boiled out of the arena from shouts and curses. The fighting circle was stained with blood that between-match soakings could only partly eliminate. Cocks jumped and clashed and there were feathers and death.

Sevilla didn't know what he would do if Ortíz never left his seat. Eventually Ortíz rose. He spoke to one of the bodyguards. The man nodded, but didn't follow. Neither did the other. They kept Ortíz's place, the only gap in the sea of bodies funneling down to the bloodsport.

The place had two restrooms. Sevilla went to the one closest to Ortíz's side of the *palenque*. The air was heavy and humid, smelling strongly of beer and urine. One man combed his hair in a clouded mirror over the sinks. Another used the piss-trough. Sevilla took a stall, but didn't sit.

Ortíz came in afterward. He said something to the man at the piss-trough that Sevilla didn't catch, then undid his fly. Another man entered and took the stall beside Sevilla.

Sevilla waited until he heard the sound of water before he left the stall. He had the impact baton in his hand. It clicked open and Ortíz turned toward the sound. The first blow caught him on the side of the neck and he spilled over, falling into the piss-trough and cursing.

When Ortíz put up his hands, Sevilla broke his wrist. He battered Ortíz's upraised arm until the man couldn't lift it any longer. Ortíz lost his balance, tumbled free of the piss-trough and collapsed on the floor. Sevilla struck him across the back three times until he thought he heard one of Ortíz's ribs break.

The door of the bathroom opened. Sevilla turned. The man stood framed there for a moment, seeing Ortíz, seeing the baton and seeing Sevilla's face.

"Get the fuck out of here," Sevilla said. The man obeyed.

"*¡Pinche cabrón!*" cried Ortíz on the ground. The concrete was pitted and filthy from dirty boots and cigarette ash and men too drunk to hit the trough on their first try. "Goddamm you."

Sevilla put the baton away. He brought out the pistol. His back twinged when he bent over Ortíz and put the muzzle in his face. "Shut up until I tell you not to," Sevilla said. "You hear me? Do you understand?"

Ortíz had blood on his face and on his lips. His eyes rolled like a horse's in panic. The second stall door opened and the man inside emerged. He flinched once as if Sevilla were striking at him and then fled for the door.

"Sebastián Madrigal," Sevilla said. "You know him, yes?"

"*¿Que chingados quieres?*" Ortíz asked.

"I asked you a question!" Sevilla thundered, and kicked Ortíz as hard as he could. The blow made Ortíz cough blood for a long minute and Sevilla regretted it. "Sebastián Madrigal."

"I know him," Ortíz managed to say.

"How do you know him?" Sevilla gestured with the gun for emphasis.

"Parties," Ortíz replied. "I arrange… please don't kill me."

Sevilla raised the gun and brought it down across Ortíz's skull. The man's scalp split and blood gushed. Scalp wounds were the bloodiest. The white material of Ortíz's suit jacket was stained red, black and dirty yellow. "What parties? Where?"

"*There is one tomorrow!*" Ortíz cried. There were tears.

"Tell me where."

The restroom door burst open. It crashed against a wastebasket and sent it crumpled to the floor. Used paper towels spilled on the dirty concrete. The bodyguard filled the frame.

Sevilla fired two shots into the man's chest. The black material of the bodyguard's T-shirt exploded wet and he toppled backward out the door. The door was blocked open by dead legs and outside the crowd was in a sudden panic. The noise of men and voices changed from celebration to terror.

He caught Ortíz crawling toward the nearest stall. Sevilla's heart raced and his vision throbbed. Every cut on his face pulsed with angry heat in time with the beat. He pulled the trigger again and Ortíz's leg was soaked in blood.

"The parties!" Sevilla demanded. "Where?"

Ortíz told him through mucus and tears. Sevilla strained to hear above the shouting. He glanced back once and saw the bodyguard had not moved. Sevilla felt nothing for the man's death.

The confession did not end. Ortíz grasped at the concrete until his palms were black with filth and his nails were encrusted. Breath hitched in his throat. Blood from his head wound mingled with puddles of water and piss. The smell of cordite and waste made Sevilla gag, but he listened.

And then it was done.

"Please don't kill me. *Por favor,* for the love of God," Ortíz pleaded.

Sevilla was ill, but not from the sight and smell of this place. Everything from Ortíz's mouth was bitter, poisonous and curdled in Sevilla's head. Ortíz lolled onto his back and put his stained hands in front of him. He had grime on his teeth.

"*No me mate, no me mate,*" Ortíz said.

Sevilla wiped his mouth with the back of his forearm. "I didn't kill you," he said. "You killed yourself."

He left the restroom when he was done with Ortíz and joined the throng jamming the exits. He didn't see the second bodyguard until he spilled out with the rest into the parking lot. Police vehicles were there, strobing the lot with white, red and blue. The bodyguard stood shouting into a cell phone near the big pick-up, the engine running, waiting for passengers that would not come.

The police tried to put up a cordon, but there were too many men in the *palenque* and not enough cops. Cars and trucks pulled away and could not be called back. Others slipped away into the night and would come back when the chaos was over and the police had given up. Sevilla was among these, walking nearly a mile to where his car was parked.

The shaking didn't begin until he was behind the wheel. In the middle distance he heard sirens, and flickering above the rooftops of houses and buildings there was the dry lightning of police and ambulances. People were out of doors despite the hour, comparing theories, but soon even they went indoors. More death in the city of the dead. It was not worth interrupting a quiet evening at home.

Only when the tremors retreated into his chest and his breathing and heart were calm did Sevilla touch the ignition. He drove a half-mile without turning on his headlights before he remembered them, and then the rest of the way with the slow care of a man twenty years his senior. He was intensely aware of the pistol against his body. When he passed a policeman on the way he tensed, but the car was gone in moments.

He went to an all-night liquor store near the tourist district and bought a fresh bottle of Johnnie Walker. He didn't wait to get home before he drank from it. Half was gone by the time he reached the door and the other half he guzzled in the shadow of his unlit kitchen. He fell into bed fully clothed and slept until past dawn.

FIFTEEN

SEVILLA DIDN'T DREAM OF ORTÍZ, but Ortíz was the first one he thought of when he opened his eyes. The feelings he had for the man were not those of pity or sadness; Sevilla had a blank inside himself where Ortíz rested because he could not summon the energy necessary for anything else.

A headache blazed behind his eyes and his mouth tasted like death. Sevilla ate breakfast in the kitchen wearing the fancy sunglasses that hadn't fooled the Madrigals, burying a handful of aspirin beneath a slurry of juice, fruit, milk and toast. Eventually he knew the only way to make the hangover go completely away was to treat it with more whisky, but for now he resolved to keep a clear head despite the pain.

He tried to call Enrique, but the call wouldn't go through. He imagined Enrique somewhere in the American desert well away from any town or settlement, blessedly ignorant of what had transpired over the last twenty-four hours. Then Sevilla imagined what Enrique would say when he knew. There was nothing to be done about that.

Sevilla showered with the bathroom light off and the door open for illumination, resting his eyes against the onslaught of the day. When he was done he dressed and put the impact baton in his pocket where he'd begun to get used to its weight. He reloaded the .45 from a box of shells kept in the bedstand. The weapon had the fresh, peppery smell of cordite still clinging to it.

It was almost noon before he left the house, careful to double-lock the door behind him, and stepped out onto the street. Saturday was a good day in this neighborhood, when children played outside and families met in their little courtyards to share food and stories and good company. He saw a pack of kids on bicycles down by the corner in intense discussion about where to ride. The cross street was busy with Saturday traffic. Shops were prime destinations on Saturdays, parkings lots turned into open-air markets. Farmers came into the city with a portion of their crop to sell at near wholesale prices. There were clothes and toys and all manner of other things crowded along sidewalks all over Juárez.

"*Hola*, Señor Sevilla," one of Sevilla's neighbors called.

Sevilla smiled and waved to the old woman. Her daughters and seven grandchildren visited every Saturday. Once Ana and Ofelia had gone over to spend time with them, but only once. "*Hola,* Señora Pérez."

"Be careful!" Señora Pérez urged.

"I will. *Gracias.*"

He drove off the block past the children and their bicycles and joined the ebb and flow of cars and trucks, headed easterly away from his home toward an address given him once by a man about to die on a restroom floor.

He found the building in a place where apartments and businesses freely mixed in a dingy clustering of old buildings stained by age and little upkeep. Auto-repair shops spilled battered vehicles into lots ringed with storm fencing and double curls of barbed wire. There were machine works cradled between decaying apartment blocks. It was not a neighborhood of restaurants and *grocerías* and the occasional little house left over from some generation gone by. The predominant colors were dead gray and rust of corrugated aluminum and stained concrete.

The first time Sevilla passed it, the place was so plain and much like the others around it. The building hunkered down on heavy foundations, a block of cement and cinder blocks with six-paned industrial windows that could hinge out in a block to vent hot air from inside. Once there had been a long metal sign above the truck-sized rolling doors at the head of the structure, but only a corner remained bolted to the building's face. The doors themselves were chained shut. An entrance for men stood off to one side, the windows beside it boarded over.

Even having found it, Sevilla circled once more. He looked at the other buildings nearby, particularly a three-story corner apartment building fifty yards away on the other side of the street. There were windows there that offered an angled view of the place. This was something Sevilla put away for later.

He parked along the curb near those apartments and walked to his destination. Somewhere he heard the insistent scree of metal on metal, the sound of machineworks, but he could have his pick of a half-dozen places where the sound could be coming from. Work in Ciudad Juárez never stopped, even for the delights of Saturday, and paused only a little while on Sunday before heading back to the job.

Unlike his neighborhood, this one had deserted streets. A vacant lot sprouted thickets of grass, obscuring the squares of what might have been concrete flooring for some long-destroyed building. A few other cars dotted the curbs, but the atmosphere of abandonment was nearly total. They were not far from an industrial park for two large *maquiladoras* and Sevilla estimated he could reach Kelly's apartment in twenty minutes if he knew the right turns.

For a long time he stood before the building. He didn't want to go inside as much as he knew he must. He wished for an open window on the ground floor, but there were none. Sevilla walked the edges of the structure and passed down a narrow alley between this building and the next. The ground was packed so densely here that even grass struggled to grow. He found another boarded-up window.

The back of the building fronted a long, open expanse of grassy field. Recognition hit Sevilla so sharply that he put a hand on the wall to steady himself. A distant line of brown and white marked the apartment complex where Kelly used to live. As for the field itself… Sevilla had seen Paloma's body there. He tasted something acid and he felt anger.

Twin tire ruts came away from another set of rolling doors at the back of the building, curving away into the field. It hadn't rained in a while, but the tracks here were gouged into the earth deeply as if they had been muddy then. Sevilla tried to remember the weather in the days leading up to Paloma's discovery, but the recollection would not come. He cursed under his breath. He went on.

The fourth face of the building adjoined the vacant lot. An exterior staircase snaked up to the second floor. The metal grating underfoot flaked rust as Sevilla mounted the steps. The door at the top was the same deep red-orange. Double links of chain strung through the handle kept it secured, though there was no lock. Sevilla pulled on it once, vainly hoping the chains would just magically disintegrate, but they didn't give way.

He completed the circuit and went back to his car. He drove away and was back within the hour with a pair of heavy-duty bolt cutters with the price sticker still on them. Sevilla felt exposed on the street with the long-handled tool, but he spotted no one watching from any high window and no car disturbed the near-perfect silence.

Cutting the chain was easier than he expected. Hardened steel cut through one set of links and then the next. The chains snaked out of the handle and fell at Sevilla's feet, making a noise that sounded like a hundred tons of metal collapsing. Sevilla squeezed his eyes shut, listened for commotion from inside. There was nothing.

The door opened onto a small room half-filled with corroded barrels leaking something that stank of benzene. Sevilla's shoes splashed in the stuff. Overhead the simple aluminum roof had exposed beams and holes that let in sunlight. Birds had made their nests up there, though the fumes must have eventually driven them away.

Sevilla tried an inner door and found it unlocked. He left the bolt cutters there and ventured through.

It was impossible to know what had once been housed in the building. The second floor was a warren of rooms in different sizes, some still storing what looked like machine equipment and others empty. He found one with a naked mattress on the floor and short tables thick with candle wax that dripped into heavy stalactites and pooled white on the concrete below. Steel eyehooks were fixed to the wall with rope loops dangling from them.

Sevilla's mouth was dry. He swallowed three times to get the flow of spit going again, but the flavor of his mouth did not improve.

He went downstairs.

The high windows angled light into the large space on the ground floor like some plain cathedral without stained glass. DayGlo spray-paint graffiti marked the cinder block walls. The corners were littered with broken or discarded beer bottles. Someone had tried to gussy up the industrial space by hanging tarps in an approximation of tapestries, but the tarps were dingy-colored and sometimes spattered with something that might have been dark paint.

The fighting arena was the dominant feature. Lengths of thick rope marked off the space, strung from metal pillar to metal pillar and lashed in place with wire and bungee cords. It approximated the size of a boxing ring, but there was no matting here. Plain cement was scattered with a thick layer of sawdust, some of it clotted together with unmistakable blood.

Facing the ring was a long table, a feudal lord's banquet space with a large chair in the center such as the lord himself would occupy. A dozen men could sit and watch the battle, and though the table was bare and rough and even splintered it would be transformed by a feast.

In another, smaller space in the back corner there was a dog-fighting pit. Brown-stained carpeting marked out the space, knee-high pressboard all around it and scarred by claws. Finally he found another large mattress, this one still clad in cheap sheets.

Others were scattered around. Sevilla breathed deeply through his nose and out through his mouth but the growing nausea wouldn't go away.

He fled up the stairs and back to the room with the barrels. He threw up in a corner there and gagged still further until there was nothing his stomach could give up. The stink of it was nothing compared to the petroleum reek of the barrels themselves.

Sunlight didn't cleanse him. He felt the inside of the building crawling on his skin, beneath his suit, in his hair. Again he heard the metallic screech and he clung to the sound because it was normal and ordinary and brought him back to a place where men worked and had families and never came near a place like this.

After a long while he picked up the cut chains and strung them through the handle of the side door. No one looking closely would be fooled, but from a distance of just a few feet it was identical to the way Sevilla found it. He realized he'd left the bolt cutters inside, but he retreated down the steps and across the street not caring. He sweated more than the day's heat demanded.

SIXTEEN

TWO MILES AWAY SEVILLA FOUND A drug store that seemed unchanged since the 1960s. It still had a lunch counter and an old man who jerked sodas from an ornate fountain with chromed spigots. Sevilla ordered food he did not want to eat and forced himself to bite, swallow and chew until the whole plate was empty.

He put down payment and a tip. His phone rang.

"Sevilla," he answered.

"It's Palencia."

"Enrique," Sevilla said. He hoped he did not sound so utterly spent on the other end of the line. "Where are you?"

"I'm coming back. I saw Rojas."

Out in the sun, Sevilla's eyes were hurting again. The headache was back. He had a bottle of aspirin in his pocket and he took two, grinding them between his teeth and tolerating the horrible bitterness because at least it was better than concentrating on the pain in his head.

"Are you there?" Enrique asked. "Can you hear me?"

"I'm here," Sevilla said.

"I spoke to Rojas. He knows about it, Rafael. He knows all about it. Ortíz—"

"You don't have to tell me," Sevilla interrupted.

"What do you mean? What's going on there?"

"I killed Ortíz," Sevilla said.

Nothing but silence greeted him on the other end of the line.

Sevilla heard the crackling of an unclear signal and the ghost whispers of other callers somewhere hundreds of miles away. Finally he heard Enrique clear his throat. "What happened?"

"He told me everything," Sevilla replied.

"What *happened?*"

"I've seen the place. I've been inside. I saw where they do it, Enrique. It's done in plain sight, all of it. They aren't afraid of anything."

"The Madrigals—" Enrique started again.

"It doesn't matter to you anymore. Listen to me, Enrique. Listen carefully: I want you to walk away from this. You don't want to be a part of it anymore. There's no good that can come of it. Put your nose back into your paperwork. You're safer with La Bestia."

Sevilla caught the sound of a car's engine in the background. He heard anxiety notching into Enrique's voice. "What are you going to do?"

"It's too late for me," Sevilla said, and he closed his phone.

Enrique called back three times, but all three times Sevilla ignored the call. He took a walk with only his thoughts for company, moving through sidewalk vendors and farmers' stalls until he was back at his car again. Back where he began with nothing to show for his effort.

He wanted to talk to Enrique because there was no one else. A part of him thought he should return to Kelly because he might not have a chance to explain himself. When Kelly woke — *if* he woke, Sevilla reminded himself — there would be no one to tell him the story of Paloma. But perhaps it was better that way. If Kelly woke they would put it all on him. El Cereso would seem a paradise compared to the hole they'd find for an American who raped and murdered a Mexican woman.

This time when he came to the neighborhood he parked in front of the apartment building he'd noted earlier. He considered hiding his car, but it seemed like there was no point; no one knew him here and no one would be watching.

There were seven apartments in the little building, each one marked with a little slip of paper and a buzzer. Sevilla pushed the buttons for the units on the second and third floors and said nothing if someone answered. A third-floor unit unlocked the front door without calling down. Sevilla went inside.

The hallway was narrow and the little space near the mailboxes smelled heavily of old cooking. A building this old had no elevator, so Sevilla mounted the stairs one at a time. He heard television sounds and radio sounds and the warble of people talking loudly to one another. On the third floor he found the foremost unit and knocked on the door.

Sevilla waited until an ancient man answered. The man peered through the space between jamb and the edge of the door at Sevilla's battered face. A brass chain held the two together. The man looked Sevilla up and down. "What do you want?" he asked.

"*Policía*. My name is Sevilla. Here is my identification. Open the door."

The ancient man squinted at Sevilla's badge and ID. Sevilla saw an idea skitter across the man's face — slam the door and call the police — but eventually he undid the security chain and let Sevilla inside.

The apartment was small but drenched in light from the casement windows at the front of the unit. The ancient man had an equally antiquated black-and-white television set and a portable record player on a folding table. Playing cards were spread out across an undersized coffee table opposite a threadbare couch.

"I have done nothing wrong," the ancient man said.

"You aren't in trouble," Sevilla replied.

He looked out the front window. His car was below and then the street and then the terrible building. The angle was not perfect and Sevilla could not see all three sides of the structure, but it was good enough for what he needed that he didn't think to complain.

When he turned back to the ancient man, Sevilla saw fear on the man's face. "Don't worry. I'm not going to cause any problems for you. But I will need to stay here for a while. I'm sorry."

"What are you looking for? I have nothing here."

Sevilla motioned the ancient man closer. In his pocket his phone began to vibrate. It was Enrique. He paid the call no attention. "Come here," he said. "You see that building over there?"

"Yes."

"Have you ever seen anything happening there? People coming and going?"

The ancient man thought for a while and then nodded. "Sometimes I've seen many cars. At night when everyone else has gone home. Fancy cars. But I don't pay such things attention, *señor*. I mind my own business."

"Of course you do. When do the cars come?"

Again the ancient man considered. "Sometimes every month. Less when it's cold."

"They are coming again tonight," Sevilla said. "I will watch for them."

"Are they *narcotraficantes*? I watch the news. I know they are everywhere."

"They are," Sevilla lied. "And if all goes well tonight, you'll never see them again."

"Good," the ancient man said. "We don't need their kind here."

Sevilla prevailed upon the ancient man to bring him a chair to put by the window and another of the little folding tables on which to put his notepad and his phone. Without being asked the man brought Sevilla something to eat, and though he was still not hungry Sevilla made himself finish this meal, too.

They had nothing else to say to each other. The ancient man went back to his game of solitaire. From time to time he shuffled, the cards purring in hands with big knuckles that looked as though they were arthritic but clearly were not. Sevilla looked at the man and saw himself in twenty years if he would live twenty years more. It was not as terrible as he thought it might be.

"What is your name?" Sevilla asked the ancient man at last.

"Rudolfo."

"Thank you for this, Rudolfo."

"*De nada.*"

From time to time a car would pass down the lonely street and Sevilla would tense, but these never stopped. The sun tracked across the sky, bleeding away the afternoon and shifting the shadows. Finally Sevilla saw a Lexus sedan turn the farthest corner and cruise to a slow stop before the building.

Two men emerged with a third still behind the wheel. Sevilla wished for a pair of binoculars but he had none, so he squinted to make out faces. He did not recognize them, but he couldn't see them clearly, either.

One of the men undid the chains that bound the front doors. He pushed one half of the entrance aside and the Lexus slipped inside. The door closed behind it. A few minutes later the little entry door opened and another blurry-faced man stood outside for a smoke.

Sevilla's heart jumped when he saw the city police unit turn the same far corner and crawl along the block. It was the first such car he'd seen all day and his pulse sped up still further when it came to a slow stop in front of the building.

One cop got out. The smoking man greeted him. Sevilla saw them talking but it was silent here. The cards purred between Rudolfo's hands as he shuffled once again.

Another man came out of the building to speak with the cop. Sevilla leaned forward as if he could catch word of what they said, but it was an unconscious gesture and pointless. His phone vibrated again and for an instant he wanted to smash it.

The second man produced something white from his jacket pocket, an envelope, and passed it to the policeman. The policeman put the envelope away. He saluted both the men and got back into the cruiser. They stood aside and let the cops drive off.

Sevilla let his breath out in a rush. He didn't realize he'd been holding it.

That was how they did it. The place was remote and the building without anything remarkable about it. And to keep the streets secure they paid the locals to stay away as they went about their business. Of course it was so simple; it needn't be any more complicated.

SEVENTEEN

WHEN THE SUN FELL LOW IN THE west it was in Sevilla's face and he squinted against the glare behind sunglasses. Rudolfo abandoned the couch and retreated to the apartment's little kitchen to begin preparations for the evening meal. Though they did not speak, Sevilla got the impression that the ancient man enjoyed the company because he had so little otherwise. Sevilla was sure there would just happen to be too much food for one man and he would have to share. He still had no appetite.

At half past seven a van approached the building. It pulled up to the great sliding doors and honked its horn. The entrance was spread wide. Sevilla could make out a telephone number on the side of the van, but not the text above it. He called the number. No one answered, but the machine told him it was a business that rented sound systems for parties and dances.

Eventually Sevilla saw the van leave and it was quiet until sunset. As he expected, Rudolfo brought him a complete dinner to eat at the little folding table.

"How old are you, *señor?*" Rudolfo asked Sevilla while they ate.

Sevilla told him.

"I have a son your age. He lives here in the city, but he never comes to visit. His mother and I raised him in this apartment from when he was a little boy. He never comes."

Sevilla had nothing to say to that. He merely nodded.

"Do you have children?"

"I have a daughter," Sevilla replied. "She lives with me and her mother while she studies. I'm very proud of her."

"You are a lucky man."

"Very lucky. I have a granddaughter, as well. When I hold her, I feel twenty years younger. It's as though I have my baby daughter back again."

"Grandchildren are a blessing," Rudolfo agreed.

Sevilla cleared his plate. He brought it to the kitchen himself. The space was cramped and the sink small. When he returned, Rudolfo was watching him.

"Do you want to see your daughter and granddaughter again?" Rudolfo asked.

"Yes."

"Then you should go away from here."

Sevilla went to the window. He saw two cars with their headlights on against the gathering darkness. They stopped at the building and disgorged their passengers. He saw one woman among them in a bright dress. She looked like a whore. The men were all in jackets and shirts as if they were headed for a night on the town at restaurants and casinos. They went in through the little door by the boarded window.

"I have to stay," Sevilla replied at last. "These men… they must be stopped."

"If you wanted to stop them, you would not be alone. I'm old, *señor*, but I am not blind. You are here to die."

Rudolfo's words made Sevilla look away from the street. The ancient man was on his couch again with the deck of cards on the coffee table untouched. As he regarded Rudolfo, the man switched on a lamp and yellow light spilled around the room.

"I'm not here to die," Sevilla said.

"Aren't you?"

"No. I've come too far with this to die before it's done."

More cars came and more still until there was a crowd of them along the curb in front of the building and across the street. Sevilla saw more women, more prostitutes and some that even from a distance and in the dark he could see were not whores. The acid feeling in his stomach increased again and made the food there like stone.

"These men you seek, they aren't *narcos*, are they?"

Sevilla took up his notepad. He began to scribble instructions on them, then slowed himself deliberately so his handwriting would be clear; Rudolfo would have to follow them and so they must be legible.

"Who are they?" Rudolfo asked again.

"You don't want to know what kind of men they are," Sevilla replied.

Now Sevilla did hear something from the street. He paused and turned his ear to the night and heard it again: the thudding pulsebeat of loud electronic music. Lights shone through the spots and cracks in the corrugated aluminum doors and out of the windows high above. Someone had opened them to let the party noise spill out.

He finished writing and came to Rudolfo on the couch. "Listen to me," he said. "When I'm gone I want you to wait fifteen minutes and call the number. This number here."

"My telephone doesn't work," said Rudolfo. "They are supposed to repair the lines on Monday."

Sevilla flinched, and then he went into his pockets. He pressed his phone into the ancient man's hands. "Here. This is my phone. You know how to use a phone like this?"

"Yes."

"Good. It also has a clock. Wait fifteen minutes by the clock and call the number. When you are put through, give them my name and then tell them exactly what I've written here. Every word."

"Who am I calling?"

"The Policía Federal," Sevilla told Rudolfo. "When they come, close your windows and go to your bedroom. There may be gunshots. I don't want you to be hurt. Stray bullets go far."

"You are going in there?"

"Yes, I am."

"What good do you think you can do that the *policía* cannot?"

Sevilla put his notepad in Rudolfo's lap. He clasped his hands around the ancient man's, the cell phone clutched between those strong old fingers. "I can do one good thing. Only promise me you will do what I ask. I thank you for everything, but do what I ask now."

"I will do it."

"*Gracias, señor. Muchas gracias.*"

He left the apartment and waited long enough to hear Rudolfo put back the chain and lock the door behind him. The stairwell was dimly lit, but it was illuminated enough for Sevilla to check his pistol one last time. He was breathing too quickly and the edges of his vision glowed white. He made himself relax and then he took the stairs.

Out on the street he could better hear the music. It thudded louder and louder as he closed the distance to the building until his heart beat in the same rhythm and his nerves steadied. He did not wish for whisky.

There were bodyguards out on the street. Sevilla thought one of them might have been Ortíz's man, but he did not want to make sure. He cut across the vacant lot, crouching low with the line of the tall grass, making no sound that the music didn't cover. He heard a burst of cheering from inside as he passed around the back.

Light poured out the gap in the building's rear doors. Sevilla pressed his eye close. He saw the Lexus parked close at hand, the trunk up. The heavy bass of the music seemed to push air against his face. There were flashing strobes and somewhere a mirrored light cast a thousand little spots across the gloomy interior of the structure.

The edge of the fighting ring was visible, but Sevilla couldn't see more, or the great banquet table with its oversized chair fit for a baron. He moved on, circling around to the building's far side and then up the rusty steps to the chained side door. No one had disturbed it. Sevilla gathered the links in both hands and set them down gently.

As earlier, the hinges on the door squealed, but it was so loud inside that it swallowed up the noise. Sevilla could not hear his own thoughts, and in a way that was good because he did not want to hear the fresh fear scratching at the back of his mind or the echoing response that would make him shake and piss himself.

He pulled the door shut behind him. He stayed in the dark among the reeking barrels for a long time, half-waiting for someone to throw the interior door open. Light would wash over him and he would be exposed, crouched in a puddle of leaking benzene, blinded and trapped. Bullets would follow and he would be cut down. No one would come.

The interior door remained closed. Sevilla's eyes got used to the darkness and he saw the bolt cutters waiting there. Though his feet did not want to move, he crept across the room. He put his head to the jamb and eased the door open so slowly it seemed to take hours before the first light came through the crack.

Wider until his head could push through and he could see if anyone waited outside. Wider until he was able to turn sideways and move crablike into the building proper. The men below cheered, but they were not cheering him.

From here he could see the ring fully. He saw naked young men circling each other. Not naked completely, but wearing loincloths that made them look like some kind of Mayan warrior. Their bodies weren't painted, but each had a colored tassle just above the bicep of the right arm marking them blue or red. There was more red besides.

They fought bare-knuckled and already the skin of their fists was broken and bleeding. The blue fighter's lower face was painted crimson from a freely oozing nose. He had more blood on his opponent and their faces were welted.

It was not boxing: they used their feet and as Sevilla watched one kicked the other in the thigh with his shin. He heard the whack of bone on flesh even above the throbbing music. They circled and struck and punched and kicked and grappled and there was no bell because this was bloodsport fought with men instead of animals.

The gentlemen watched from their chairs. A purple cloth was thrown over the rough-hewn banquet table and the top was laden with food and drink. An enormous pile of white powder was at hand.

The whores mingled among the men, touching them out of sight or whispering in ears or sharing bestial kisses that came before open rutting. The other girls, the ones who were not prostitutes, watched the fight with disgust and fear on their faces. Sevilla singled out one who argued with the man next to her. The man held her upper arm and held her in her seat and then just as suddenly smacked her across the face hard enough to leave a deep mark. Another girl cried silently in her chair, staring forward at nothing.

Rafa Madrigal sat in his chair at the center and led the cheering when a particularly brutal blow was landed in the ring. He ate with his hands as if he were some kind of medieval king. Sevilla looked for Sebastián, but Sebastián was nowhere to be seen. This was as Ortíz said: the younger made the arrangements while the elder enjoyed the spoils.

Sevilla saw the other old men from that luncheon at Misión Guadalupe and the fourth from their golf session. They did not seem younger among the others despite the way they carried on beneath the party lights.

The one called Hernández, the one who asked after Sevilla's charity work with hospitals and the police, rose abruptly from the table and dragged one of the girls with him. He bumped against her in a parody of dance and held her when she tried to shrink away. One of the young men joined him and the two of them ground the girl between their hips while she cried openly. Sevilla gritted his teeth.

One of the fighters went down and the other leaped onto him, straddled his hips, rained punches down on upraised forearms. The fighter beneath had his skull cracked against the sawdusted concrete three times until his scalp split and there was gore everywhere. Madrigal and the others roared their approval. A whore fell between Madrigal's legs and vanished beneath the table.

Hernández and his companion wrestled the girl away from the table, toward the stairs to the second floor. The girl's clothes were torn from Hernández's grasping. Up the stairs they went and Sevilla suddenly realized he would be seen if they came to his level. He went back the way he'd come, hiding behind a door and hoping they had no reason to go all the way to the end.

They didn't come to his door. Over the thunder of the music he heard thin cries. His heart would not slow down. Out of his hiding place he came again, and slowly he advanced along the walkway. At the first door he stopped and pressed hard against the wall, sweating. He risked a glance through.

Hernández and the other man bore the girl to the sheets like wolves, biting and clawing. Hernández's bare buttocks were turned toward the ceiling. He humped and there was screaming that no amount of music could drown out. Sevilla felt heartsick.

On the warehouse floor the fight was over. One man lay motionless on the sawdust while the other reeled. Madrigal saluted the fighter from his chair and then the man collapsed from exhaustion and lost blood.

The girl was still crying out. For her mother, for God. Sevilla's eyes stung and he knew he was crying. He trembled all over.

Sevilla drew his pistol. This was not the way he imagined it. He did not want to be so afraid. But he could not stop the sounds of the girl's rape or of the bacchanal on the warehouse floor as men indulged in good-time girls and wine and drugs.

He took a breath and then moved.

When he entered the room, the men didn't see him at first. Sevilla saw the girl eclipsed by Hernández. His companion masturbated furiously. As his eyes lifted to Sevilla, he never stopped grasping his cock.

Sevilla's mouth was dry, but he forced himself to speak. "Stop," he said too quietly. "Stop this."

Hernández took notice and rolled halfway from the girl beneath him. Now Sevilla could see her face, her tears and the desperate hollow in her eyes that could only be filled with more pleading. "What the hell is this? Who are you?"

"I'm police," Sevilla said, and he raised his gun. His voice was steadier now. "Get away from her."

"Fuck you, you're the police," Hernández said. "What kind of a joke is this?"

Sevilla pointed his gun at Hernández's face. "I said get away from her. Now."

"I said fuck you, *pinche cabrón!*"

Once again Sevilla glanced down at the girl. Afterward he would not remember telling himself to fire. The bullet entered the center of Hernández's face and crashed out the back of his skull. The man flopped off the mattress completely. There was blood on the girl.

The man called Julio made to run out of the room. Sevilla shot him, too. This time he was splattered.

The music was still booming, but Sevilla thought he heard shouting. The girl was paralyzed on the mattress, her dress torn and dirtied. Sevilla had to leave her. He rushed from the room.

Every eye was raised from the floor of the warehouse and settled on him. Sevilla froze with the gun in his hand.

"*¡Policía!*" he heard.

Suddenly the big doors at the head of the building were shoved apart and two of the bodyguards spilled in crying panic. Red and blue lights flashed outside in the street and then there was chaos.

Down on the floor of the warehouse the men and their whores fled toward the exits but were turned back by a flood of spotlights from outside. Loudspeakers blared orders to surrender. Some headed for the rear doors.

He wanted to do something for the poor girl at his back, but the time was now. He was on the steps now headed down.

Gunfire sounded on the street and a stray bullet shattered the pane of a high window. Bodies swirled around the great banquet table and at the center there was Madrigal, standing alone. He did not flee. His face was stone because he was not afraid.

He saw Sevilla. Sevilla saw him. The gun was in Sevilla's hand.

"I know you," Madrigal said over the noise.

Sevilla put a bullet through Madrigal's eye.

The federal police poured in through the open doors of the building. Sevilla was already on his knees, his gun on the floor and his identification held over his head. Men in black armor were everywhere, charging up the steps to the second level, swarming around the girls where they lay violated and the bodies of the dead fighter and Madrigal.

Out on the street it was a stroboscopic explosion of clashing lights and black-and-white vehicles. Someone wrapped Sevilla in a blanket and steered him toward an ambulance. Once he saw the girl, the one Hernández violated, being loaded into another, but the glimpse was short and he had no chance to speak with her.

He looked toward the apartment building. He saw Rudolfo's window illuminated with yellow light. The ancient man was silhouetted there, and as if he knew Sevilla was watching, he raised his hand in greeting.

EIGHTEEN

IT WAS DAWN AGAIN AND HE WAS SET free. There were questions, so many questions, and he answered them all with half-truths and outright lies. In the end they had no choice but to turn him loose; the evidence was there, the men in custody, the bodies catalogued. He asked one of the *federales* to take him back to his car.

Behind the wheel, he steered himself to the Hospital General. He signed in at the front desk and went to Kelly's room. It was empty.

Sevilla went to the nurse's station. "Excuse me, I came to visit Kelly Courter. He was in that room just there."

The nurse furrowed her brow. "Who?"

"Kelly Courter. He was being cared for here. Just there. That room."

"You mean the American?"

"Yes, the American. Kelly Courter. Where has he gone?"

"One moment, *señor*." The nurse used the phone. She spoke with her back to Sevilla and glanced once over her shoulder at him in a way Sevilla did not like. When she returned she was polite. "Please wait for Señora Garza. She is the head nurse."

Sevilla looked into Kelly's room again as if he might be there again and it would all be a mistake, but the bed was empty and the sheets fitted tightly. The quiet machines that ensured his breathing and monitored his pulse and kept track of the functions of his body were all gone. The room seemed emptier still than just of life.

"*¿Señor?* Pardon me."

He turned away from the room. The head nurse was there in her whites.

"I'm looking for Kelly Courter. He was in this room."

"He's been moved."

Sevilla could not describe the sensation that rushed through him. It was more than relief or happiness but something akin to both that made his face flush and his skin tingle. He gripped Señora Garza on the arm and felt himself nearly cry. "Is he all right?"

"Yes. He's been moved to a bed in chronic care. Follow me."

They went away from the intensive care unit to the third floor. Kelly was held in a long room with many other beds, some occupied and some empty, the only real division between them being curtains hung from sliding tracks in the ceiling. Kelly seemed smaller here, lighter and paler, but he was real and he was alive.

"Thank you, *señora*," Sevilla told the head nurse. She left them there.

He could not sit far away from Kelly here, but was so close that his leg touched the bed. This close he could hear Kelly breathing on his own, see the stubble of beard that the hospital staff kept down with trimmers and smell the odor of a man bathed every other day with a sponge as he lay motionless.

How to begin?

"Kelly," Sevilla said. "I came to... I wanted you to know."

There was no reason for him to hesitate. Things were no different between them, though Sevilla felt changed. It was the place, open enough that anyone could hear Sevilla talking and draw judgments that only Kelly was qualified to make. Sevilla did not want to speak here, to tell the things he knew and what he'd seen.

Sevilla put his hand on Kelly's. It was surprisingly warm and soft the way boxers' hands were always soft, steamed inside tape and gloves for long sessions before the bag. His own hand trembled and then his whole body shook, his breaths shuddery and his eyes suddenly filled with stinging tears. He held onto Kelly and cried until the urge was passed and then he rubbed his eyes with the edge of his sleeve.

"It's all right now, Kelly," Sevilla said. "It's all right now."

AFTERWORD

*T*HE DEAD WOMEN OF JUÁREZ IS A
work of fiction and the Ciudad Juárez of the novel has been semi-
fictionalized to fit my purposes as a storyteller. That said, the
problem of the *feminicidios*, the "female homicides" of the *real*
Ciudad Juárez, is not some feat of morbid imagination.

Since 1993 more than four hundred women have gone missing in
the city or been found raped and murdered. A handful of the cases
have been tried in court, but to a one the suspects have complained
of fabricated evidence, torture, forced confessions. For a recent (and
excellent) examination of the facts, I refer you to *The Daughters
of Juárez*, written by Teresa Rodriguez with assistance from Diana
Montané and Lisa Pulitzer.

In recent years the *feminicidios* have been overshadowed by an
outrageously violent war between drug cartels that has plagued
the state of Chihuahua and the city of Juárez in particular. This
doesn't mean the problem has gone away. If anything the situation
is worse because the attention groups like Amnesty International
and the Inter-American Commission on Human Rights managed
to direct to these women has now been taken away. The drug war
trumps all.

It is my hope that this novel can in some small way shine a light
on the femicides. Many dozens of families hope daily for *justicia*.
Some would be happy just for the opportunity to bury their dead.
Until the police and the government of Mexico do something
substantial, that will never happen.

The group Mujeres Sin Voces in the novel is inspired by the real-life organizations Voces Sin Eco (Voices without Echo) and Las Mujeres De Negro (the Women in Black). I urge you to get involved with the issue through Amnesty International. In the end, this problem will be solved not with a bullet, but by bringing all those responsible for the abuse and murder of Juárez's daughters to judgment before the law.

—*Sam Hawken*

Other Serpent's Tail Titles of interest

They Shoot Horses Don't They

Horace McCoy
Introduction by John Harvey

'Aficionados of hard-boiled fiction who think that Hammett, Cain, and Jim Thompson set the standard ought to take a look at Horace McCoy' *Kirkus*

'Horace McCoy shoots words like bullets' *Time*

'A spare, bleak parable about American life, which McCoy pictured as a Los Angeles dance marathon in the early thirties . . . full of the kind of apocalyptic detail that both he and Nathanael West saw in life as lived on the Hollywood fringe' *New York Times*

'Captures the survivalist barbarity in this bizarre convention, and becomes a metaphor for life itself: the last couple on their feet gets the prize' *Independent*

'I was moved, then shaken by the beauty and genius of Horace McCoy's metaphor' *Village Voice*
'It's the unanswerable nature of the whydunnit that ensures the book's durability' *Booklit.com*

'Takes the reader into one of America's darkest corners . . . The story has resonance for contemporary America and the current craze for reality television. How far are we from staging a dance marathon for television?' *readywhenyouarecb.com*

Beer in the Snooker Club
Waguih Ghali
Introduction by Diana Athill

'*Beer in the Snooker Club* is one of the best novels about Egypt ever written. In the protagonist, Ram, a passionate nationalist who is nonetheless an anglophile, Waguih Ghali creates a hero who is tragic, funny and sympathetic. Through him we are presented with an authentic and acutely observed account of Egyptian society at a time of great upheaval' Ahdaf Soueif

'This is a wonderful book. Quiet, understated, seemingly without any artistic or formal pretensions. Yet quite devastating in its human and political insights . . . if you want to convey to someone what Egypt was like in the forties and fifties, and why it is impossible for Europeans or Americans to understand, give them this book. It makes *The Alexandria Quartet* look like the travel brochure it is' Gabriel Josipovici

'A plainspoken writer of consummate wryness, grace and humor, the Egyptian author chronicles the lives of a polyglot Cairene upper crust, shortly after the fall of King Farouk and thoroughly unprepared to change its neo-feudal ways . . . This is the best book to date about post-Farouk Egypt' *Los Angeles Times*

'Ghali's novel reproduces a cultural state of shock with great accuracy and great humor' *The Nation*

'A fantastic novel of youthful angst set against a backdrop of revolutionary Egypt and literary London. It's the Egyptian *Catcher in the Rye*' *Lonely Planet Egypt*

The Piano Teacher
Elfriede Jelinek

'In this demented love story the hunter is the hunted, pain is pleasure, and spite and self-contempt seep from every pore' *Guardian*

'A dazzling performance that will make the blood run cold' Walter Abish

'A brilliant, deadly book' Elizabeth Young

'Some may find Ms Jelinek's ruthlessly unsentimental approach – not to mention her image of Vienna as a bleak city of porno shops, poor immigrants and loveless copulations – too much to take. Her picture of a passive woman who can gain control over her life only by becoming a victim is truly frightening. Less squeamish readers will extract a feminist message: in a society such as this, how else can a woman like Erika behave?' *New York Times Book Review*

'With formidable power, intelligence and skill she draws on the full arsenal of derision. Her dense writing is obsessive almost to the point of being unbearable. It hits you in the guts, yet is clinically precise' *Le Monde*

The Piano Teacher (2001) was directed by Michael Haneke, and starred Isabelle Huppert and Benoit Magimel. It won the Grand Prize of the Jury and Huppert and Magimel were awarded the Cannes Grand Prix as Best Actress and Best Actor in 2001. On DVD from all good retailers & online.

We Need to Talk About Kevin
Lionel Shriver

'This startling shocker strips bare motherhood . . . the most remarkable Orange prize victor so far' Polly Toynbee, *Guardian*

'Once in a while, a stunningly powerful novel comes along, knocks you sideways and takes your breath away: this is it . . . a horrifying, original, witty, brave and deliberately provocative investigation into all the casual assumptions we make about family life, and motherhood in particular' *Daily Mail*

'An awesomely smart, stylish and pitiless achievement. Franz Kafka wrote that a book should be the ice-pick that breaks open the frozen seas inside us, because the books that make us happy we could have written ourselves. With *We Need to Talk About Kevin*, Shriver has wielded Kafka's axe with devastating force' *Independent*

'One of the most striking works of fiction to be published this year. It is *Desperate Housewives* as written by Euripides . . . A powerful, gripping and original meditation on evil' *New Statesman*

The film of *We Need to Talk About Kevin* is in production, for release in 2011, directed by Lynne Ramsay, and starring Tilda Swinton and John C. Reilly.

Shoedog
George Pelecanos

'A model exercise in dysfunction and doomed American cool'
Guardian

'The coolest writer in America' *GQ*

'The kind of book you are always hoping to find but rarely do' James
Sallis

'Pelecanos has carved out a territory – the seedier suburbs of
Washington, DC – and a language of danger and sadness all his
own' *Chicago Tribune*

'A consummate stylist with a rare sense of contemporary slam-bang
and angst' *Time Out*

'Washington DC's Zola' *Publishers Weekly*

'George Pelecanos has broken with tradition in so many ways, it
feels as if he has launched a category of his own. Partly, it's his
convincing evocation of an unfamiliar setting but mainly it's the
feeling that we are definitely in the present – here is your first turn-
of-the-century crime writer' Charlie Gillett

'Snaps with authentic street talk and with a switch-hitting plot . . . has
something important to say about trust and treachery' *Washington
Post*

Serpent's Tail

'Serpent's Tail is a consistently brave, exciting and almost deliriously diverse publisher. I salute you!' Will Self

'Nobody else has the same commitment to the young, the new, the untested and the unclassifiable' Jonathan Coe

'Serpent's Tail is one of the most unique and important voices in British publishing' Mark Billingham

'Serpent's Tail has made my life more interesting, enjoyable, exciting, easier' Niall Griffiths

'Serpent's Tail is a proper publisher – great writers, great books. If you want a favourite new author you've never heard of before, check their list' Toby Litt

'You're a good deed in a naughty world' Deborah Moggach

'Thanks, Serpent's Tail, for years of challenging reading' Hari Kunzru